THE MONDAY NIGHT HEARTBREAK CLUB

JANE LOVERING

Boldwood

First published in Great Britain in 2025 by Boldwood Books Ltd.

Copyright © Jane Lovering, 2025

Cover Design by Alexandra Allden

Cover Images: Alexandra Allden and Shutterstock

The moral right of Jane Lovering to be identified as the author of this work has been asserted in accordance with the Copyright, Designs and Patents Act 1988.

A CIP catalogue record for this book is available from the British Library.

Paperback ISBN 978-1-83533-260-3

Large Print ISBN 978-1-83533-261-0

Hardback ISBN 978-1-83533-259-7

Trade Paperback ISBN 978-1-80656-023-3

Ebook ISBN 978-1-83533-262-7

Kindle ISBN 978-1-83533-263-4

Audio CD ISBN 978-1-83533-254-2

MP3 CD ISBN 978-1-83533-255-9

Digital audio download ISBN 978-1-83533-257-3

This book is printed on certified sustainable paper. Boldwood Books is dedicated to putting sustainability at the heart of our business. For more information please visit https://www.boldwoodbooks.com/about-us/sustainability/

Boldwood Books Ltd, 23 Bowerdean Street, London, SW6 3TN

www.boldwoodbooks.com

In a departure from traditional dedications, this book is for all my fellow Boldwood authors who dashed in to support me when I had a (very minor) Valentine disappointment of my own. This was the book that came out of their suggestions. So, thanks, guys, I couldn't wish for a nicer group of authors to belong to!

1

I was well on my way to discovering that, unless the question was 'what is the best way to screw up your life totally', alcohol was, most definitely, not the answer. Alcohol *did*, however, mean that I read the poster tacked to the wall of the wine bar through the kind of pink fug that only a three-daiquiri haze could inspire, which made all the letters blend together, as though it had been left out in the rain.

'Wazzat say?' I asked the equally blurry barman, who was polishing glasses in front of me with the dedication of a man trying to remove DNA evidence from a crime scene.

'What does what say?' He barely even looked up.

'That. There.' I stabbed a finger in the approximate direction of the poster. 'The one with...' I squinted and leaned closer. The poster swam and seemed to be made up of cut out letters, like a ransom note. 'The big heart thing. With the knife in the middle.'

The barman looked across me and put down his polishing cloth. 'It says, "Was your Valentine's Day a big disappointment? Want to meet like-minded people and discuss where it all went wrong? Inaugural meeting of the Disappointed Valentines' Club here, Monday 8.30 p.m. Ask for Margot.'" He picked up the cloth again and got started on some espresso cups. 'Are you interested?'

'Dunno.' I had two attempts at getting up onto one of the high stools in front of the bar, failed at both and decided to go home. 'Might be.'

'Are you a disappointed Valentine?' He wasn't looking at me but was buffing the china with a lot more concentration than it needed, unless he wanted the pattern to come off.

'Yes. No.' I thought as deeply as the daiquiris would let me, skimming the surface of emotions. At least alcohol was good for something. 'I'm just disappointed,' I managed, finally. 'Thass all. Disappointed. In. Life.' I punctuated each word with a stabbed finger on the bar.

'Life is what you make of it, you know,' said the surprisingly philosophical barman, throwing me a bright glance.

'Well, the only thing I'm making is a mess.'

'And Valentine's Day is a commercial construct,' he said, polishing again as though the tiny cup had personally affronted him. 'People should think about their romantic partner all the time, not make an effort on one day of the year. If they are really in love.'

Nice sentiment, if not applicable to me. 'I think,' I said with all the dignity I could muster, which, after three strawberry daiquiris drunk *very* quickly on an empty stomach, wasn't very much, 'that being thought of at all is better than being ignored. Or... or used like a... y'know. Thing.'

Then, with that Wildean witticism, I cannoned off a table, hit my head on the glass door and finally managed to walk out of the bar, where I promptly fell off the edge of the pavement.

The barman had followed me. 'Are you all right?'

"S'fine. 'S'all good.' I clambered back to the pavement again. "M'just a bit, you know. Drunk thing. Don' need help.' I realised I was talking to a lamppost and turned around. "M'fine,' I repeated.

'Can you get home? You live across the road, don't you? Would you like me to help you?'

I shook my head and the daiquiris spun the world. 'When's it Monday?'

'Today is Saturday.' He looked as though he was about to take my arm, but changed his mind.

"S'no help.'

'Day after tomorrow.'

'I'll see you then.' I staggered a few more steps forward. 'Gonna join the club. Dis... disapp... thing club.' I looked blearily into the barman's face. He was younger than I'd assumed and wore round-framed glasses which, combined with the alcohol I'd drunk, made him look like a smeared owl. 'Men,' I said confidently to his name badge, which I couldn't read, 'are all bastards, you know.'

He smiled. 'If you say so. My opinion may differ, of course.'

I tried to look stern but I'd lost the use of my eyebrows. 'Yes. Bastards. All of 'em.'

Those round-framed eyes blinked down at me. 'Sounds as though you need that club. Now, you get home and sleep it off. Are you sure you'll be all right?'

"Es,' I stated, gravely. Then I walked into the wall, turned around and, with a certain amount of alcohol-driven dignity and legs that contained more rum than the average limbs, took myself home.

Monday morning crawled over me like a slug. I woke, late, to find it sitting on my face and had to rush to get ready for work with a banging headache and an inability to find one of my shoes. After my Saturday night exploration of the potential for cocktails to improve my life, I'd fallen back on the cheaper standby of wine. This had not made a notable difference to my situation but it had meant that I'd yet again failed in my weekly mission to tidy up the flat.

Life improved only slightly once I got to work and hid behind my desk to conceal the fact that I was wearing one trainer and one slip-on deck shoe. Demi was in. Demi was my only friend at this godforsaken outpost of slavery and she usually worked from home. Actually, Demi was my only friend, full stop.

'Morning, sweetie,' she said, pulling up at the desk opposite. 'You look dreadful. Bad weekend? Has Dexter called yet?'

'Demi, we're over. I wouldn't have him back if he had his willy replaced with diamonds.'

She winced. 'Ow.'

'Yes, not the best metaphor, now I come to think of it. But you know what I mean.' I remembered that poster, strobing into my head in the wine bar, and the idea that had come with it. 'I'm going to join a club. To help me get over him.'

Demi twisted her lips. Her filler needed redoing, I noticed, and she'd compensated by using a brighter shade of lipstick which didn't suit her. It also strobed through my head, reigniting the headache which had only just begun to respond to paracetamol. 'Hm.' She looked at me sideways. 'You two break up more regularly than a well-used Lego set.' Demi had children, so I forgave this simile. 'You always say you're going to get over him, but you always take him back.'

'Not this time.'

'You always say that, too.' Demi seized her headset. 'He's an utter waste of space; he's a criminal thug and I still have no idea why you ever got together in the first place.' She smiled, a somewhat impersonal smile. 'I'm only telling you this because I'm your friend, remember.'

Rub it in, why don't you, I thought, clenching my jaw without meaning to. Dexter had, at the very least, stuck around, presumably for reasons of his own. I remembered my resolution that this time... *this time,* I'd grab the tattered edges of what little self-esteem I had and pull it tight around me. 'This is a support group. For disappointed Valentines.' I pulled on my headset. I needed to be on top of the calls this morning or I'd be put on performance management, I'd been warned.

But this time I'd find my inner strength. *This time* I wouldn't turn into that weak and helpless woman, scared and overridden and shouted down until I backtracked and apologised and made promises that I knew would be impossible to keep. I *wouldn't*.

Resolution was all very well but selling household insurance down the phone to unwilling customers gave it a good testing. After an eight-hour shift of unanswered telephones, shouting, one engagement in conversation with an elderly lady who thought I was calling about her cat, and the return of the headache, I was on the point of just going home and going to bed.

'Have a lovely evening,' Demi chirruped, flipping off her headset and picking up her bag. 'Let me know when Dexter comes round. I promise not to say *I told you so* when you take him back. Honestly.'

I found I was narrowing my eyes as I trailed out after her, lurching slightly in my mismatched shoes. Demi's certainty that I'd have Dexter reinstalled by Tuesday morning at the latest gave my resolve a poke in the conscience.

I just needed some help. Some support. Which was why I was back in the wine bar. It was surprisingly quiet, and the same barman who had offered to help me home on Saturday night was still polishing glasses. They might even be the same glasses.

'What can I get you?' He put the cloth down and then recognised me. 'Ah. It's you. Are you wanting that Valentines group thing? They're over there.' He pointed with the stem of the wine glass. 'Can I get you anything? Orange juice?'

The light was reflecting off his little round spectacles, so I couldn't see his eyes, which meant I didn't know whether he was being sarcastic or not.

'I'll have a large Sauvignon Blanc, thank you.' I pulled out my phone and tried to find a card that might have some money on it. 'And where are they?'

'Table in the corner. Three others, so far. Funny that, I'd have thought the place would be rammed with people wanting to badmouth the opposite sex.' He put the glass of wine down on the counter and my mouth watered. 'It does seem to be a popular sport.'

That was way too cynical a comment for a Monday night, so I didn't answer him.

'Potential Disappointed Valentines' Club member?' As I reached the table, one of the women stood up. She was tall, blonde, with impeccable make-up and very blue eyes, which reminded me distressingly of my old head teacher at school. Her manner was similar too, very direct, and her delivery was clipped, as though she bit the words off longer sentences. 'I'm Margot. Welcome to our first meeting. The club was my idea.'

The other two women looked up at me; both had varying degrees of hopelessness behind their eyes. I suspected that I, too, radiated despondency – in fact, I knew I did. It was, after all, how Dexter had hooked me. Well, no more. I set my mouth into lines of 'stiff upper lip'. But then, a club for disappointed anything was hardly going to be made up of smiling people full of outgoing enthusiasm, was it? The clue was in the name. I gave my lip permission to sag, just a little.

'I'm Annie,' said the greying-haired lady in the beaded top. She looked nervous, as though wine bars weren't really her thing, and was twirling a tall glass in which a single slice of lime bobbed amid bubbles.

'And I'm Wren.' This person was younger than me, mid-twenties, perhaps. Pretty, soft-voiced and nursing a cocktail which made me jealous. Then I looked around me, remembered that daiquiris had propelled me to this in the first place, and decided that sticking with wine was probably less likely to make me behave unwisely. Margot did not appear to have a drink at all. I went and sat down on the seat furthest from her.

'I'm Phoebe,' I said, trying not to wince at the sound of my own name. My parents, I'd always thought, hadn't bothered with much of a discussion; they'd let the name book fall open and stuck a pin in it. 'Sorry, yes, I know it's a dreadful name. I'm usually just called Fee.'

The two women nearest me chorused a downbeat 'Hello'.

Margot eyeballed me sternly with a look that made me want to hang my head and mutter about the dog eating my homework.

'Phoebe is a lovely name,' she said, definitively, as though my view of my own name was completely wrong. 'Classical. If I'd had children, Phoebe would be at the top of the list for names. For girls, obviously.'

She obviously hadn't had to spell it out for everyone. My background was not 'classical' and I'd worked hard to leave it behind. Well, I'd *tried* to leave it behind by educating myself through reading, although evidently quite a lot of it still tiptoed in my shadow.

At the table by the window, two men incongruously playing dominoes clacked away. Their conversation sounded a lot more lively and fun than the one I was currently enduring and I wondered whether I could suddenly discover that I was no longer a disappointed valentine but had a previously undiscovered passion for table games and Cinzano.

No. I was here to make good my decision to never take Dexter back. While the domino players looked fun, it would be a 'cloth cap and Norman Wisdom' type of fun and I wasn't quite ready for Christmas cracker jokes and guffawing yet.

At my table, everyone looked at their glasses. Nobody seemed to know what to say, so I drank my wine in short, jerky sips. Wren wasn't drinking her cocktail, I noticed, just twisting the glass between her fingers. Annie was staring into hers, glumly watching the lime slice bob up and down amid the bubbles. They all looked less thwarted in love and more as though they'd received a life sentence.

Margot turned her wrist and looked at her watch. I hadn't seen anyone wear an actual watch for years. 'Well, as it's eight thirty-five, I think we should start now,' she said, in a 'chairing the meeting' voice. 'Anyone else will have to fit in around us.'

Now all four of us looked over at the rest of the bar. Even for a Monday night it was quiet. Outside the windows, the Yorkshire night was drawing in against the glass as though wanting some comfort from the light within. The men playing dominoes sat in their corner, as though this were the pub it had once been before rebranding and a desire to take the small town upmarket had seen its dark-painted interior and sticky floor replaced with pale wood and parquet. The pub clientele had all moved up the road to the still-sticky and convivial Black Horse, and the wine bar was mostly frequented by tourists. And me. But, in late February, the tourist season hadn't yet started. So tonight it was occupied solely by disappointed women, two old guys who couldn't be bothered to hike up the steep hill, and the barman, who seemed to be the only person who worked here.

I wondered if he'd ever thought of installing a juke box. Then I tried to imagine Dua Lipa playing into this solemn atmosphere and almost smiled for the first time in days. Even Harry Styles would have had a job on to lift the mood in here.

'Shall I go first?' Margot leaned forward across the table, seemingly filled with an almost indecent desire to share her story. I wanted to say *If you must*, but didn't, mostly because the wine was doing its work, blunting the edges of life.

'My husband told me he wanted a divorce the day before Valentine's,' Margot said, matter-of-factly. 'I'd been planning a long weekend. Val d'Isère, I thought, really terribly popular just now.'

I thought that was the name of an opera singer, so I was quite pleased when Wren said, 'For the skiing?' and stopped me looking like a total culture-free idiot.

'Of course,' Margot replied, as though there were no possible reason for anyone going anywhere unless it was to slide down mountains. 'I was going to surprise him with it for his birthday.

His birthday is 17 February, you see,' she added. 'But he sat me down and told me that as far as he is concerned our marriage is over and he wants a divorce.'

She stopped speaking suddenly, as though the reality of the situation had only just dawned on her. 'He wants a divorce,' she said again, more softly. 'After thirteen years.' Those bright blue eyes clouded and she blinked rapidly.

We murmured consolation. Margot seemed to have come to an end, so Annie, the greying-haired lady, took over. Her top swung and the beads clattered against the edge of the table with a noise that made my teeth want to chew my wine glass. 'I think my husband is having an affair,' she said, in a monotone that made the words seem free from any emotion. 'He forgot Valentine's Day this year, for the first time in forty years.'

Margot cocked her head. There was an interrogative shine in her eyes now. 'Any other signs?' she asked.

Annie sighed. 'Oh, the usual ones. Secret phone calls, lost weight, he's bought himself some new clothes, taken up going to the gym. All the clichés. He's snappy with me, short tempered, you know. He's sixty, we'd been saving so he could retire this year, but he's suddenly stopped talking about all the plans we'd made – it doesn't look good.' She took a deep breath. 'So I'm joining this group because I think I'm going to need support when it all comes out.'

She looked around at the three of us. 'I don't have many friends,' Annie went on. 'It's always been just me and Eddie. If I lose him...'

I swallowed hard. I'd been thinking that this group would be a bunch of women like me, who wanted to meet up every so often, drink, shout about what a bunch of bastards our exes were, sing two verses of 'I Will Survive' and try to pick up a man at the bar. I'd not considered that real emotion might come into things.

Everyone nodded, as though committing Annie's betrayal to memory. I wanted to skip past this bit and get to the part where we all bought another round of drinks and possibly managed a chorus of 'Respect', but there didn't seem to be any hurrying anyone. Plus the lack of juke box would mean we'd have to go a cappella, which might be a little cold-blooded, even for me.

'I mean,' Annie added, 'I've got my groups of course. French lessons, crochet club, bowls on Wednesday...'

We carried on nodding.

'...reading to the elderly on a Friday, knit and chat alternate Tuesdays, supporting refugees – but that's only once a month of course – collecting for the Red Cross, Daffodil club...'

Our nodding had slowed somewhat.

'...the WI, our baking group, and organising outings for the playgroup.'

There was a pause as we all waited to see whether she'd run out of associations.

'But I don't have many what you could call real *friends*,' Annie went on, rather begging the question as to why she bothered with all these activities. 'Oh, there's Sally of course, but all she wants to do is talk about her grandchildren.'

After a slightly stunned moment of silence, when Annie failed to reveal fifteen more friends of varying realities, attention switched to Wren. Like her namesake bird, she was small and tidy and somehow... brown. Her hair, her clothes, everything was over-washed with a kind of mental sepia, forcing her into the background even though she was currently the centre of attention.

'Jordan didn't bother with Valentine's Day,' she said, looking down into her cocktail. 'Nothing. I'd bought some chocolates, thought we'd go out for dinner, you know, that sort of thing, but I got...' A shrug. 'So I asked why – I mean, surely, even a voucher, would that be too much trouble?' She took a deep breath. 'I got "I appreciate you every day, why do you want me to do something extra just because some card shop says you have to spend money? That's capitalism at its finest." Or something like that. So I ended it.'

I remembered the barman expressing similar sentiments when I'd been falling over my own feet on Saturday night and glanced over at him to see if he was listening. He seemed to be sorting out money in the till and was therefore presumably not in a position to appreciate anti-capitalist rhetoric.

Wren sighed again and Margot leaned forward across the table to lay a hand on Wren's wrist. 'Typical bloody man,' Margot said, in a tone so laden with vitriol that it ought to have burned a hole through the table. 'Taking women for granted. Not wanting to spend so much as a fiver if it means inconveniencing themselves.'

'Er,' said Wren, looking even smaller and browner.

'No, no, I understand how you feel.' Margot's conversational juggernaut was rolling forward, squashing all objection. 'We do everything for them. We cook, we clean, we organise their lives. We're like social secretaries, housekeepers and sex workers all rolled into one, and all we ask is a little bit of gratitude now and again. But oh no, it's too hard for them to even go online and order a bunch of flowers once a year to say, "Thank you for all you do". Honestly. Men!'

'Jordan is a woman,' Wren said quickly, obviously trying to squeeze this vital information into the conversation before Margot dug herself in any deeper.

We all looked off in different directions in the resulting silence. Over in the corner, the barman was now doing something to a gin bottle that made it look as though he was trying to earwig on our conversation. Although why he would want to listen to four women doing Sad Face and complaining, I had no idea. He wore an all-black uniform too, shirt and trousers and a tie, which made him look like a formal ninja.

'How about you, Fee?' Margot was using me to distract everyone from how deeply her foot was currently in her mouth, obviously. 'What made you want to join our group?'

Three pairs of eyes swung my way. Four, actually, because the barman was looking over now, still uncoiling a roll of plastic which had inexplicably sealed the gin into a pirate-ship-shaped parcel.

'I dunno,' I said, awkward at being the focus of attention. 'My ex walked out on Valentine's Day. I mean, he was always walking out, but he usually came back. This time...' I shrugged. 'This time I really don't want him back. I know he's not... good for me,' I finished rather lamely.

I saw Margot and Wren make eye contact and both raise their eyebrows.

'Did he say why he left this time?' This was Annie, a gentle question in her soft, Yorkshire tones.

'Not really.' I thought back to that night, but absolutely wasn't going to admit that I'd declined his offer of sex and he'd decided to go back to Leeds and knock on the door of someone more available. 'Nope. He upped and left in the middle of an episode of *Our Flag Means Death*. Threw his stuff into a bag and walked out.' I didn't add that it was something I'd grown to expect, Dex walking out to find either his dealer or another woman, because that made me sound desperate. After all, why would I want to hang on to a man like that? Why *would* I?

I didn't tell them about the yelling and the screaming and the accusations, about how hard I had tried to keep Dex because I thought this was what I wanted, what I *deserved*.

'Oh, Fee.' Annie's eyes were bright. I thought this was very generous of her, given that she had an unfaithful husband. 'That's awful, love. Not even to give you a reason or a chance to talk.'

I couldn't think of anything to say to that. How did I explain the strange feeling that came so close to relief, after Dex left? The kind of relief you feel when a boil has burst, when you hope the worst is over but suspect it's just going to build up again. My new resolve never to take him back again was just the pin I sat with in readiness. He was a boil I was determined to prick.

Thoughts about boiling his prick weren't totally alien to my nature either.

I finished my wine and tried to catch the barman's eye to order another. He was now pretending not to listen but standing right up at the end of the bar, as close to us as he could get. He had his dark curly hair pulled back into a small tie at the back of his neck and his glasses kept catching the light, making his eyes look like white circles of reflected light. I still couldn't read his name badge.

'So.' Margot cleared her throat. 'Looks like we're all in this together, do you all agree? I'm getting divorced, Annie's got suspicions, Wren has been taken for granted and Fee's been abandoned.' She sounded perkier now and I definitely saw her rub her hands together almost as though she were gleeful at the prospect. 'But we can all support each other.'

'How?' I asked, but nobody seemed to have heard me.

Annie gave a rueful smile and Wren nodded earnestly. 'Can we meet every week?' Annie asked.

'Well, I *was* thinking monthly...' Margot began.

'Only, like I said, I've got nobody else. Nobody to talk to, there's no one who knows what I suspect and I'd really like to be able to, you know, chat. I can't talk to Eddie, obviously, and, well, it's always been just me and him.'

None of us felt able to mention the crochet club, the WI or any of Annie's other numerous hobbies and groups.

'Oh yes!' Wren bobbed in. 'Me too. Now Jordan and I aren't seeing each other any more I need a good distraction. Something to stop me moping and texting everyone in my contacts list.'

They were all looking at me again now. I looked at my empty glass. Well, there were worse things, weren't there, than a once-a-week chance to sit in a bar and drink wine? If the alternative was to sit in my living room and mope? At least here it was warm and convivial and I didn't have to listen to the terrible karaoke coming up through the floor from the neighbours underneath and think about how I seemed to not only have missed the boat on life, but to be rowing after it in a leaky barrel. 'I don't mind,' I said, sounding more grudging than I felt. Margot and Wren didn't seem the kind to need the acclaim of others or a relationship just to feel like acceptable members of society, and even Annie admitted to chiefly needing support to get through her husband's infidelity. I was the only one who wanted an excuse to get out of the house. The incongruity, and the memory of the barman's cynicism, made me ask, 'But what's it *for*?'

'For?' Margot stared at me. Annie and Wren gave me little covert glances, as though they wondered whether I was about to launch into an agenda filled with corporate speak. 'What do you mean?'

'The club.' Caught in the spotlight of so much attention I wished I'd voted to go monthly and never raised the issue of what the club might achieve. 'Er. Sorry, but shouldn't we be *doing* something? Something...' I rummaged around in my brain. The condemnatory words of the barman, when he'd assumed the club would just be women sitting around badmouthing men, had sunk into my psyche and given me something to prove. Although why I wanted to prove anything to a man whose entire career seemed to comprise polishing glassware and shelving bottles, I had no idea. 'Something proactive? Something that might cheer us up? Rather than sitting and talking about how shit life is.'

'Talking can be useful, you know,' said Wren.

'But it doesn't change anything, does it?' I said, rather limply. I knew that drinking lots of wine didn't change anything either, it just made dreadful situations easier to bear, but I wasn't ready to give up on that aspect of the club yet. Talking, however, I could make a case against. Talking was the thing that you did when it was already too late. I didn't know what actions we could take that might be more cheering than reiterating our desperate situations, but there had to be some. I tried to remember Annie's list of activities. 'Maybe we could take up crochet?'

'I suppose we...' Margot began but was interrupted when the bar door opened and a man came bursting in at speed, as though the night had propelled him through the doorway.

'Is this the Valentines' Club thing?' he panted, arriving at our table. 'Sorry I'm late; the bus broke down on the hill. I had to walk the last bit.'

'But... you're a man.' Margot stood up now and stared at him as though a human-sized beetle had appeared in front of her. 'A *man.*'

The man in question, who was red-faced and puffing slightly, shrugged his shoulders. 'Yeah, and? Your poster thing didn't say your club was just for women, did it? "Disappointed Valentines", you said, and I'm one of them. So I reckon I can join, right?'

He and Margot eyeballed each other across the table while Annie, Wren and I tried not to meet one another's gaze. Everyone seemed to have forgotten my suggestion that we use the club to help ourselves, and I had the dreadful urge to laugh at how ridiculous this all was. In fact, they looked shell-shocked.

I glanced, for no reason I could come up with, over at the bar again. The barman was looking directly at me, one eyebrow raised.

Margot visibly gathered herself and her tone became 'dinner party host soothing difficult guest'. 'You're right, of course,' she said. 'I was a little taken aback because our poster definitely said eight thirty and now' – another glance at that slim watch – 'it's nearly half past nine.'

'Eight forty-five bus,' said the man. 'They only goes every hour. And then it broke down and...'

'You had to walk the last bit, yes, you said.' Margot glanced around at Annie, Wren and me and the headteacher stare was still in evidence. 'Well? Do we admit another member?'

I had an odd feeling then. A kind of warm burst somewhere near my stomach that spread out to cuddle round the other women as though I tried, invisibly, to draw them closer to me, and it dawned on me that this was the first time I'd felt *included* in so long that I couldn't remember when it had happened before.

Demi tried to include me, of course, although her cute house and kind husband all stood in such stark contrast to my life that I always felt – although I would have died rather than told her – like the hired help whenever we were together.

Here, Margot was treating me like one of the club. I *was* one of the club.

I looked at the sweaty-faced man, in his *Star Wars* T-shirt and badly fitting jeans, and experienced a moment of fellow-feeling. 'Why not?' I said. 'He's right, you didn't say it was just for women, Margot, and if he's a disappointed valentine then he's as much right to join as we have.'

Margot gave me an appraising look which I tried to block out by pretending to finish the last of my wine. In reality, the wine had gone about ten minutes after sitting down, but in the face of nobody else reordering, I hadn't felt I could fetch myself another drink and I couldn't afford to buy a round. 'What do you think?' she asked Annie directly.

'Oh!' Caught clearly by surprise, Annie jumped. 'Well, yes, I suppose, I mean... Fee is right, we didn't say women only.'

'Wren?'

A shrug. Wren didn't seem to care one way or the other, although her shoulders had curled forward.

'All right then.' Margot sat down, leaving the man standing. 'But we've finished our meeting now; you'll have to come back next week. Same place, same time.'

'Okay. That's fine. Great.' On his chest, Chewbacca and Luke Skywalker were patchy with sweat. 'I'll get the earlier bus. I lives over the other side of town.'

There was a moment of silence. Overhead, the trendy pendant lamps swung ominously in a draught, and one of the dominoes men cleared their table, counters clacking into their box like a death rattle. Nobody seemed to want to be the first to move, so we all remained in stasis, like the closing scene of a bad play, waiting for the curtain to come down.

Finally, the barman came over and began wiping the table. He smelled nice when he leaned alongside me to pick up my glass and I took a furtive glance at his name badge, stark and white against the black uniform.

'Thanks, Flynn,' I said. For some reason I wanted to use his name, perhaps to discomfit him a little. He had a slight air of superiority that I wasn't sure I liked, listening in on our discussion and only giving me a small glass of wine when I'd asked for a large.

He didn't miss a beat, just wiped a cloth over the table and said, 'You're welcome,' without meeting my eye.

'Cheers, mate,' said as-yet-unnamed man, Luke Skywalker now showing definite signs of clothing abuse.

Flynn nodded and walked off, carrying our empties. Margot seemed to gather herself. 'Until next week, then.' She picked up a rather nice bag which had been out of sight under the table and stalked off towards the door, followed in a slightly raggle-taggle format by Wren, Annie and then me.

'Don't suppose anyone can give me a lift back down the road?' came the plaintive voice of the nameless club member, drifting through the door as it closed behind us.

3

On Saturday Demi texted to tell me she was moving to Peterborough.

> You'll have to come and stay all the time.

In Peterborough? I wanted to ask. *Why the hell would I come to Peterborough?*

> Yes, of course.

I texted back.

> Good luck. I'm sure we can have a drink before you go.

> We move on Thursday.

There wasn't much I could reply to that. Her life was going to go further and further towards the house, big family, reliable husband and a spaniel that she'd had it pointed at when we'd first met. Mine... wasn't.

I put the phone down and stared around the flat.

It echoed with emptiness. Also a little with the argument breaking out downstairs, which seemed to be based on Him looking at Her again, you know Her, the one with the lips and the bum, not that they're natural so you needn't get any ideas. I slumped at the kitchen table and stared out of the window, which looked out over the main street and directly across to the wine bar, where Flynn was pulling a couple of tables out onto the small pavement area and trying to make the town look like Paris.

I watched him for a few moments. Then I opened a bottle of wine.

* * *

I was the second to arrive on Monday evening. Margot, of course, had got there first and was neatly arranging her handbag and some A4 pads when I swung through the door.

'Ah, hello, Fee!' Her use of my name made me feel odd, a little as though she was greeting me like an old friend, not like someone I'd only met once before. 'How are you today? How's life?'

'Don't worry, I'm still single,' I muttered.

Flynn, behind the bar again, poured me an unasked-for small glass of wine. 'Never mind,' he said. 'Being single isn't that bad. Sometimes better than the alternative.'

I thought of Dex. He might not have been perfect partner material, but at least he'd *been there*. He'd shown that I could have a normal life – a flat, a boyfriend, a job – despite everything I'd always been told. I'd been *doing it*, having a life. Now, everything was gradually seeping away from me, leaving like heat evaporating from a warm bath. I was floundering in the cold water already.

'Very gnomic.' I picked up my glass. 'They should hire you to write T-shirt slogans.' Being bitchy to Flynn distracted me from feeling sorry for myself. Then I looked at Margot. She was a little paler than she had been previously, her make-up just a touch less perfect. 'Are you all right?'

As though my question surprised her, she jerked her head up and stared at a corner of the ceiling. This went on for so long that Flynn and I made eye contact and pulled faces, indicating that we were unsure as to whether or not interrupting her upward stare might result in a tirade.

Finally, she brought her eyes back down to the table. 'Yes, thank you, Fee. I'm fine. The divorce is going ahead. Bruce has agreed to all my terms. I'm having the house, of course, and half his pension.'

Flynn and I widened eyes at each other now. 'Wow,' I said. 'What does he get?'

'Oh, he's having the place in Spain.'

'Well, that's...'

'And the cabin in Scotland. Plus the boat, of course.'

There was a pause. I didn't know what to say to any of that, other than another *Wow*, but I thought the previous one pretty well summed things up. 'And are you happy about that?' I asked eventually.

Margot sighed. 'I shall miss the cabin. The Highlands are so wonderfully relaxing out of season, I find.'

I hadn't meant that. I'd really meant to ask her how she felt about her husband wanting a divorce. She'd already mentioned not having children and I wanted to know if that had been the bone of contention or whether she had been replaced with a younger, blonder model. I wanted company in my misery, basically, and her resolute attitude wasn't giving me the All Men Are Bastards vibe that I was after.

The door jingled and our newest recruit, the bloke who'd been wearing the *Star Wars* T-shirt, came in. 'Just a pint, mate,' he said to Flynn, who had half-heartedly begun to sort bottles in the racking.

'This is a wine bar,' Flynn said levelly.

'Pint of wine then,' said Luke Skywalker, and guffawed, as though this had been one of Stephen Fry's best-ever comeback lines.

Flynn sighed and poured a large glass of white wine. Tonight his hair was loose and hung around his face, which made him look like a student working his evening job, although I knew he must be older. I wondered what else he did, apart from working in here. Or maybe this was all he did?

Mr Star Wars saw Margot and me and came bouncing over, balancing his wine carefully. 'Didn't get to introduce myself last week, did I?' He stuck out the hand not holding the wine. 'I'm Fraser. Fraze-the-Haze, the boys call me.'

'Do they?' Margot shook hands, looking a bit faint. 'Why?'

Fraser's face scrunched up in thought. He had a very round face; the fringe of beard did nothing to disguise its rotundity and made him look like a baby in fake facial hair. 'Well, well... haze, it's like fog, isn't it?' he asked, uncertain in the face of Margot's stringent questioning. 'Like – stops you seeing?'

Her expression became one of intermediate clarity. 'Oh. I *see*. Airborne pollution. Obviously. Silly of me, really.'

Fraser-the-Particulates-in-Suspension sat down, looking a bit stunned, and took a large mouthful of his wine, which made me warm to him a bit.

'I'm Fee and this is Margot,' I said. Then, in a spirit of mischief, 'And the onlooker is called Flynn.'

Flynn waved.

'Our other two are Annie and Wren. I'm sure they'll be here in a minute.'

'Wren called to say she may be a little late.' Margot was fiddling with the notepads again. 'I gave her my number last week, I should give it to you too, Fee. In case you can't make a meeting or something.'

'Can I have your number too?' Fraser glanced over. 'In case I'm late.'

Margot paused. 'I'm not sure that's appropriate,' she said. 'I don't give my number out to men I don't know.'

'Well, that's discrimination then, isn't it?' He sounded confrontational. 'What do you think I'm going to do with it? Unless you reckon all men are drunk-diallers who're going to phone you up, pissed, and send you dick pics.' The confrontational tone was diluted somewhat when he swigged another mouthful of wine as though it were lager.

He did have a point.

'Why the notepads, Margot?' I asked, to break the tension. 'Are we doing exercises?'

Fraser put his glass down. 'I don't do writing,' he said. 'I'm dyslexic, me.'

'No, no.' Margot waved vaguely at the pads and pens. 'It's for making notes, scribbling ideas. I always think a meeting looks so much more *finished* if people make notes, don't you? Besides, Bruce's company produces stationery products, so I've got literally millions of these at home and I ought to start clearing out some cupboards. I'll write my number down on them.' She picked up a pen. 'So you *all* have it.'

Another small pause while she wrote, and Fraser and I tried to avoid catching one another's eyes. Thankfully, Annie and Wren chose that moment to come in together, letting a little of the night's chill in with them. Through the open door I could see the windows of my flat opposite. There were no sudden flickers of illumination in the kitchen or bathroom to show that someone was moving from room to room, no strobing blue indicating that the TV was on. Only that one single bulb trying to light up my whole life.

I drained my glass.

'Wren! Annie! Over here!' Margot called, sounding slightly imperious and making one of the old men – who were playing poker tonight, for furtive pennies – look up and say something, which made the other laugh.

There was a bustle of coats and bags and moving of chairs. Fraser sank himself down into his T-shirt neck; tonight's featured the slogan 'Pigs Might Fly' accompanied by an unlikely picture of cartoon pigs smoking joints. Fraser was not giving me 'joint-smoking' vibes and he now seemed to be rather intimidated by the volume of women he found himself surrounded with.

Margot indicated the notepads. 'Just a little "giveaway" for the evening,' she said. 'In case anyone wants to write things down – future dates, useful contacts, that sort of thing. I've written my number on the inside, so everyone has it.'

Annie smiled politely, but Wren thanked Margot and tucked the pad inside her tote bag. Wren, I thought, looked a little less brown tonight. She was still make-up free but wearing a bright yellow scarf tied loosely, which contrasted with her hair and made her skin glow. Annie looked ruffled. She was what Dex would have called 'built for comfort', well-upholstered and with the softness of limb and face that made her look older and happier than she probably was. She was dressed older too, in a pleated blouse and the kind of trousers that were advertised in Sunday supplements as 'slacks'. I wondered about Eddie's evident affair – had he found himself a younger, slimmer version of his wife? Or gone completely off-piste and started seeing a dynamic organiser type? I *really* hoped he wasn't going to turn out to be having an affair with Margot. That kind of neatness wasn't what I expected from life these days.

I sat somewhere between Wren and Margot in looks. Older than Wren but younger than Margot, tall but I didn't have Margot's imperious height. I dressed not to be noticed and had hair of the neither curly nor straight persuasion. In any given gathering I looked as though I was there to make up the numbers.

We all regarded one another glumly across the table. Except for Fraser, who had slumped even further and seemed to be trying to avoid everyone. 'Well,' said Margot eventually. 'How are we all?'

'We all' chorused that we were fine, thanks, against all available evidence.

'Fraser,' Margot barked his name, making him flinch and try to slide even further under the table, 'why don't you tell us about yourself? What brought you to our club? Were you dumped?'

Fraser took another big mouthful of wine and shook his head. 'Not really,' he said.

'Did you dump her?' Annie leaned forward, unknowingly putting one elbow in a spill of the tonic water she'd ordered.

Fraser shook his head again. All the swagger and blokey mateyness he'd shown when it had only been Margot and me was gone, as though, faced by a wall of women, he had lost all confidence. 'I didn't have a date for Valentine's,' he said. 'Nobody wanted to go out with me.' Then he pushed himself a little more upright in his chair and straightened his shoulders. The pigs undulated. 'But that's all right though, isn't it, cos I'm a disappointed valentine too.'

Flynn came in over my shoulder, wiping up Annie's spill. He smelled good again, and there was something rather pleasant about the gentle press of him against me as he moved his cloth over the tabletop.

'How many women did you ask?' Margot arranged her face in lines of concern in front of Fraser.

He slumped even further. 'I don't know any women,' he muttered. 'There weren't anyone to ask.'

The remaining four of us did a kind of round-the-table stare.

'But I'm still disappointed,' Fraser went on, his tone becoming a little more wheedling, a little more self-justifying. 'I mean, not having anyone to shag don't make me exactly happy with my life, know what I mean?'

The stare went round the table again, like an unclaimed bill.

'I'm not sure,' Margot began carefully, 'that you are quite grasping the nature of this group, Fraser. We're meeting as a support group for those who suffered romantic disappointment, not a generalised dissatisfaction with life as a whole.'

'Well, that's not right then.' Fraser stuck out his round chin. 'That's trades discriminations, that is. Just because I'm disappointed all year round, it don't make me ineligible for the club. Makes me *more* eligible, if you asks me. We should change the name.'

'Of the club?' Margot looked taken aback.

'Yeah. It's not just, like, for people who've had a bad Valentine's, is it? Not really. It's for...' He frowned, seeming to mentally grope for a definition. 'It's for *us*,' he finished, with a lack of clarity that made his nickname of Fraze-the-Haze suddenly become obvious.

Wren cautiously raised a hand. 'We're all heartbroken though, aren't we?' she offered. 'Maybe The Heartbreak Club?'

Fraser snorted. 'Sounds like a country and western band.'

I thought of Dexter and felt everything inside me clamp down. 'I don't know,' I said. 'I wouldn't mind dealing out a bit of heartbreak.' Then, in a spirit of honesty, I added, 'If I had anyone to deal it to, of course.'

Margot doodled for a moment, then looked up. 'How about – this?' She'd drawn the same heart that I'd seen on that very first poster, with the knife through the middle, but now it was surrounded by blocky letters spelling out *The Monday Night Heartbreak Club*. 'We can leave it to onlookers to decide whether the heartbreak is being suffered or occasioned by us. Makes us look a little less hopeless, don't you think?'

'What's that supposed to say, then?' Fraser asked. Margot read it out and he curled his lip. 'Bugger me, that's even worse! Now we sounds like a Taylor Swift song.'

Annie raised a cautious hand. 'Something happened to me,' she said. 'I'd like to know what everyone thinks.'

Our attention switched to her so fast that we all got whiplash. 'Of course,' Margot said. 'Go ahead, Annie. We can discuss the naming of the club another time.'

'Well, Eddie went off to work on Wednesday but he forgot his bag – he works over at the meat-packing factory and he always takes his own lunch. He's in the offices, mind, not on the factory floor, so it's sometimes hard for him to get to the canteen. So I rang the main switchboard, just to tell them to let him know that I was putting it in the fridge for tomorrow. And they said...' Her words half-choked off, as though she didn't want them said.

Margot and Wren were leaning forward in identical postures of suspense. Fraser was picking his nails.

'They said he wasn't in.' Annie finally got the words out but with her head pulled back towards her chest, defensively. 'They said he'd booked the day off and he must have forgotten to tell me. Well, I pretended that I'd been daft, and of course he'd told me, I was just having a bit of a senior moment and everything.' Now she looked up at each of us in turn, and her slightly faded hazel eyes were clouded with worry. 'But I really hadn't. He never mentioned it to me. And, if he did have the day off, *why did he make himself a lunch*? It could only be so that I didn't suspect anything.'

'Does he have any hobbies?' Wren asked. 'Might he have taken the day off to do one of those? Golf, or something?'

Annie shook her head sadly. 'His only hobby is watching *Escape to the Country*.' She took a deep breath. 'It's an affair. Of course it is. I don't know why I'm being so silly, trying to find reasons for everything. It's practically textbook, the daft old bugger can't even be original about it! Going to the gym every day...' She looked wistful for a moment. 'He's got some lovely biceps now, mind.'

'Any idea who the other woman is?' Margot was colouring in the corner on her notepad. 'Any suspicions?'

Annie seemed to feel better now that she had put words around her fears. 'Nope. Not a one. I mean, he's an overweight sixty-year-old administration manager who deals with pork by-products; he's hardly Richard Armitage.' Then her face drooped. 'But I love him,' she said, more quietly.

It must be nice, I thought, watching her press her hanky to the corners of her eyes in a genteel dabbing motion, to feel that way about someone. To actually love them so deeply that the thought of losing them caused you pain. *Or to have someone feel like that about you*, whispered the tiny, treacherous voice at the back of my head which sometimes liked to remind me that nobody loved me or ever had. The best I could say about Dex was the fact that he closed the bathroom door when he was in there and he liked the same music as me.

But I'd had someone, a job, a best friend and a life. Now, gradually, everything was falling away from me like when you peel an orange and let those slivers of peel slip to the floor.

'He's talking about taking up cycling,' Annie went on. 'Cycling! Maybe he just wants to show off his legs – he's got very good legs has my Eddie. But I can't be married to a cyclist, not at my age.'

'Are you all right, Fee?' Wren closed the gap between us at the table. 'You're looking a bit aghast.'

'Just thinking,' I muttered. 'I mean, I feel a bit of a fraud really. Poor Annie...' I lowered my voice a little more, but Annie was still busy talking to Margot and showing her pictures of her garden, as far as I could tell. Eddie was, apparently, a demon with the lawn-mower. Fraser was listening in, clearly at a loss for anything to say, twisting his wine glass between his fingers, as though he wished it were a pint.

'But you're heartbroken too,' Wren said urgently. 'There's nothing that makes one experience more valid than another. I mean, *I* ended my own relationship. Jordan would quite happily have carried on seeing me. Does that mean I shouldn't be here?'

I looked at her. There was nothing remarkable about Wren: she was a generic pretty, small, young woman, almost the blue-print for what you'd produce if someone asked you to sketch 'woman in their mid-twenties'. And yet here I was feeling that weird 'included' feeling that I'd had on the first night – as though, somehow, someone *saw* me. 'Of course not,' I said, surprised.

'None of us are happy. Well, except Margot, who doesn't seem as cut up about her divorce as I would have thought...' Wren trailed off as we both looked thoughtfully over at Margot, who was showing Annie photos now. From the exclamations, I think it might have been the Highland cabin. Or the boat, it was hard to tell. 'And you can't quantify unhappiness, can you?'

'I suppose not.'

'How shit does life have to be before you're allowed to say it's shit?' Fraser put in suddenly, surprising us. 'That's what you means, isn't it?'

'Succinct, but true.' Wren smiled at him and, to my astonishment, Fraser blushed. His whole face gained the colour of severe sunburn, he thrust his empty glass onto the middle of the table, stood up and said, 'Got to go, bus to catch, same time next week?' and fled the bar as though we'd threatened to tie him to the table.

'That was unexpected,' Margot said, after a pause in which the surprise at his sudden departure died down. 'Young Fraser doesn't seem to quite know why he's here, does he?'

'I think he thought it would be like shooting fish in a barrel,' I said, rather bitterly. 'Lots of women disappointed in love, gagging for a...' My brain strained for nouns that Fraser might use, but all the ones I could come up with made me sound like a twisted anti-male woman who's convinced anyone with a penis is bad news. '...bloke.' I came up short. 'Maybe he thought joining the club would be a shortcut to getting a girlfriend.'

'He's lonely,' Wren said, again showing more depth of character than I'd had her down for. 'We're all lonely. Aren't we? Isn't that why we're here? It's not so much the disappointment about Valentine's Day, or that we're all heartbroken, it's the fact that we're all on our own now. Apart from you, Annie, of course.'

'And my marriage is looking to be more and more a temporary state of affairs,' said Annie darkly from inside her glass of tonic water.

Gradually the meeting broke up. Annie wanted to get home to check that Eddie had eaten the meal she'd left for him, Wren had work to do and Margot – well, Margot probably wanted to shake Bruce to see if another cottage fell out or something. But they all departed, leaving me sitting at the table and reluctant to head over the road.

I hadn't even had chance to discuss my idea of us actually

doing something useful with the club, whatever we were going to call it.

I bought another glass of wine, and Flynn leaned on the bar towards me. 'You live up there, don't you?' He nodded towards my flat.

'Yes.' I grasped my glass as though it were a lifeline. 'Although "live" is a bit stretched as a term.' I was talking too much; wine did that to me.

Flynn pursed his mouth. 'You were watching me putting the tables out the other day.'

I had a horrible moment where I wondered what else he'd seen at those windows. 'I wasn't watching *you*. I was looking out. At the street.'

He nodded. 'And you lived with that big guy sometimes. Is that the one you split up from right before Valentine's?'

'No, he was just one of my harem. I keep a cupboard full of men up there and swap around,' I said, snappishly. I was disconcerted by this man seeming to know so much about my life and my comings and goings. Had *he* been watching *me*?

'Yes, I used to see him going in and out, during the day, when you were at work,' Flynn went on, fumbling with the card machine. 'He'd have someone different with him every time. Women, sometimes. Does he have a lot of sisters or something?'

My phone slipped from my hand and slithered down behind the bar. Flynn bent to retrieve it, giving me time to compose my expression. I had it smooth and unbothered by the time he came back up again. 'No,' I said evenly. 'No. No sisters.' I drank the wine down in two gulps. 'I have to go now.'

'Would you like me to walk you back?' Dark eyes. He had dark eyes I'd not noticed before behind those gold, round-rimmed glasses. Dark eyes, dark hair and that black uniform, like a shadow of a man moving through the world. Only the white tag on his shirt that proclaimed his name – also in black – gave me something to focus on.

'No, thank you,' I said to his badge. 'I'm fine.'

But neither of us moved. 'So, then. What's the point of your club?' Flynn asked eventually. 'I heard you trying to steer them towards something, last week.'

'I don't know,' I said, tiredly. 'At the moment it's a bunch of us who've had a rubbish time lately, getting together to chat, and they seem happy with that.'

'Hmm.' Flynn picked up the bar towel again and began wiping the surface free from wet rings and scattered peanuts.

'And what does "hmm" mean? What point do you *think* we should have?'

He looked meaningfully at my empty glass. 'I dunno. Some self-help? Something to get you over your romantic disappointments? Otherwise aren't you just reinforcing your own misery?'

'Have you ever thought about being on TV? Because with the level of trite aphorisms you come out with, you'd be an absolute winner on the daytime circuit.' I propped my empty glass carefully in the middle of his newly wiped surface. 'And I'm going home now.'

Flynn nodded. 'Goodnight, Fee,' he said quietly. 'Take care.'

I'd closed the door very, *very* carefully behind me before it occurred to me to wonder what I was supposed to be taking care *of*.

4

I woke in the night thirsty and thick-headed, and groped my way into the bathroom for some paracetamol and water. Fortunately it wasn't far to go: the flat was tiny, converted from an old chemist's shop into three flats over three floors, in which nobody had enough storage space or a bathroom with an opening window. My flat comprised a kitchenette, which looked out over the backyard where bins bred and feral felines yowled the night away, and a miniscule bathroom too small for a bath, and where the shower cubicle rocked if a door slammed. Then the one main room, where our... where *my* bed was supposed to be folded back to make a sofa during the day, but in reality I never bothered and watched TV from the pillows.

I blundered into the bathroom, ran the tap for a few moments and fumbled a couple of tablets out of the pack. The floor wobbled under my feet, giving me a moment of wondering whether the hangover was worse than I thought before I remembered that I'd pulled the bathmat over the loose floorboards so I could ignore them. The landlord wouldn't do anything about it – see rocking shower, electricity that tripped out when it rained, etc. – so there was no point in mentioning it. I'd bought the flamingo-patterned mat to try to cheer up the flat last time Dexter slammed out of my life but it really only made the bathroom floor look as though someone had had a spectacular nosebleed all over it that hadn't washed out. My metaphorical bathmat was equally bloodstained and Gothic, but a lot less easy to replace.

I finished my analysis of the flooring, took my glass of water and went back through to sit on my bed and swallow the tablets. I hadn't drawn the far curtain, which meant I could see out of the window across the street to the wine bar, which was shrouded in darkness now, with only one small blue bulb indicating that a machine was still switched on somewhere inside. I supposed Flynn was happily tucked up in bed somewhere now, sleeping the sleep of the blameless. Probably wearing jet black pyjamas, I thought, making myself smile. I wondered if he took his name tag off at night, or whether he kept it on to help his sleeping partner remember his name.

That made me think about our 'club'. It gave me a kind of itchy feeling in the back of my head, almost as though I could see us all projected five, ten years into the future, all still sitting around that table, sticky drinks and sympathy. Why *were* we meeting? To tell one another horror stories about our dreadful relationships? Misery loving company?

Perhaps it was an overspill from the pep talks at work, all the constant cries for achievement, forward motion, targets – I think someone had used the word *synergy* at one point, and I still didn't know what that meant – that made me want to *do* something. Those little chats did seem to have instilled in me a desire for some kind of results. Funny that, I'd not even really taken much notice when I'd been sitting in that room with fifteen other 'team members' and a whiteboard, but now, in the middle of the night, a desire for targets and an end goal seemed to have crashed over my head and was stopping me sleeping.

Or it may have been the hangover, of course. Alcohol-anxiety, a killer headache and the twisting little knife of guilt at having once again drunk more than I should, all ganging up in the back of my mind to needle me with how insipid I was, how inefficient. How uselessly, pointlessly *dull*.

I leaned back against my pillows, gulping down the water and remembering that warm, included feeling that I'd had earlier that night. Here were people who were offering me friendship and understanding. They weren't seeing a wishy-washy drunk, they were seeing the Fee that I *could be*. They hadn't had the chance yet to see the numerous ways in which I was a total fuck-up, of course.

A renewed sense of purpose trickled through my veins. I could *be* that Fee they thought I was, at least for the purposes of being in the club. Once a week I could pretend, couldn't I? Reinvent myself to be the purposeful, ambitious person that I might once have been, before Dexter, before... well, before conception probably. The others would believe that I was whoever I said I was – all I had to do was act like it. I couldn't give Margot a run in the leadership stakes but I could be the ideas man.

My knuckles tightened around the water glass. We could make this club something. We shouldn't be meeting to complain, to moan about our circumstances and become bitter while watching elderly men play increasingly competitive table games. We could DO something. We could help one another.

I dragged my phone out. I still kept it under my pillow, because Dexter had liked me to return all his messages promptly, although I didn't know why. Nobody was going to be messaging me during the night any more, were they? After a few moments thinking, I messaged Margot.

> I think we ought to try to help Annie. There must be a way we can find out who Eddie is having his affair with, at least. If she knows, she can take it from there.

My finger hesitated over the send button, as I had a horrible flashback to Flynn telling me about Dex and the way he'd casually dropped in the fact that he'd brought women back to the flat. I typed:

> And maybe we could get some kind of revenge on the people that made us join the club?

Then I erased that. Revenge wasn't what I wanted. It wasn't in the image of the Fee I wanted to be.

> It would give the club a kind of purpose.

And I realised that, for probably the first time in my life, I actually wanted to achieve something. Not just go through the motions or follow the crowd. I wanted to be *useful*. To have, as I'd said, a purpose. Helping Annie could be our purpose.

I was sitting rereading the message, trying to work out whether what I'd said was really what I meant, when I managed to press the send button instead of scrolling down, and threw the phone onto the bed in disgust. Honestly. It was three in the morning. Now Margot would think I sat up all night obsessing over being single, as though I didn't have an actual life to be getting on with. It rather blew the illusion that I wanted to create, of Strong, Purposeful Fee, and replaced her with Insomniac Fee. Overthinking Fee.

Bugger.

I got back into bed and lay down, trying to will the headache to disappear and, to my surprise, my phone pinged a message.

That is a very good idea. Let me have a think.
See you soon!

So Margot was awake at this godforsaken hour too, was she? Well. Okay then. Maybe I hadn't cocked up as much as I thought.

I snuggled down into the duvet, feeling curiously better for knowing that someone else was up and answering messages. It took me back to nights lying awake next to Dex, while he snored and I tried to work out how I was feeling about my life. If I'd nudged him to try to get him to talk, he would mutter something incomprehensible, grab any part of my anatomy he could reach and instantly start up the wood-chipper snore again, as though I were a human comfort pillow. I'd sometimes felt as though I was the only person alive in the world on those nights.

But now I knew Margot was awake too.

I wriggled my way around in the bed. It wasn't the world's most comfortable sleeping arrangement – the hinge that closed it up into a sofa was in the wrong place and I had to arch my lower back over it – but I'd got used to it now. As I wriggled, I saw a reflected glow in the window and realised that a light had gone on across the road, above the wine bar. Just a faint light, as though someone had turned on a small lamp down a corridor, but noticeable. After a few seconds, that went out and darkness resumed, but I was still staring at those blank, bland windows opposite.

Did Flynn live over the business? I didn't know much about the wine bar, only that it had changed hands recently and been closed for a while for the revamp. There must be a warren of rooms above, left over from when it had been the pub, so presumably someone lived there. Well, given the light, that or they had a very tidy-minded poltergeist.

I closed my eyes again. Me, Margot and – someone. I didn't

want to think that it might be Flynn, but it pleased me to imagine that dark-eyed man roaming the network of rooms above his workplace like a clockwork automaton, awake and alert and waiting for dawn. Suddenly the night didn't feel like quite such a lonely place.

I was drifting off to sleep when I jerked awake again. Had I *really* suggested that we use the club to help Annie? What the hell could we do? Shit happened, we'd all been treated badly, that was something there wasn't any real solution for. Although, I thought, as I punched the pillow and tried to get comfortable again, Annie could probably benefit from chatting to someone about the ending of a forty-year romance – to help her reframe a new future. Had I really suggested that we find out who Eddie was being unfaithful with? What the *hell*...

I slumped into sleep again, to new dreams of Inspector Gadget-type shenanigans, lots of secret following and flying cars, plots and planning and creeping around corners.

5

Work was hell. Demi was working from home again and since her bombshell about moving to Peterborough we'd not had a lot of contact. Maybe that was why I was embracing the cautiously titled Monday Night Heartbreak Club quite so ferociously. It was a fixed point now; Monday nights I knew I'd have people to talk to, and I was slightly scared of how easily it had happened and how much I was looking forward to it.

Of course, there wasn't much else in my life to look forward to. Dexter had maintained radio silence, but that was nothing new. He'd be waiting for me to text, to beg him to come back, to promise all kinds of exotic sexual practices and nightly home-cooking if he'd only – what? What had Dexter really ever brought to my life? Apart from a presence, a smell, loads of dirty laundry and constantly disturbed nights, I couldn't think of anything, and all of those things could easily be replaced if I got a Labrador. Although a Labrador probably wouldn't have all those dodgy friends or come home at three in the morning rambling incoherently and full of braggadocio, testosterone and cocaine.

My manager Had Words with me about productivity, turn-around time, length of calls and whether I was offering value for money. Since there wasn't much I could say to any of this – what did she expect me to do? – I nodded and smiled and pretended I'd try harder. All the time in the back of my mind, like a savage earworm, ran the thought that if I lost my job I wouldn't be able to afford the rent. I could go home, yes, back to my parents in York, who would receive me gratefully because, after all, hadn't I proved their point? I *couldn't* manage by myself out in the big wide world as they always said. I should stay with them, find myself a nice little job and contribute to the household, which comprised them and my feckless brother. My 'nice little job' would mean my contribution could provide him with pocket money to enable him to vanish on a weekly basis and turn up back at the house with a tottering new girlfriend who would spend several days holed up with him in his room, giggling and sending out for food, then disappear, never to be seen again, and be replaced with a new giggler in a crop top the following week.

My parents indulged my brother. It wasn't their fault. But I'd have a roof over my head.

I sat back down in my cubicle and vowed that I'd live in a tent rather than go through that again. Maybe Peterborough wasn't so bad and I could camp out on Demi's sofa for a while?

Then they switched the calls back through to me again and I was overtaken by the need to sell household insurance to people who didn't want or need it for the rest of the day.

Five o'clock meant home time. Back to the dingy flat, where the couple downstairs had progressed to throwing things and having noisy make-up sex. Back to staring out of the window.

'Hello. Are you having an extraordinary meeting?'

'No, I'm having a large white wine.'

I didn't know why I was here. Other than I didn't want to sit in on yet another evening, and I'd run out of alcohol in the flat.

Flynn poured me a small glass and then leaned on the bar as though he had all the time in the world.

'So, how's life?'

I thought about the question as I drank my wine. 'I'm not entirely sure. But I think I proposed that we find out who Annie's husband is having an affair with, so there's that.'

Flynn widened his eyes at me. 'Wow. Really? That's very proactive of you.'

'Don't, you sound like my boss. She's all about the proactive and the dynamic, and it's rubbish.' I gulped some more wine. 'I do think we should help Annie, though. If she knows more about the affair she might find it's easier to come to terms with. She'll be in a position of power.' Then, because something about Flynn's apparent disbelief that I could have any influence made me want to fly over the top of his scepticism in a vehicle made of whimsy, 'We can always offer to set fire to his trousers, if she wants.'

'Will you tell her that's what you're doing?'

'I think she'll know. The flames and the smell of scorching M&S underpants will be the giveaway.'

He stared at me silently for a moment. 'I meant, are you going to tell her you're tracking her husband, not about the setting fire to his trousers, which, as you so eloquently put it, will become obvious in time.'

'Oh.' My confidence left me in the face of his matter-of-factness and I felt myself go red. 'I don't know. I have to talk to Margot and Wren first. I just had the idea, I can't go off and do it by myself.'

'Why not?'

'Because I have a job that I absolutely will lose if I take any more time off. They've run out of sympathy. Especially because,' I admitted to the bottom of my now-empty glass, 'I'm really shit at it. I hate it. Call-centre work was the only thing I could find, though, and it covers the bills.'

'Oh dear, you are having a bad time,' Flynn said cheerily. 'I'd offer you a job here, but I don't think you'd like the conditions.'

'Working with you? Nope, you're right there. I couldn't work with a smarmy arse like you.'

'Ha.' He wandered off to go and serve a trendy young couple who were dressed to the nines. I wondered where they were off to. Then I wondered what their relationship looked like, whether he was cheating on her or she on him, or whether they were totally loved up, as they appeared to be, and a pang of jealousy hit me like sniper fire, strafing my nerve endings until I had to turn away.

Flynn didn't come back. I wasn't even sure that I wanted him to, but he got busy, serving and sorting bottles and loading the dishwasher, and I'd finished my wine, so I went home.

The silence buzzed. Even the couple downstairs had entered their refractory period. The shops were closed, there was no traffic apart from the odd car bumping up or down the hill on its way somewhere. Everyone seemed to be where they wanted to be right now. I picked up my phone.

'Margot, I've been thinking.' It was her voicemail, but better than sitting in silence. 'If we can find out Eddie's usual routine from Annie – carefully, so we don't let on what we're doing – then maybe the three of us could take it in turns to keep an eye on him? Maybe we could take photos? Then maybe we can tell Annie what we know, but we can do it in a supportive way, so that we're there when she finds out who it is, and she's got us there to talk to about what she does next? Maybe. Anyway. See you on Monday.'

I hesitated. My finger hovered over the 0 button, and I fought with myself not to delete the message which had, after all, mostly been maybes stuck together with supposition and not quite given the impression of Purposeful Fee that I'd intended. *Sod it*. I carried on. 'Oh, and of course Fraser might want to be involved too, but then again he might think it's too revengey for him, being a man. Okay then, bye.'

There. I took a deep breath and the unaccustomed feeling of accomplishment settled on my head like a crown. See, world? I *could* do it. I could have ideas...

The phone rang five minutes later. 'Hello, Fee, it's Margot. Are you free tomorrow evening? Only, I've had a bit of a think about what you said.'

All the poise and certainty plummeted. What had I said? Had I just been stupid? But it was only the club, I hadn't proposed holding strip nights in the wine bar. Was I free? A kind of bitterness scratched at the back of my eyes. 'Yes, I'm free.'

'Then let's meet in the usual place. Oh, and let's not mention this to Annie yet, shall we? I'll phone the others and ask them to come. We'll all have a little conflab and maybe come up with something? Would that suit?'

There was an eagerness in Margot's voice, as though she was looking forward to it, and it struck me suddenly that perhaps she was as lonely as I was. Newly single, having to adjust to a whole new way of life – not that it was new for me, more a recurring reality, but it was still an adjustment. I felt that glimmer of warmth again, not happiness that someone else was as miserable as I was, but a snatch of fellow-feeling. It *wasn't* just me. Other people were alone too.

'I'll see you tomorrow,' I said, knowing that I sounded jaunty and in control again and rather liking it.

'Wonderful.' And Margot hung up. I sat for a moment, staring around the flat, and then went to tidy the kitchen.

6

To my surprise, Margot arrived with Fraze-the-Haze. 'He asked if he could have a lift,' she said to my raised eyebrows while Fraser was at the bar. 'And it turns out that he doesn't live that far from me, and I know his mother slightly.' She watched Fraser, who was trying to initiate banter with Flynn, a man so far removed from banter that he was practically Trappist. 'We met through work,' Margot went on, slightly dreamily.

'Oh? What is it that you do?' I asked politely. I had Margot down as a woman who lunches and attends every work function of her husband's looking groomed and together.

'I'm a barrister,' she said, still vague, and I nearly swallowed my tongue. 'Wren should be here in a... ah. There she is.'

Wren pushed at the door, reversing in with a large cardboard box in her arms which she set down on the table with the air of one expecting a fanfare.

'What the fuck's that?' Fraser came over carrying a long glass of something for himself and a wine for Margot, which he handed over with ceremony.

'Everything I could get from Annie without being obvious.'

Wren lifted the lid. 'I popped over this morning, after Margot rang. It's all right,' she said to our intakes of breath, 'I was subtle. I didn't tell her what I wanted it for. In fact, some of it I stole off her shelf. Oh, it's all right, I'll take it back, I'll tell her I picked it up by accident.'

Wren took out a framed photograph of a man, some other loose photographs and one of the notepads that Margot had given us. 'I managed to get some details of his timetable too, so I wrote them down here.'

Margot bestowed a smile. She was the kind of woman who 'bestowed' most of her expressions, wearing them as though the front of her face was an advertising hoarding. 'Well done!'

Wren's cheeks glowed. 'Thank you. It wasn't too hard to get Annie to talk to me – she's got all those groups and clubs but she says that nobody there knows anything about her circumstances, so she can't really talk to them the way she can to us.' She glanced around at Fraser and me. 'It's really sad,' she said. 'For the whole forty years that they've been together, Eddie has always bought her flowers and a card for Valentine's Day. And this year he forgot. She said that he bought her some the next day, but it's not the same, is it?'

I thought of Dexter, who had never bought me anything for Valentine's Day. Or birthdays, Christmas or even just because. He'd always been too busy trying to break out as a TikTok-sensation MMA fighter, while making what money he did from stealing cars and drug dealing.

'She's trying to be all stiff-upper-lip about it, but she was crying when she was showing me the pictures.' Wren laid out the photographs on the table. There, all in white, was a very young Annie with a tall, handsome man on her arm, in an immaculate suit and buttonhole. She looked radiant and I had another belt of that vicious envy. Then more photos of an increasingly ageing Eddie – doing DIY, on holiday in Paris, mowing the lawn.

'How did you get these? I mean, what did you say? You can hardly wander into someone's house and empty their albums without a good excuse.' I flipped among the pictures trying to find one that didn't look like contented domestic bliss to make me feel better.

'I told her I was writing an article about marriage through the ages.' Wren put her notepad down. 'I'm a journalist. I write articles for the weekly magazine in the local paper, so I think she believed me.'

At this rate, Fraser was going to turn out to be an astronaut who did brain surgery in his spare time. I felt like such a loser suddenly, with my call-centre job and my pathetic three rooms across the road.

'And, of course, it meant I could make notes. Only they weren't really notes on what it was like to get married in 1985; I was writing down what she told me about Eddie. It's *amazing* how much people say without realising.' Wren pulled out the photograph in the frame. 'This was Eddie last month, the most up-to-date picture Annie had. He works at Drayton's out on the York road, eight thirty to five, four days a week, finishing early on Fridays.' She consulted her notepad. 'He goes to the gym every morning at seven for an hour, then straight to work.' Wren looked up at us. 'And if you believe that, you'll believe anything.'

'So he's got a bit on the side, yeah?' Fraser moved his chair over and when I looked across, I saw Flynn had come alongside him and was wiping the table in a desultory way, clearly listening in for all he was worth. 'Maybe... maybe he's not happy, yeah? Maybe she's not giving him everything he wants, if you know what I mean.' Fraser stared around at our blank faces. 'Not enough sex,' he muttered into his glass now.

'Yes, we fully comprehend your meaning, Fraser,' Margot snapped, and Fraser's ears got a bit red. 'But don't you think that a man who's been married to his wife for forty years has a duty to raise an issue if he's unhappy? To talk about it *to his wife*, rather than go off and find another woman?'

All of Fraser's visible skin had now gone so red that I was surprised the drink in his glass wasn't bubbling. 'Dunno,' he muttered, as though a favourite teacher had suddenly started to pick on him in class. 'S'pose so.'

'And if a satisfactory conclusion for both parties couldn't be reached, then he should end the marriage *first*, decently and cleanly, *before* taking up with another partner?'

Wren and I looked at one another and pulled similar 'blimey, she's fierce' faces. I wondered whether Bruce had perhaps not always been faithful to Margot, and sympathy tugged at me along with that memory of Flynn telling me about Dexter and his 'visiting women'. While I'd not really kidded myself that he'd stay faithful, bringing them to *my* flat to cheat was disgusting behaviour. And it wouldn't have occurred to him to change the bedding either.

Meanwhile, Flynn had practically cleaned the varnish off the table. 'Why don't you just sit down?' I suggested to him. 'If you're going to eavesdrop, you might as well do it comfortably.'

'He's not a Disappointed Valentine!' Margot pulled herself back from her haranguing of Fraser, who had practically crawled inside his glass by now, and stared at Flynn, who'd fetched another chair from the next table and was squeezing it in between Fraser and me with a shocking amount of eagerness.

'I am really,' Flynn said, leaning forward with his black-clad elbows on the table. 'I didn't get any kind of valentine, disappointing or otherwise. I was working in here all day and we stayed open late. Not so much as a sniff of romance, unless you count the quite frankly massively over-the-top amounts of body spray I had to put up with. It smelled like the cheap aftershave section of Boots the Chemist in here all night.'

'And we're not Disappointed Valentines any more,' Wren pointed out. 'We agreed. We're the Monday Night Heartbreak Club now.'

Fraser looked disgruntled. 'Why can't we be the Vengeance Squad?' he asked. 'That's got a ring to it, that has. Vengeance Squad. Like a film.'

'Because that sounds like it should be on an arrest warrant.' Margot gave Fraser a stern look and he reddened around the ears again.

'Or a T-shirt,' Flynn said and grinned. 'Maybe we could have club T-shirts?'

'You can't have The Monday Night Heartbreak Club on a T-shirt!' Fraser's disgruntlement had almost ignited his hair now. 'People will think I does line dancing and stuff like that and bang goes my credibility in me online forums if anyone sees me.'

We all jointly lapsed into a momentary silence, clearly wondering about Fraser's current credibility status in any given forum.

Flynn coughed. 'Anyway,' he said. 'Can I join?'

'But you didn't come to the meetings!' Margot almost wailed.

'I couldn't. I was working.'

'And he sort of did,' I added, not quite sure why I was so keen to support Flynn joining the group, other than I was tired of him making judgey remarks to me whenever he saw me. If he was going to be supercilious, he could be it to the whole group and stop singling me out. 'He was hanging over us like a cheap Christmas decoration the whole time.'

'Oy. I'm a lot of things but I'm not cheap,' Flynn said, and winked at me, which made me narrow my eyes in his direction.

'Plus, and this might be the biggie, I have a lot of free time during the day. The wine bar only opens at six, except on special occasions. Like Valentine's Day,' he added with a hint of resentment.

'All right, all right. I suppose one more member won't hurt.' Margot sounded begrudging now, but Flynn gave me a beaming smile as though she'd welcomed him in with tea and cake.

'Plus we needs another bloke,' Fraser muttered. 'I don't want to be a sex symbol.'

'Token representative member of your sex, is what you mean, Fraser,' Margot said, but not in an unfriendly way, then turned to me. 'So, as this is your idea, Fee, do you have a plan?'

I hadn't, but the way everyone crouched low over the table as though we were MI5 made me come up with one *really* fast. 'Wren says that Eddie goes to the gym every morning, yes? And it's early?'

'Seven o'clock,' Wren said and shuddered. 'Awful. Nobody should be that enthusiastic for exercise at that time in the morning. It isn't even *daylight!*'

'Do we know which gym?'

'The new one, on the outskirts of Malton, Annie said. She's always asleep when he leaves.'

'Then one of us should join the gym and be there at the same time. We can find out if he actually does go and, if he does, what he gets up to while he's there,' I said triumphantly.

There was a resounding lack of people volunteering to get to the gym before seven in the morning.

'Well, I can't do it,' Margot said. 'I have to be preparing for work at that time.'

'I don't do mornings,' Wren said sharply. 'Seriously. I don't. If you want someone to follow him home from work or find out where he goes in the evenings, I'm your woman, but mornings – nope.'

'We could really do with someone in the gym and someone watching outside too,' I said carefully, slightly upset at the turn things were taking. 'In case he gets away from whoever's inside.'

Fraser sighed. 'Right,' he said. 'I'm the token fat bastard. I'll pretend to join the gym; everyone will believe that. Besides, I could stand to do some proper exercise.' Then he glared at us, his ears shining like beacons. 'But someone has to sub me the joining fee, I'm broke.'

'I don't mind sitting outside, doing the following to and from the gym,' I said. There was no way I could afford to cover his fees, but I didn't mind being incognito in a car. 'As long as Eddie doesn't hang around; I have to be at work for nine. But I'll need someone with me, in case we have to follow him, because he might head off somewhere on foot and then I'd have to park the car.'

'I can come with you.' Flynn grinned. 'It's not that busy round here in the early morning; I think I can spare the time.'

'And I'm going to need a lift,' Fraser said. 'I haven't got a car,' he added, unsurprisingly.

'Right. So, tomorrow morning, Flynn and I will pick you up at six thirty, Fraser,' I said, far more decisively than I felt. 'We'll drop you off at the gym. We can sit outside and pretend to be...'

'We could snog,' Flynn said cheerily. 'Pretend to be a couple, you know.'

I glared at him. 'For an hour? No thank you. I'll bring a flask of coffee.'

'Oh, yes, or that.'

'Do I get a snog?' Fraser asked hopefully.

'No. What *you* get is an hour on an elliptical trainer, keeping an eye on Eddie.' Margot was glaring now too. 'I'll pay for a month's trial for you.' She had her phone in her hand and the gym website open. 'That's the shortest period you can join for, unfortunately. And if Eddie makes a break for it, you'll have to make your own way home because these two' – she waved a hand at Flynn and me – 'will be following him.'

'I'm going to need my bus fare too then.'

Margot rolled her eyes. 'Fraser, do you have any independence at all? I mean, what do you *do* with yourself? Why haven't you got transport? Why haven't you got a job?'

Fraser hunched himself down as though he wanted to become invisible. 'I has to help Mum,' he said.

'No, you don't. I know your mother; she's the last woman on earth to need any of the kind of help that you could provide,' Margot snapped.

'Yeah, but she's got my sister's kids to look after now, with my sister being, well, you know. Mum don't hold it against you, by the way, she says you did everything you could, but they'd got her holding the stuff on camera, so...'

Wren and I tried very hard not to let our eyes meet. I could see her bending her head and I was also considering the wooden tabletop as though I were performing some kind of tree ring analysis. Beside me, Flynn's eyebrows were so high that his glasses had dislodged.

'And the kids can be proper little tw—buggers,' Fraser went on. 'Sometimes Mum needs an extra pair of hands and someone who can really shout. So I helps her out. I gets benefits, cos of the dyslexia,' he finished.

Nobody knew what to say. Finally Margot came out with, 'I'm very glad that your mother is managing, and I'm only sorry that your sister got such a protracted sentence.'

'You did your best,' Fraser said, equably, clearly not having the faintest idea what a 'protracted sentence' might be, while the rest of us kept our faces very, very neutral and tried not to breathe.

'So, you live at home with your mum?' Wren said at last, as though this were a dinner party conversation.

'Yeah. Like I said, I wanted a girlfriend but I don't know any girls. I tried a few online, but they all told me to fu—to go away.'

The solid silence descended again.

'You must know some females, surely?' Wren persisted. I tried to kick her under the table but missed and hit Margot's bag. It felt as though she had bricks in there. 'Didn't you stay in touch with any of your schoolfriends?'

Fraser shrugged so deeply that it looked as though today's T-shirt – the *Star Wars* one again – was trying to eat him. 'Didn't go to school much,' he muttered. 'Dyslexia an' all. And I never meets *anyone*.'

'You met us,' Margot joined in now, breezily.

'Yeah, well, my mate Scousie...'

'Scousie the Lousie?' Margot asked, in a rather pointed way, I thought.

'Nah, Scousie's already his nickname – he's really called Gerald – well, he's my mate, and *he* said that joining a disap-pointed valentines' thing would be like shooting fish in a barrel. He said it would be full of women desperate for a bloke and I'd be in with a shout.'

More silence. This one was painful.

'You can report back to your friend, Scousie' – Margot spoke so slowly and clearly that she sounded like an elocution lesson – 'that *no* woman is desperate for a man.'

I thought about Dexter. I thought about meeting him at a friend's party, how he and his mates had gate-crashed and I'd thought it was funny and brave and when he'd homed in on me and started drinking out of my glass, I'd admired his effrontery. I'd thought it was a sign that he was a man who knew what he wanted and went after it. I didn't realise that it was a sign that he was a man who knew desperation when he saw it. I didn't say any of this to Margot or Fraser, of course. It had been a lesson hard learned and I still wasn't entirely certain that I'd taken it quite to heart.

'On the other hand' – Wren broke the awkwardness – 'it must have taken quite a lot of courage to turn up here.'

We all stared at her.

'I know *I* was nervous, coming to the first meeting, not knowing who I might meet or what it might all be about. And I'm used to – well, having to meet lots of different people, being a journalist and everything. So it must have been worse for you, Fraser.' She took a mouthful of her drink. 'I think you were very brave to turn up, whatever your reasons for coming.'

Now we were all gaping, but I could see the activity behind the eyes. My own mind was racing. I'd exceeded nineteen to the dozen and was rapidly approaching ninety to the dozen. *Brave. Walking into a meeting of new people, not knowing what might happen. Not knowing whether they might laugh or sneer or dismiss me as not disappointed enough.* I found myself sitting up straighter. *I'd been brave. For the first time in my life, I'd been brave. I'd been the Fee that I wanted to be.*

I ignored the fact that alcohol had had quite a lot to do with that bravery. Fraser was displaying a paint-chart worth of colours: his ears were red, his cheeks were practically purple and his neck had gone an odd shade of yellowish-green. The silence was now broken by the sound of everyone gulping their drinks much too fast.

'Well, anyway,' Flynn glanced over at the door, where two men in suits had come in and were pointing around at tables, clearly trying to decide where to sit, 'I'd better go back to the bar. I'll come over tomorrow at six thirty, Fee?'

I looked down at my half-finished wine and let the newly

acknowledged feeling of courage trickle through me. 'I'll be ready. Scribble me down your address, Fraser, so I can pick you up.' I looked around until Wren tore off a page of her notepad.

'Er, I can't.' Fraser entered more deeply into his relationship with his T-shirt. 'But I can tell you where I live.'

As Flynn pushed his chair back over to the table where it belonged, Margot gathered her bag from under the table and Wren squeaked about how exciting this all was and not at all what she'd expected when she'd joined the club, I wrote down Fraser's address and listened to his slightly garbled instructions as to how to find his house. None of us seemed to want to talk about Wren's insight, but, to me, it felt as though our smiles were a little broader, our actions a little bit more assured. Especially Fraser's, once his colour returned to normal.

'We've got gnomes,' he said. 'Mum's really big on gnomes, so you can't miss us. End of the cul-de-sac, down the alleyway, and I'll meet you out there. Don't want to wake the arseh—I mean, everyone else in the road.'

It was only when I went up the fishy-smelling stairs to my flat that I realised I was smiling. A proper relaxed grin sat on my face, broadening as I opened the door and collapsed onto the sofa bed. It felt odd, but very, very good.

7

'It's down this road.' Flynn had the maps app open on his phone.

'It can't be. There's nothing here.' I swung the wheel to turn the car out of the narrow lane.

'They're putting in a new Aldi,' Fraser said from the back seat. 'Mum loves a good Aldi.'

'Drive a little way down,' Flynn suggested as we sat under the breaking dawn. 'Look, there are other cars heading that way, there must be something.'

'What does Eddie drive?' I asked idly, turning the car again to follow a little Fiat down the barely made-up roadway.

'Skoda,' said Fraser, promptly. 'Scala. New one. What? I knows about cars and it was in one of them pictures that Wren had.'

We bumped a bit further on, until we could see a brightly lit building up ahead. It bore an astonishing resemblance to a tin-roofed barn, but had huge full-length windows down one wall, emitting the kind of glow that made it look as though a gigantic UFO had set down in a car park.

'That'll be it,' Flynn said, as we stared, our retinas frying. 'Fraser, you're on.'

Fraser hesitated. 'I don't really know what to do,' he said, holding his rolled-up towel, which contained his 'gym kit'. 'I've never been in one of them places before.'

'Margot's got you an induction session,' I said, checking my messages. 'You just have to go in and ask for Minnie, and she...'

'Or he,' put in Flynn, and Fraser winced.

'Or he, will get you going from there. You'll be fine. And the place will be full of women, so you might get your chance to chat some of them up.'

Fraser muttered, 'Huh', but he got out of the car and began crossing the car park to the behemoth of a building, with his towel under his arm, like a child off to their first swimming lesson.

'Do we have to do this every day?' Flynn asked, breaking the awkward silence that resulted.

'Until we can find out something, yes.' I yawned. 'So I really hope Fraser is going to be able to give us something to go on this morning. I can't take this early start for too long.'

We jointly gazed at the nuclear-standard illuminated building in front of us. Through one of the windows, I could see a row of fixed bikes, two of which were being ridden by men with very serious faces, and a very slender girl was running on a treadmill to one side while doing something on her phone at the same time.

'I'm going to park around the side, out of the way,' I said, starting the engine. 'We don't want to be spotted, especially if we're going to be here the whole month. People might get suspicious.' Besides, I didn't think I could stand to watch everyone dedicatedly getting fit, not when I was craving a Mars bar.

'There are other cars.' Flynn indicated the car park, which was studded with cars and bikes.

'But not with people in. We look like parents waiting at school pick-up, and I don't think Fraser would get away with looking like a five-year-old on his first day.'

'Fraser,' Flynn said carefully, after a moment. 'He's a bit... He doesn't seem to know much about women, does he? Has he asked you out yet?'

'No!' I fumbled behind me, found the flask of coffee that I'd made in the pre-dawn darkness and pulled it out. 'Why would he?'

'Because Wren is gay, Margot's old enough to be his mother and Annie's married.' Flynn took the cup I handed him.

'Wow. I'm clearly not even the best of a very weak bunch.'

'I didn't mean that.' Flynn looked at me. 'You're very eligible, even though you don't seem to think so.'

In the resulting quiet, a distant bass beat throbbed. The girl on the treadmill was texting, one handed. Another car drew into the car park and I put my coffee down. It was a Skoda being driven by an older man. 'I think that's Eddie.'

Flynn and I watched as the car was reversed several times in order to place it neatly in the middle of the parking space, and a middle-aged man got out. He had a holdall with him which he swung jauntily as he crossed the car park and entered the gym, where, I noted, he was greeted by the guy on reception as though they knew one another.

'Well, at least he was telling the truth about the gym.' Flynn drained his plastic cup.

'We'd better keep an eye on the door in case it's a ruse. He might turn straight around and come out again.'

But Eddie didn't. Flynn and I drank coffee and discovered a mutual love of obscure nineties bands, scented surface cleaners and the local supermarket, and a joint hatred of build-it-yourself furniture. All of this turned our early morning excursion into a moderately pleasant experience. Flynn wasn't quite as cuttingly sarcastic as I'd imagined; he was at times genuinely funny. But even so, we ran out of conversation after an hour and I'd slumped down into the driver's seat in a got-up-too-early daze, when Flynn nudged me.

'Fraser's coming. Quick, look as though we've had a miserable time, otherwise he's going to be jealous. Blimey, he's pink!'

Fraser was indeed trudging down the entryway of the gym, in the company of a woman who looked as though she could have lifted him with one hand. Her tan glowed, her leggings were sprayed on and her eyelashes were so long that I could almost feel the updraught from here.

Fraser looked as though he'd eaten a radioactive vindaloo. He was scarlet all the way down and blowing like a cart horse after a heavy day's ploughing. He got into the back of the car and instantly lay down across the seat. 'Get me out of here before she kills me,' he said.

'We have to wait for Eddie.' I handed him my coffee cup, which he couldn't take because his hand was shaking so badly. 'We need to know where he goes from here.'

'Eddie,' said Fraser, with heavy emphasis from his prone position, 'is in there going like a McLaren round the Nürburgring. Minnie says she's never seen such good progress.'

'And what's Minnie like?' I asked.

'The Spanish Inquisition, with added torture.' Fraser sat up slowly. 'Bugger me sideways, my head's spinning.' He breathed carefully for a moment. 'She says she's looking forward to seeing me tomorrow,' he said, glumly.

'On the bright side, Eddie might be heading for his girl-friend's house right now.' Flynn pointed at the doors to the gym, where Eddie was bidding the young man on reception a cheery farewell. 'So you might not have to come back.'

'Margot made me promise to use the full month,' Fraser said, even more dolefully. 'She said she wants her money's worth.'

'Great, does that mean I'm committed to this for the whole month too?' I yawned, a jaw-creaker of a yawn.

'We do need to find out what Eddie's up to,' Flynn pointed out. 'And it would be extraordinarily convenient if we established it on our first day.'

'Oh God,' Fraser and I groaned, in a Greek chorus of misery.

We followed Eddie's car at a careful distance as he drove out of the car park and straight to Drayton's. We didn't follow him all the way in but turned for home at the entrance. 'Bit of a bust, then,' Fraser observed. 'Unless he's bonking someone at work,' he added, hopefully.

'Well, I'm not putting on a funny walk and pretending to be a factory inspector.' Flynn gazed out of the window. 'How would we find out?'

'Wren says he can't be, because Annie knows everyone who works there.' I checked again on my page of handwritten notes that Wren had given me. 'He's worked there for nearly forty years and they haven't even had any new female staff for the last ten. Plus, someone would have told her; she's very friendly with the managing director's secretary, and *she* wouldn't have hesitated to spill the beans.'

'You've got a crib sheet?' Flynn took the notes from the centre console. 'Wow. You're all really going into this full throttle, aren't you?'

'Something to do, in't it?' Fraser piped up. 'Otherwise, I'm just home gaming in my bedroom.'

'I think Margot and Wren are using it as a distraction from their own circumstances too.' I steered towards home. I was going to drop Flynn and Fraser and go straight to work. 'And you offered.' I snatched my papers back from Flynn.

'So, what's your excuse?' He was giving me that look again, an almost heavy look, as though he and I were in on some secret that mustn't be spoken aloud.

'I'm bored,' I said, surprising myself. 'Work is rubbish, my best friend is moving away, and Dex – well, I've not seen him since Valentine's Day and I don't want to see him anyway,' I added honestly. 'So I'm at a lot of loose ends.'

Fraser and Flynn shared the last of the coffee as I drove back to town, with the sun climbing its reluctant way into the sky, using the grey clouds as a ladder. Dex still hadn't tried to text me – obviously I had him blocked, but he usually messaged me through any app he had and I hadn't blocked him on all of them; I needed to know when he wanted to come back. This time, it seemed, he didn't. Or he was punishing me by maintaining radio silence; that thought had also occurred to me. Perhaps he thought I'd miss him more and be so apologetic that I'd let him trample all over me if he didn't speak to me for a while.

Who was I kidding? I always let him back. It was just that this time I didn't seem to be missing him as much as usual. By now I'd normally weakened and messaged him in the middle of the night, halfway through my second bottle of wine, begging him to come home, but I realised with a gut-punch that I hadn't even *thought* of him for a couple of days, except in a negative way.

I let the men out at the wine bar. Fraser was going to wait to get his breath and the bus back, and I immediately turned around and headed for work, where I was five minutes late.

My manager looked at me with raised eyebrows. I mouthed 'sorry,' and sat down, putting on my headset, logging in on the computer and wondering how long I could keep this up. Getting up at five thirty in order to be showered, dressed and ready for work, and then sitting in a car park for an hour while Fraser worked himself into cardiac arrest was not sustainable.

Maybe we could force Eddie's hand somehow?

'Phoebe, your light is on.'

I shook my head and took the call, yawning as I did so.

Eddie went to the gym, then straight to work. At least, he'd done that *today*. Perhaps he had to maintain a presence at the gym in case anyone checked up on him; everyone there clearly knew him and would vouch for the fact he went. But maybe there were days when he *didn't* go...

'Phoebe!' The voice came from behind me and made me jump. 'I think we'd better have a word, don't you?'

Damn. My caller had hung up without my even noticing. I sighed, stood up and followed my supervisor into the dreaded Back Office.

8

'So they've fired me.' I slumped over my arms on the wine bar counter. 'Which, in a way, is a good thing, because now the worst has happened. But in another way, obviously, it's a very, very bad thing indeed.'

Flynn was mixing cocktails. It was cocktail night at the wine bar, although this little market town tucked into the dip before the land rose to the bleak heights of the moors wasn't exactly inundated with mixology connoisseurs. 'Have to keep my hand in,' he said, as I watched him doing something fancy with strawberry syrup. 'The tourists love this stuff.'

'I've got the flat for another month, because I pay a month in advance,' I said, still with my head down on the bar. 'After that, I'm out.'

'What will you do?' A deft flick and he added ice cubes.

I sighed. 'Tent on the roundabout?' I thought briefly about my parents, the too-small house in York where photographs of my brother concealed the wallpaper in every room. Walking into their house, you wouldn't even know I existed from the evidence. 'You said you could offer me a job?'

'Did I? I think I also remember saying that you wouldn't like the conditions.' Flynn shook the concoction until his hair bounced and his glasses slid sideways.

'You're not that bad. I can put up with you.'

'What sort of job would you *really* like to do? If you could choose?' A stream of slightly pink liquid foamed out into a wide-rimmed glass as Flynn poured and then pushed the results across the counter to a couple of young women, who giggled.

'I dunno.' I talked to my forearms.

'What do you like doing?' He smiled at the girls and they giggled even more, nudging one another and making 'he fancies you' faces.

'I like cooking,' I said. 'I make great soup.'

'Right. Anything else?'

'Not really. I used to be good at poetry,' I said, before I realised that he was talking to the cocktail-buying girls and sighed deeply again. 'Right. I'd better go to bed to be ready for tomorrow's early start. Six thirty at mine?'

But Flynn had already gone, chopping mint and chatting with what looked like a hen party, although why a hen party would bother our tiny corner of North Yorkshire, I wasn't sure. Maybe the hen was a pheasant? No, that was tiredness clouding my brain, I thought, sliding off my stool and heading for the door.

I looked back over my shoulder before I stepped out into the chilly evening. It was strange, but the wine bar, with its careful, subtle lighting and laughter, felt more like home now than the chilly flat. But then, if I didn't do something about getting another job soon, the flat wouldn't be home either for much longer. I was seized with a sudden fondness for the smell of fish on the stair-case as I walked up to my front door, and for the way the key didn't properly turn in the lopsided lock. It wasn't the fondness born of appreciation for the conditions, more a kind of 'I'm going to lose all this soon' anticipatory nostalgia for having a roof over my head.

But I couldn't worry about that now. I had to get some sleep.

Worry about my future and the threat of losing the flat ought to have meant that I sat awake half the night, fretting and chewing at my nails. But the imminent disaster that was my life imploding was counteracted sufficiently by that morning's early start to mean that I plummeted into a deep sleep as soon as I climbed into bed. So the banging on the door made me jerk upright, uncertain as to where I was or what was happening.

'Girl! You'd better be in there!'

It was Dex. He'd clearly bypassed the text to tell me he was coming back and gone for direct action.

'Open this door, now!'

I could hear the couple in the flat below waking up. The 'plink' sound their overhead light made as it switched on and the buzz from the bedroom floor was the giveaway, but I could also hear their voices, muted by midnight.

I sat up in bed and pulled the covers to my chest. I could *not* do this right now. I had to be up in – a quick glance at my phone told me – three and a half hours, to pick up Flynn and Fraser. If I let Dex in now, he'd want to keep me awake for the rest of the night, alternately telling me what I'd done wrong and engaging me in noisy sex. Plus, he'd probably want me to stay here, in bed with him, tomorrow too, and I had promises to keep. *Plus*, it was dawning on me slowly, I *really* didn't want Dexter back in my life. Following Eddie had become more important than having a boyfriend.

'Phoebe! Open this door!' A stream of epithets that made me wonder whether Dex actually *had* a vocabulary or whether he just strung together loads of swear words, brought my downstairs neighbours to their door.

'Shut the fuck up, you nutjob! People are trying to sleep!'

'She's locked me out of my own home!' Dex yelled back, lying on both counts. He *had* a home, somewhere in the arse end of Leeds, and he wasn't locked out, he'd never had a key to the flat. He hadn't needed one; he knew I'd always let him in. Then, in a slightly quieter voice, he added, 'My stuff is in there.'

This was a huge lie. Dex never left *anything* here, apart from the odd paracetamol packet and some Tiger Balm. He didn't live with me, he'd made that very clear; he stayed with me as long as I made it worth his while. Or, more likely, when he was too broke and off his face to get back to where he *did* live. I didn't reply. Before, I would almost inevitably have opened the door to him, grateful and wary in equal measure, missing perhaps two days of work as a result while we got drunk and ate our way through the output of the pasty shop on the corner.

This time it was different. I had things to do. People were counting on me to do something other than sell them insurance. Annie needed answers, and that was down to us.

And now I had an 'us', whereas before it had just been Dex and me, with Demi as an occasional presence and a voice on the phone. I tried to imagine Margot's reaction to Dex turning up in the night, or Wren's, or even Annie's. Any of them would be sending him away, not only with a flea in his ear but an entire circus of bloodsuckers loose about his person. I couldn't see any of them standing for this kind of treatment. Only Fraser, who would, presumably, never be in this position, and would have invited Dex in for a drink and a round of *Call of Duty* should he have shown up at two in the morning.

'Well keep it down!' My downstairs neighbour clearly was not in the mood for sympathy. 'Any more noise and I'll call the police.'

I tried not to breathe.

'You'd better be in there.' Dex was muttering now. I knew he was sick of being arrested. 'Because if you're shacked up with someone else, I'm coming after the pair of you.'

I almost laughed and wanted to shout, *If I'm not here, then I can't hear your threats and they're pretty pointless, don't you think?* but I didn't. I stayed, rigid, with the bedclothes clamped to my chest like armour, trying to keep my eyelids from making a noise when I blinked.

I stayed that way for ages, even after I was fairly sure Dex had left. I didn't dare make any sound in case he was sitting there outside the door, either waiting to hear me or waiting for me to come home from wherever he thought I'd been. My mouth was dry and gritty with a lack of saliva, but I didn't even dare to lick my lips in case it made a sound. I breathed in little shallow gasps so that the bed didn't creak and give me away. Eventually, though, I must have fallen asleep, because I was woken by a tapping on the door.

'Fee? Are you ready?'

It was softly called through the door and I leaped out of bed, where I'd slept sitting up, disorientated and slightly panicked. 'Flynn?'

'Yes. Who were you expecting? Only it's six thirty and you weren't outside...'

'Two seconds.' I flung on yesterday's clothes, grabbed my keys and phone and ran to the door. Then I hesitated and asked, 'There's nobody else out there, is there?'

'Like who? It's a bit late for Father Christmas.'

I opened the door. Flynn, looking irritatingly composed for this time in the morning, stood on the threshold. 'You look dreadful.'

'Disturbed night. Sorry I kept you waiting.'

'It's fine.'

We were both whispering. I was worried about the people downstairs waking up again, twice in one night might well have them calling the police for real, rather than as a threat.

Flynn put a hand on my shoulder. 'Are you all right?' he asked. 'You seem a bit twitchy.'

'My ex turned up in the middle of the night,' I said, biting down on my lip to stop it wobbling. 'It was a bit of a shock.'

I led the way down the stairs and out to where my car was parked on the street. I looked at it, sitting there in its slightly bent-bumpered philosophical way, and wondered if I ought to sell it now I didn't need it for work. It might raise enough for another month's rent.

'Sounds it. Does he often do that? Turn up out of the blue?'

The morning was chilly and the door had frozen shut. I had to tug really hard to get the seals to allow me in. 'He used to.' I opened the passenger door. 'I'd always take him back, you see. But now I've decided... well, it really is over. I don't even know why I kept it going so long.' We pulled away from the kerb, my car reluctantly biting its way onto the frosty surface of the road.

Flynn gave me a long look. 'He was dreadful,' he said quietly. 'Absolutely awful. What were you *thinking*, Fee?'

'You don't know him!' The presumed insult to my intelligence stung. 'He could be quite... He sometimes...' The indignation drained away and left me with the backwash comprising acceptance and a surprising feeling of culpability. 'No, you're right. He was rubbish. I'd been single a long time and I didn't really feel up to a long selection procedure.'

'You were acquiring a boyfriend, not a street dog,' Flynn observed mildly.

'My friend, Demi, was a bit obsessed with baby things. She was pregnant with her second and Alfie was only nine months old, and everything was a bit heavy going for her, so we sort of drifted apart and I just wanted... someone.'

Flynn wasn't looking at me. He seemed, from the direction his face was pointing, to be watching the dark lines of roadway, creased by tyre marks in the heavy frost. 'Where did you meet him?' he asked, as though making conversation was painful.

'In a bar.'

'Ah.'

'What?'

Flynn sighed. 'Alcohol does not make the wisest choices, Fee. I think you know that.'

'Bit rich coming from a guy who's earning his daily crust selling the stuff to anyone who'll buy,' I said snippily. Then, as the annoyance at his presumption drained away, I sighed. 'I know. I really do. There isn't anything else, that's all. My life looks – empty.' I tried not to over rev the engine; my car could be surprisingly noisy in the dark of the night. 'I'm not good at friends,' I said finally to the black windscreen.

'And yet, here you are, driving out at this ridiculous hour to try to help Annie? That sounds like friendship to me.'

I didn't say anything. I steered us to Fraser's, where he was waiting at the end of the road, his rolled-up towel under his arm. 'Thought you weren't coming,' he said, falling into the back seat. 'I *hoped* you weren't coming. Fuck me, I can hardly walk today.'

'It's all in a good cause, Fraze,' said Flynn, surprisingly matey.

Fraser sniffed and lolled his head against the seat back on the journey.

The gym was, once more, lit up like a landed spaceship. Fraser reluctantly peeled himself out of my car and limped to the reception desk, where Minnie was already waiting for him, wearing flesh-coloured leggings which made her look distressingly as though she were naked from the waist down. Fraser looked back over his shoulder, like a child being sent on an outward bound course, and Flynn gave him a cheery wave as Minnie led him off into the bowels of the building.

The two men were back on the static bikes, pedalling away in silent unison.

'Why don't you have friends?' Flynn had brought sandwiches. Sandwiches! At seven in the morning! I hadn't even had time to make the flask of coffee. He pushed a foil-wrapped parcel at me and the prospect of food took away any annoyance I was working up for his resumption of our previous conversation.

'I do have friends!' There was Annie and Margot and Wren and if the total needed adding to, I was even prepared to feel warmly towards Fraser. 'I just don't have a lot of time, with work and... work.'

The glasses wriggled. I presumed his eyebrows were creeping up his forehead again.

'What about family?'

'I have a family too.' I unwrapped the foil. Cheese and ham with a token bit of salad, carefully wrapped in kitchen roll, not too offensive for this time in the morning. I hadn't had anything to eat last night either, had I? I tried to remember the contents of my fridge, which mostly seemed to be small bottles. 'Do you?'

'Neat reversal.' For a moment we both chewed, staring out through the show-off windows at the motivated individuals inside the gym. 'I didn't spring fully formed from the loins of a wine bar,' he said, and then, as though seizing gratefully on a chance not to talk about his family and letting his sandwich drop onto his lap, 'Is that Eddie?'

'Is what Eddie?' A piece of lettuce had slithered from my sandwich onto my leg and I was trying to retrieve it when Flynn's hand came onto my wrist.

'Over there!'

I jerked my head up. The Skoda had been in the same place as we'd seen him park yesterday when we arrived, as neatly centred in the space as before, so we'd assumed Eddie was busily doing whatever it was he did in there. Now, here he was, jauntily coming out of the reception area, waving his cheery farewell to the young man with the lanyard and carrying his holdall.

Flynn and I both ducked, which caused considerable sandwich dispersal. 'He must have been early today! Annie said he was always regular as clockwork,' I hissed in a whisper, although I didn't know why, as Eddie was half a car park away and couldn't have heard us. Our sub-par detecting was as cheesy as the sandwiches and if he'd looked up, he'd have seen us, hunched low in the car, but he didn't. We watched Eddie fussily arranging his bag in the boot of the Skoda, carefully folding a rug to fit it in. 'Which seems to fit his profile,' I continued.

'Oh, he has a profile now, does he?' Flynn straightened back up and began to reassemble his sandwich.

'I've got a computer. I read,' I said shortly, shrugging sliced bread off my shoulder and hesitating over the ignition key. 'Should we follow him?'

'We'd better. It's what we're here for, after all. Fraser's got his bus fare, he'll be fine.' A pause. 'Annoyed, but fine.'

But as Eddie got into his car and started the engine, Fraser came flying out of the building, towel flapping, wearing the tightest shorts I'd ever seen and the *Star Wars* T-shirt. Minnie was sprinting alongside him, clearly offering advice as he came.

'He's going!' He puffed, hitting the back seat. 'Drive!'

I drove, my back door waving to Minnie until Fraser could slam it shut, like a getaway vehicle after a bank raid.

'What did you tell Minnie?' I asked, as we trailed Eddie's car at a suitable distance through the quiet streets of Malton, hoping he hadn't seen our frenzied leaving.

'Said I'd got the runs.' Fraser leaned forward between our seats. 'These shorts really chafe.'

'You need bigger ones.' Flynn looked behind him for a second. 'Honestly.'

'Yeah, I know that now. Minnie says...' Fraser stopped. 'Can I have that sandwich?'

'Help yourself.' The packet went into the back and there was some noisy chomping, while the world's slowest and most sensibly driven vehicle pursuit went on. 'Where's he going?'

Eddie had turned out onto the main road to York. Away from the gym, away from Drayton's.

'Minnie said he sometimes does a short session and then gets away by seven,' Fraser said indistinctly, around cheese. 'About once a month, she says.'

I met Fraser's eye in the rear-view mirror. 'Wow. You didn't let her know we were following him, did you?'

'Nah.' Luke Skywalker gained a lettuce hat. 'We were just chatting. About making progress and all that. Minnie says I've got the legs of a footballer,' he added proudly, then, in a slightly more downtrodden tone, 'It's all the rest of me that lets me down.'

Other cars were making their way along the dual carriageway and I had to concentrate to keep the Skoda in sight. 'What else did she say? I don't suppose he sometimes turns up with a gorgeous model-type on his arm?'

Fraser shook his head and more lettuce rained down upon the blameless Luke. 'Not much. Just that Eddie's really put his back into training; he's lost loads of weight and he goes to the gym five mornings a week like he's some kind of addict. She does his assessments.' Chew chew. 'He's fitter than most blokes half his age, she says. She's all right, is Minnie. For a masochist. She's going to put me on the cable machine tomorrow, if the runs are under control.' Chew chew. 'What the fuck is a cable machine?'

'He's turning in here.' Flynn pointed ahead. We'd reached the outskirts of York, where large, expensive houses had begun to pepper the fields, surrounded by grazing horses and wildlife ponds.

'Should I follow him?' I hesitated over flicking on my indicator.

'Looks like a private house. Better not.'

We drove past as slowly as possible while in a stream of traffic. Eddie's destination was where house building had become more serious, on a street of similar but widely spaced large, detached houses with driveways. This one, my rapid sideways glance told me, led to an Edwardian construction of the type that I always imagined would be lived in by a pre-war doctor. Nice gravel sweep, overhanging trees, what looked to be an extensive garden at the back. Little wooden summerhouse to one side, all very affluent and *Homes and Gardens*. The sort of place that Demi aspired to, I tried not to think bitterly.

I turned the car around in a nearby side street and we drove back, Fraser and Flynn hanging over their seats to try to get a good look as we passed the house, heading in the opposite direction.

'There's a porch light on, and some lights at the back,' Flynn said. 'Someone's expecting him.'

'Looks like a woman,' Fraser had wound his window down and stuck his head out as far as it would go. 'Standing there waiting in the porch.' He pulled his head back in. 'He's bloody got a woman! In a posh house.' Fraser stared for a moment as we drove away, getting a last glimpse of the place. 'Wonder how he did it?' he asked, thoughtfully.

We all looked at one another. 'Should we take photographs?' I asked hesitantly. What had previously seemed a fun little conceit, something to keep us busy, had suddenly all become very real.

Eddie was clearly lying about going to the gym every day and I wondered what Annie would say, whether this would blow her marriage up completely when she realised her worst fears were true. Forty years they'd been together, and he was throwing it all away like this. Maybe I wasn't missing anything by staying single; falling in love looked as though it might be a shortcut to a nervous breakdown, and I certainly wasn't going there over Dexter.

'Once a month in't much of a shag,' said Fraser, the Hugh Hefner of the bench press.

'They might meet elsewhere the rest of the time. There was that day he didn't go to work, after all.' I carried on driving, heading back home. It suddenly dawned on me that there was no rush – that I had no job to go to. The day stretched as a painful space of time to fill.

Suddenly Fraser piped up. 'Can you take me back to the gym? I'll tell Minnie I'm full of Imodium.'

Flynn and I turned surprised eyes on him. 'You sure? You didn't seem over-keen on the place.' Flynn asked.

'Yeah, well, Margot's paid for a month, might as well use it. And there's some well fit lasses in there I gets to stand behind, and Minnie does this thing where she touches my leg...' He trailed off into his own private musings.

'Just go steady in those shorts.' Flynn began rewrapping the sandwiches. 'You'll do yourself a mischief.'

I drove back down to the gym, where the car park was now much fuller, as those who started the day at a sensible hour put in their exercise. The two men on the bikes were still there, I noted.

'Don't enjoy yourself too much!' Flynn called as Fraser got out. 'And you'll have to get the bus back!'

Fraser's farewell was a lot cheerier in the daylight. He didn't exactly bounce his way into the gym but he limped in a more convincing way.

'I hope he's not going to turn into a gym bunny,' I said as we watched him go. 'Well, maybe not a bunny,' I added, as Fraser's stocky form scuttled up the entrance steps. 'A gym wombat, possibly.'

'It's good for him. Social contact,' Flynn said. 'You and Fraser have a surprising amount in common.'

'Shut up. No, we don't.' I turned the car again. I wondered if I could ask Margot for petrol money; all this running up and down was sending my fuel gauge lower than I liked it.

'You both need to get out more.'

I rounded on him. 'Who made *you* God?'

Flynn looked taken aback for a second, scrunching foil. 'What?'

'All this telling me what I am and what I'm not and what I ought to be doing with my life! Maybe I'm happy with it the way it is, all right?'

I oversteered and the car wobbled into the middle of the road, incurring a beeped horn of warning from an oncoming driver.

'I'm sorry,' Flynn said quietly. 'It's weird, working in a bar. People come in and tell you their problems and it's awful when you can clearly see what's wrong but you're not allowed to say anything other than "have you ever tried a Cancun Mobcap?"'

'That's not a real…'

'No, no it isn't. It was for illustrative purposes only.' He sighed. 'But you seem like a nice person and I hate to see the way you're… You're right. None of my business if you want to work some grotty job and date awful men. Up to you. Obviously.' Another sigh. 'I like you, that's all.' Flynn took his glasses off and polished them on the cuff of his shirt. Without them he looked a lot less sarcastic – almost naked to the world.

'Oh.'

'And I really would like to offer you a job. I need someone else behind the bar.'

I stared at him and the car wobbled again. Things like this didn't happen to people like me, getting offered a job out of nowhere. I'd practically had to beg for the call-centre role. 'Are you allowed to hire people like that? Don't you have to check with the owner or something?'

The polishing upped in tempo. If his glasses had been that dirty, it was a wonder he'd been able to see Eddie at all. 'I... well, I am the owner. Technically. Sort of.'

'How can you be *sort of* an owner?' I felt a bit weird now. I'd been assuming that Flynn was like me, working the kind of job that most people do at the weekend, making just enough to get by. But he was the owner of the bar? Or was he spinning me a line – like Dex had when he'd told me he was an 'entrepreneur'? But then, admitting that your main job is dealing drugs would be a hard sell, even on Tinder. I straightened myself up a bit, as though I had my boss in the car.

'My dad.' Flynn began to examine his spectacles now, holding them up to the light and twisting them this way and that, almost as though the distraction was helping him through the conversation. 'He owns quite a few bars, bistros, that sort of thing. I'd come back from Melbourne – I was out there managing some of his wine bars – and he'd bought this place to renovate but didn't really know what to do with it. I had some ideas, so he made the place over to me. To prove myself, I guess.'

Without his glasses on, I could see that Flynn wasn't quite as young as I'd assumed. There were faint lines and creases around his eyes and the morning stubble that outlined his cheeks made him look older, too, and more serious.

'That must be nice,' I said, meaninglessly but aware that my voice was tight and the words sounded bitter.

He shrugged and slipped his glasses back on. 'It's life,' he said. 'I've not really known any different. Anyway.' He shook his head. 'I could offer you a job, but there is one absolute deal-breaker...'

I pulled the car into the same space as I'd pulled it out of. Life hadn't really got going in the little town yet this morning, none of the shops were open and the street was almost devoid of any action, apart from a little knot of binmen who had clustered into a doorway and were smoking furtively. Did I really want a job that came with conditions? From a man I'd assumed was on my level? I had to admit to myself that I'd have treated Flynn differently if I'd known that he wasn't only a bartender in a tiny Yorkshire town. I would have been wary of him, for a start.

I looked up at my flat. It was grim, the stairway smelled of week-old cod and I had to watch TV in bed. I could move. I could head for the city and find myself another minimum-wage job that would only pay me enough for a room in a house share. But at least I wouldn't have Dexter turning up on the doorstep whenever he felt like punishing me.

'What's the deal-breaker?' I asked, cautiously.

Flynn, still sitting in the passenger seat as though oblivious to the fact that we'd stopped and I'd turned off the engine, grinned, and it made him look young again, almost like the student I'd assumed him to be. 'You can't drink,' he said. 'I won't have anyone working with me drinking. It's too easy to slip up, to short-change, to get into arguments. Believe me, I've seen it happen. Would that...' He stopped, frowned, then started again, with weighted words. 'Would that be a problem?'

I wanted to say, *No, of course not!* But then I thought of sitting in the wine bar without a glass of wine, of my fridge with its contents of single-glass bottles of cheap Chardonnay. 'I don't always drink,' I said quietly.

'Never said you did.' I saw him purse his lips as though there were words straining to come out that he thought were better kept contained.

'And I never drink at work.'

'Uh-huh.'

'It's just that…'

'I could hear you, you know.' Flynn had evidently decided to let the words out now. 'Sometimes. You and Dexter. When I was outside, doing the windows or sorting out a delivery.'

'Ah.'

'I mean, it wasn't deliberate or anything. I wasn't listening in.'

'Not at all like you have a track record for nosily hanging over people having a conversation or anything,' I said, snippily. 'Which has led us to the unfortunate circumstance we now find ourselves in. You can get out, by the way. I've stopped moving.'

Flynn did not get out. He did start staring at the smoking binmen though. 'He encouraged you to drink, didn't he? I could hear the yelling.'

Suddenly all I could think of was my father, sniffing at my breath when I came in and shouting to my mother that I'd been drinking alcohol, and what kind of a daughter did she think she was raising? And my brother, lying on the sofa sleeping off yet another hangover, laughing uproariously, as though his sister being berated was the funniest thing he'd ever heard. How I'd thought I might as well be hung for a sheep and started drinking more and more, because it made the nights shorter and the shouting ignorable.

How I'd stormed out one night, battered by their demands and accusations, and the words. How they'd told me I'd be back in a week, I couldn't manage without them and anyway they needed me back because my brother had lost his licence and needed me to drive him to work.

Then I'd met Dex, and his brand of control had felt like love. He'd told me that I was no fun without a drink inside me, probably because when I was sober, I pulled him up on his behaviour. I'd been driven to drink on both sides, but I shouldn't console myself with that fact. I'd chosen it. Chosen the tipsy tolerance of Dex's behaviour, his casual violence, his chauvinistic assumptions that I would cook and clean and never ask questions, and his neglect of me as a person.

I told Flynn all of it, sitting there in my car as the little town woke up and began its day around us. When I started to cry, he raked around but couldn't find anything handkerchief-like, so he handed me a bit of the kitchen roll that had been wrapped around the sandwiches, and I ended up with a face covered in cheese slivers. But I couldn't stop talking. Even when a piece of soggy tomato dropped onto my chin, I just ate it and carried on.

Finally, when I'd hiccupped myself to a standstill, Flynn spoke.

'So, you drank because your life was shit, then your life became shit because you drank?'

I liked the way he'd put it into the past tense, as though that wasn't me any more.

'Sort of. I didn't really drink that much until Dex – well, it wasn't a great relationship, put it that way, and alcohol made it… fuzzier. I didn't mind so much when I was a bottle of wine in.'

'Oh, Fee,' he said, rather hopelessly.

'And then sometimes Dex *didn't* want me to drink, because I had to be able to drive him around and he didn't have a car. But I *had* to drink, because otherwise being with him was – difficult. So, he'd shout and I'd shout back and it all got messy. As you heard,' I added.

Now Flynn shook his head. The hopelessness seemed to have robbed him of words. Over in the doorway, the binmen had started showing one another stuff on their phones. 'But he's gone now? You're definitely over?' he asked, at last.

'Yes.' Well, that sounded firm, at least. I thought of Dex, his muscle vests and his tattoos, and the only image I could call to mind was last night, his thuggish insistence that I be in the room. That wasn't love. It wasn't even friendship. He'd never even asked me about my family, knew nothing about my golden-boy brother. Flynn had got more of my background in twenty minutes sitting in this car than Dexter had in two years. I was far closer to the Heartbreak Club than I'd ever been to Dexter.

'Then maybe you could put in a couple of shifts for me? Only temporarily, until I can... well, until I can be certain. Like I said, I won't have people drinking on my watch. What you do in your own time is up to you, but I need someone sober and with-it behind the bar. And definitely no "have one yourself".'

'Right. Yes. Thank you.' I didn't sound very grateful. I wasn't even sure that I *was* grateful. I was glad to have the whisper of a job that might keep me from having to return to my parents. I was happy that Dex was out of my life. But I wasn't sure that I liked the idea of being beholden to Flynn, or any man, for life's necessities. I would have felt better if I could have found myself a job – and I still wasn't entirely sure that Flynn wasn't stringing me a line with his 'my dad gave me this place to manage'. I'd been told one too many 'make myself look important' lies by Dexter and his associates, and I couldn't *quite* believe that anything could come this easily, just from a friend. I strongly suspected that a morning would come when Flynn would have to admit to having massaged the truth somewhat, and I would be back on the street with nothing. But, for now, anything was better than nothing and I didn't exactly have stellar references.

Flynn grinned again. 'Okay. I'll see you at six this evening when we open and I'll run through everything with you then.' He got out of the car, bending back in to gather the detritus of sandwiches and sobbing. 'And we can also talk about what Eddie might be up to.'

'Eddie,' I said blankly. My mind was full of other stuff, it hadn't the capacity to dwell on Annie's faithless husband right now.

'Yes. We might need to work out how we find out who he's seeing, now we know he's sneaking off from the gym.'

'I'll have a think.'

'Right, see you later then.' Flynn was gone, hustling himself off down the pavement to the side door of the wine bar, and leaving me to haul myself back up to my flat to lie on my bed, exhausted and feeling oddly deflated.

The weeks rolled around and Flynn gave me the evenings off to attend the club meetings. I had to admit that he showed every sign of being a bar manager – there had been paperwork and forms, and he'd walked me round the equipment and showed me what I needed to know, just as though it was a real job. And, I reassured myself, even if his 'dad' did turn out to be an absent owner who turned up angry at this casual hiring procedure and threw me out, at least for now I could pay my rent, and Flynn let me eat any out-of-date crisps, and he'd call me into the back room for an omelette or some chips to take home when we closed, so I wasn't starving.

Not drinking wasn't as hard as I'd thought it might be, either. With the stress of having no money somewhat alleviated, no sign of Dexter revisiting the flat and Flynn's ultimatum of no job if I drank, I gradually stopped bothering. I found that keeping busy helped and I was less and less inclined to pour myself a drink when I got in after my shift.

After some frantic messaging between us, the group had decided not to mention to Annie what we'd been doing, and besides, Eddie had blamelessly been attending the gym every morning, as advertised. Apart from that one visit to the posh house on the outskirts of York, he'd not put a foot wrong. Flynn and I had been sitting in my car, drinking coffee and chatting aimlessly, while Fraser had bought himself some new shorts and was apparently learning how to use the treadmill without sailing backwards off the end, while keeping an eye on Eddie. We'd kept Margot and Wren updated on the lack of action, but how we were going to avoid mentioning anything to Annie, I wasn't sure.

Wren arrived first on this Monday, giving Flynn and me a complicit smile as she came in and looking around carefully to check that Annie hadn't arrived. 'Nothing to report this morning?' she asked in the kind of whisper that would alert anyone in a five-mile radius to the fact that we were up to something.

'Nope. Gym at seven on the dot and then off to work. Anything on the evening shift?' Wren and Margot had been checking up on Eddie's after-work doings, which sounded even more boring than the morning stint, but at least it lacked the necessity of seeing Fraser in shorts.

'Nope. Straight home every night. Oh, he went to the pub one evening to meet some people, but they were all men. Margot and I had a fish supper and a gin and tonic – all very good, by the way, I thoroughly recommend the place – and then came back. He was watching the football. Oh, there's Margot now, and Fraser.'

Fraser had cadged another lift with Margot and was obviously telling her all about his gym exploits because she wore the kind of expression usually only seen by someone who is having the offside rule explained to them in painful detail. 'Ah, good, you're here.'

'And then there's this really big machine, right? You has to pull on this handle...' Fraser continued. 'Minnie says I'm a natural.'

Minnie, I thought, wanted shooting. But I did have to admit that Fraser's *Simpsons* T-shirt looked a little bit less tight around the stomach regions, and Homer's face didn't look quite as prominent as it had.

Annie wasn't far behind, and I felt the atmosphere change as soon as she came in. We were all biting our tongues as hard as we could not to let anything untoward escape.

'Maybe tonight we could talk a little bit about what went wrong in our relationships?' Wren suggested when we'd all sat down and Flynn had come to lurk at our end of the bar. 'I've been doing some thinking and it would be good to get some opinions.' Plus it would give us a topic of conversation that wouldn't veer quite so heavily towards the 'Eddie' end of the spectrum, I thought. I gave Wren a small smile, which she returned.

'Well, Eddie...' Annie began, and we all instantly began to talk over her.

'Bruce and I were more like housemates...'

'I know that I pushed Jordan, but she was so helpful to everyone else!'

'Dex came round to the flat the other week and I wouldn't let him in.'

'Minnie says another couple of sessions and I'll be ready to try the rowing machine.' We all stopped and looked at Fraser. 'What?'

'You said Jordan was helpful to other people?' As Wren had had the idea, I thought she should be the first to pick up on the topic. Anything to prevent Fraser from giving us chapter and verse on the workings of every machine in the gym was welcome. He'd started giving demonstrations that were beginning to attract the attention of people passing in the street outside. He looked like Torquemada miming the effects of his latest torture instruments.

Wren seemed to realise that her idea meant she'd become the centre of things. For a moment she looked hesitant and glanced towards the door as though trying to work out whether she could bolt or not. Then she sighed.

'Yes, I felt that Jordan seemed to take me for granted,' she said, putting her elbows on the table. 'I *did* want some kind of sign on Valentine's Day that she was serious about our relationship – that she *saw* me, if you know what I mean.'

We all murmured assent, even Annie who was still looking a bit cheated of her opportunity to offload more worries about Eddie.

'She was so certain that she did thank me every day, but it wasn't what I heard. I felt as though she was just saying thank you so automatically that it didn't mean anything, she was only paying lip service.'

Fraser made a 'hur hur' sound, but someone must have kicked him because he went quiet almost instantly.

'Jordan worked at a dementia clinic, and she couldn't do enough for her clients. She'd make cups of tea and chat to them and remember their favourite little treats. She'd remember everything they said about their families and their pasts and she'd talk about those for hours with them, to help them calm down when they got a bit overwrought.' Wren looked wistfully down at the table. 'Then she'd come round to mine and she couldn't so much as make me a coffee or talk to me about what we were going to do at the weekend.'

'My mum had dementia,' Annie said softly. 'It's a dreadful disease.'

'Yes, yes it is.' Margot came in now. 'Do you think, perhaps, that Jordan just didn't have anything left to give?'

'I... How do you mean?' Wren, to her credit, didn't sound

dismissive or as though she were justifying anything, more as though she really wanted to know.

'Working with dementia patients has to deplete your emotional reserve, I would have thought,' Margot went on. She wasn't looking at Wren; instead, she was picking away at the edge of the table. 'Perhaps she didn't have enough left to give you what you wanted.'

Wren stared at her for a moment. 'I can be a bit of a princess, I have to admit. And I think you're right, I wanted too much attention. Jordan wanted peace and tranquillity to help her deal with what she went through every day, but I wanted fun and excitement and a girlfriend who put me first. Jordan couldn't do that. Her clients came first for her.' She glanced at Margot. 'I had a better time with you, eating fish and chips in the pub while we...' The collective expression of panic that I saw dashing across everyone's face and which I was sure must have broken out on mine, stopped her blurting out why they'd been there just in time. '...when we... err... met in town,' Wren went on, limply, 'than I'd had with Jordan for ages. I wanted attention and company and she didn't have anything left to give. We'd stopped laughing,' she finished and her lip wobbled. 'And I've always thought, when you can't laugh together any more, it's over.'

Margot looked across the table at Wren and I was surprised to see the faint glitter of tears in her eyelashes. I hadn't credited Margot with the ability to cry. I thought she'd had all her emotion taken out and replaced with fifty-pound notes. 'That,' Margot said, and even her voice had lost its usual strident tone, 'is so right. It sounds as though you needed different things from the relationship and neither of you could give the other what you wanted. I'm sorry, Wren.'

Annie leaned across the table and patted Wren's arm. 'That's very honest of you, dear,' she said.

'Yes, well.' Wren swallowed hard. 'Now I'm honest and alone.'

Across the bar, the Monday night men, who were back to dominoes again, laughed at something and we all bristled, even though I was fairly sure they couldn't hear us.

Flynn came over bearing a bowl of crisps and pulled up the chair which had carefully been left spare. 'It must have been hard for Jordan too,' he said as though he'd been part of the entire conversation. 'Mentally exhausting job and trying to fit in a real life.'

Wren smiled at him. 'I've come to that conclusion, yes. Nobody's fault, not really. Mine, more than hers, if I'm honest.'

Margot looked around the table and her expression was fierce. 'I don't think I should have to tell anyone that all conversations here – everything we do *as part of the club*,' and this was added with extra spin, directed towards Fraser, Wren and me, 'is confidential? It goes no further than this table?'

'Absolutely,' I said.

Flynn nudged my shoulder.

'That goes without saying,' Wren put in.

'I don't know who I'd tell.' Annie's soft voice came across the table. 'Eddie is...'

'I'm a virgin,' said Fraser, surprising no one, but stopping Annie in her tracks. 'And if that gets out, I'm dead, so, yeah. No further than this.'

'So, we can say anything here?' Margot went on. 'I needn't remind you all that I am trained in law, so should anything happen to become public gossip, I would sue for slander, and possibly defamation.'

We all mumbled acceptance. I really didn't think anyone had enough dirt on anyone else to be a real danger, but I did take her point. Some of this was personal. It hurt. We were making ourselves vulnerable – I'd already had my turn earlier, spilling my life story to Flynn, and that had been hard enough. Now we were basically laying our faults and fears bare in front of people we didn't know that well, and that was scary.

I admired them all for it.

Margot took a deep breath, but then paradoxically whispered, 'It was sex. It was all about sex.'

I saw Fraser open his mouth, but the under-table kicker must have been at work once more, because he closed it again, went slightly pink and nodded wisely, although what he was wise *about* I wasn't entirely sure.

'It wasn't so bad when we were younger,' Margot went on, still in the peculiar whisper as though she were afraid that the glasses racked on the wall behind the bar might be listening in. 'I could do it then. But as we were together longer and longer, I found I... couldn't.'

The whole table had gone quiet now. Fraser appeared to be holding his breath. Even the dominoes team were reduced to clacking tiles and clinking glasses.

'I knew Bruce wanted to... more often, but I had to bring myself to do it, and as we got busier and busier I began to find it – yes, almost *repulsive*. Oh, not Bruce, no, he's a very handsome man,' Margot put in hastily, with evident pride. 'Very successful. A perfect husband in many ways. But not...' she lowered her voice still further, '...*in that way*.'

'Was it kinky sex?' Annie asked in a more normal tone of voice, and slightly surprisingly. 'Did he like it all fancy in the bedroom? Stockings and suspenders and fantasies about watching you with other men?'

All the rest of us, who had seen Eddie and knew him to be a slightly overweight, balding and possibly prissily concerned with detail middle manager, busily rewrote our mental images.

'Oh, not that Eddie ever goes in for that stuff,' she went on, and we all silently scrubbed our visions of Eddie in suspenders, wielding a whip. 'But he's told me about some of his workmates. Well! You wouldn't *believe* what goes on! My Eddie is strictly twice a week, lights out, thankfully.' And then, obviously remembering her fears, 'At least, that's what I thought,' she added sadly. 'I might be wrong, of course.'

'Er.' Margot was off balance. I suspected she had shared our musings over Eddie's predilections. 'No, no, nothing like that. Very... straightforward. Bruce is a man of simple tastes.' Now she looked down at the table. 'I just couldn't comply with any of them. We hadn't had... intimacy for three years. I loved him very much, of course, and he was exceptionally talented in... in the bedroom when we were younger. But I began to feel taken advantage of, a little as though we were going through the motions and I just lost the urge. It came as a blow to poor Bruce, of course. He suggested counselling. I refused. That's when he asked for the divorce.'

More silence. Beside me, Flynn shifted his chair slightly.

'Had you seen a doctor?' Annie again. Her soft Yorkshire burr made the words feel sympathetic, not as accusatory as they might have done. 'They can do wonders, there are creams and all sorts.'

'I am *not* being medicalised into having sex with my husband!' Margot snapped, more loudly than she obviously intended, because the silence extended across the room and the dominoes fell dormant again. 'It's not a medical problem,' she went on, voice lowered again. 'I simply don't want sex. That was the deal-breaker, as far as Bruce was concerned. Sex or divorce. I chose divorce.'

Now Margot's face crumpled. It seemed as though saying the words had drained her of the unemotional sternness that kept her skin taut. 'It's dreadful.' She fumbled in her handbag and drew out a packet of tissues. 'Truly dreadful. I love him, of course

I do, but I couldn't love him as he wanted. I thought we were all right, we were planning for our anniversary, and then...' she trailed off, words lost to sniffing.

'It's all right.' Wren slipped a consolatory arm around Margot's shoulders. 'We understand.'

I thought of Dex and some of his more extreme sexual requests – the arguments that had resulted when I wouldn't go along with whatever porn-inspired ideas he'd come up with, the feelings that I was letting him down that he played on. Then, my assertions that I wasn't a performing seal or blow-up doll for him to act out his fantasies on. I gave a little shudder.

Beside me, Flynn shifted again. I wondered if he knew what I was thinking. Some of this had come out in my teary collapse, but not all. Not by any means all. Maybe he could imagine the rest.

'I drink... *drank* too much,' I said, feeling I should offer something. 'I made stupid decisions and Dexter was one of them. There's a lot of boring backstory, but that is the crux. Too much wine, trying to make myself feel better and only managing to make myself feel worse. And I feel a bit of a fraud being part of this club, because the only person who's broken my heart is me. I brought it all on myself by getting with a chauvinistic thug like Dexter.'

All eyes were on me now. Under the table, Flynn's leg rested against mine for a second.

'You say you drank? In the past?' Wren's frown made her look like the worried little brown bird I'd taken her for when we'd first met. 'Have you given up?'

I thought of Flynn's 'conditions'. Of the headaches, the hangovers, the disturbed sleep and the gaps in memory. The feeling that I needed to drink just to cope with Dexter and his behaviour. Then I remembered last night's single small bottle. 'Nearly,' I said. 'I'm working on it.'

'Still reckon Vengeance Squad is a better name,' Fraser muttered.

'Eddie's booked another day off,' Annie said quickly, as though she worried she wouldn't get her fears out into the open if she didn't say it now. 'He hasn't mentioned it to me, not a word.'

A look went around the table, all of us trying not to look at one another yet desperate to catch the eye of someone to communicate the internal *ah-ha!* that we were clearly all thinking.

'How did you find out?' Margot asked eventually.

'Nikki, she's the person who manages their diaries, she rang me to let me know. I asked her to, after last time. I said that Eddie was getting a bit forgetful and he'd only tell me last minute when he had a day off. So I asked her to tell me next time, and she did. Oh, I pretended I already knew, of course.' Annie's tone was sad. Lying clearly didn't come easily to her.

'Will she tell him that she told you?' Margot asked.

Wren was making notes on her phone, I could see. I hoped Annie wouldn't guess what she was up to and just assume that Wren was callously using this time to text her friends.

'I asked her not to. Said he was getting a bit self-conscious about his memory lapses – oh, I made him sound a right nellie! But having nursed Mum with the dementia, I know how it can start, just the odd "forgetting". Poor Nikki, I think she thinks I'm worrying over nothing! But she knew Mum, they all knew how it was, so I think they're putting it down to me being a little bit over-cautious.'

I glanced at Margot, then Flynn. How did I ask the question? I didn't want to make it sound obvious.

Fraser came to my rescue. 'He's probably going to watch the football,' he said. 'Is it next Wednesday he's got off? There's a big match on, kick-off's at three.'

I had no idea whether this was true or not, but had to admire Fraser's quick thinking.

'No, it's a week on Thursday,' Annie said and I watched Wren tap the date into her calendar app. 'He watches most matches on catch-up when he gets home. Nobody's allowed to mention the scores at work!' She laughed, but there was an undercurrent to her laughter that showed how worried she was about what Eddie was really up to.

'Ah well,' Fraser said. But there was a pink glow to the tips of his ears – he knew he'd been clever.

'What about you?' Margot suddenly rounded on Flynn, who'd been sitting there eating crisps all this time. 'You want to be a member of our club, you didn't have a Valentine's Day date – why not?'

Flynn withdrew his hand from the crisp bowl, startled. 'Me? Oh, I dunno. Like I told you, I had to work.'

That 'headmistressy' tone was back in Margot's voice now. Perhaps she wanted us all to forget her moment of weakness. 'Yes, but as you say, this place doesn't open until six. You had all day.'

I turned to him now. The light was reflecting off his glasses and his eyes were hidden behind the bobbing white bulbs, but I could feel the stillness that had descended over him. His hands were balled in his lap and he'd pulled his shoulder away from mine. 'I wondered about that,' I said. 'You could have had a daytime date.'

He shrugged. 'Nobody I felt like asking.'

Then, to his evident great relief, the dominoes men approached the bar for refills and with some questions about hiring a space for a dominoes tournament, and Flynn had to get up and go across to them.

The Monday Night Heartbreak Club talked about holidays, then, until it was time to go home. We seemed to feel the need for general chat after the emotionally charged nature of our previous conversations, and hearing Margot casually mentioning Mauritius, while Fraser debated the merits of Pontins with Annie, was the normality we wanted. I didn't have much to add to the chat, having not had a holiday since 2014 when my parents took us all to Center Parcs and I was shouted at for not letting my brother beat me down the water slide, so I found myself letting much of the talk flow over me, while I wondered quietly about Flynn.

It felt as though he was hiding something. He was evasive, not to an offensive degree, but he'd duck and weave away from direct questions as though he didn't want to give anything away. Why couldn't he have found himself a date for Valentine's Day, if he'd been that keen? He certainly didn't seem to be heartbroken either. I glanced over at the bar, where he was serving red wine to two women. He wasn't bad-looking, I supposed, he was socially acceptable and seemed easy enough company.

Flynn looked up suddenly from pouring the wine and caught my eye, which hadn't been hard because I'd been staring. One eyebrow raised above his glasses' frame, giving him that lopsided look again. What *was* the deal with him? Then it occurred to me that if he was lying about being the owner of this place, the more people he told the lie to, the more chance there was of the real owner getting to hear it. Unless it *wasn't* a lie and he really did own the place? But that would mean financial backing, and surely someone with a sound and monied background could find a date? Women would be scrambling over themselves for a good-looking, solvent man. But Flynn didn't have a date. Or, it appeared, anyone else.

I looked again at the dark figure, who'd stopped giving me the sarcastic glances. There was something rather lonely about him, now I came to think about it. Maybe he'd attached himself to our club to have people to talk to? After all, he'd volunteered to sit for hours in my car while we waited for Eddie, and, by extension, Fraser. Perhaps he just wanted company.

The thought that he might quite like *me* was easily dismissed. Apart from listening to me trot out the miseries of my life amid much snotty crying, and giving me a job when I was clearly desperate, he'd shown no sign of it. He hadn't asked me out and hadn't demonstrated any signs of attraction – there had been no attempts at groping, no thoughtless patting of my bum when I passed him behind the bar. And – I faced the idea with a burn of acid up my throat – I would have been the easiest person to get drunk and involved in a casual overnight tumble, wouldn't I?

Flynn had done none of these things. He had, in short, been a gentleman. Or, putting it another way, he'd been a man who was kind, listened, talked to me and who had no overt interest in simply trying to get me into bed. Which was, I thought, in the quietness of my flat as I was tidying up before going to bed late that night, the definition of *friend*.

We put in another week of following Eddie, which kept to the same pattern as the previous ones. Early start, pick up Fraser, then Flynn and me sitting outside the gym in my car eating whatever we had to hand. I quite often fell asleep as soon as we parked in front of the brightly lit gym. The late nights were getting to me. Flynn didn't seem to mind and I'd wake up, bleary and with one or two of the door-opening mechanisms embossed on my shoulder, to find that he'd undone my seat belt to aid my unconscious slump, or moved the sandwich I'd been eating from my lap.

I'd straighten up, embarrassed, but Flynn just grinned at me and offered me a night off to catch up on my sleep, but I wouldn't take it. Nights off meant sitting alone in the flat, and I had enough of that during the day. Sitting up there on my own meant the pull of the alcohol was strongest. I could avoid it during the day, knowing I had to work later, but when the evenings stretched long and boring, sometimes the temptation was too much. After work I could get through without breaking open one of the small bottles in the fridge – by the time we'd washed up, cashed up the till and swept the floor, I was too shattered to do anything apart from fall into bed, hence the falling asleep in the car. But a night off might mean I slipped, and anything that kept the urge at bay was to be seized and held.

On my days off, I started a grand tidy-up of the flat, which helped to fill the time – I'd found several of Dexter's cast-off socks, two forgotten lighters under the table, and I'd chiselled months of grime off the cooker. I had even nailed down those loose floorboards in the bathroom. The place still smelled of fish, though. I managed to ration myself to only one small bottle on those nights, using the physical exhaustion of scrubbing and DIY to prevent me from opening more. It worked. Mostly.

Eddie continued in his routine, apart from the Friday morning, when a gym newcomer had parked in the spot he usually occupied, causing him to drive twice around the car park and Flynn and me to sit alert as whippets. Two circuits seemed to reassure Eddie that no other parking spaces were explosive, and he parked, precisely as usual, two spaces to the left of his usual haunt.

Other than that, nothing unusual happened.

Flynn didn't mention my sobbing all over him in the car that morning, and the situation wasn't repeated. I carefully kept the chat light: last night's TV, the customers we'd had in, how much less pink Fraser was looking now when he came out of the gym, and how much we both hated hearing every single detail about his performance improvements and Minnie's words of wisdom.

We had the weekends off. According to Annie, she and Eddie went to Asda on Saturday, then he mowed the lawn, and on Sunday they sat and read the papers together and cooked a big roast. I got 'green draylon and toilet roll covers' vibes about the whole thing, but she seemed happy with it. At least it meant she had eyes on him all day, so we were excused from following him and, to Fraser's relief, the gym.

'Do you think she'd forgive Eddie, if he is having an affair?' I asked. It was Sunday afternoon, the March sun was managing to muster a little heat, and we'd taken chairs out into the garden at the back of the wine bar. It wasn't much of a garden, more of a yard, but Flynn had done his best with a couple of barrels filled with soil, in which sad leaves occasionally emerged and were instantly stripped to sticks by the slugs.

Flynn stretched out his legs and picked up his tea mug. 'I'm not sure,' he said. 'She's more of a tough cookie than she lets on, I think, our Annie.'

There it was again. That tiny hint of warm inclusion in the phrase 'our Annie'. I felt the warm blanket of belonging over my shoulders; I was part of something here. 'But he might want to leave her. Set up with his affair partner, start a new life.'

We both stared into our tea, pondering the duality which could make fussy, routine-obsessed Eddie, whose gym obsession seemed to have shaped him, according to Annie, into someone who could have qualified for the next Olympics, manage to keep another woman.

'Maybe it's a man?' I turned my face up to the sun. Mostly what I turned my face up to was the mossy overhang of the guttering, where the flat above the wine bar jutted out into the yard, but it was better than nothing. Better than my place, where the sun only highlighted the mould in the grouting. 'Maybe Eddie is secretly gay and leading a double life?'

Flynn made a 'could be' face over his mug rim. 'Fraser's definite it was a woman he saw standing outside that house in York, and I'd bet my business on Fraser's ability to tell a woman from a man. It would be sad though, don't you think, if Eddie were gay and he'd never felt able to come out and be his real self?'

'I'm sure Annie's roast dinners make up for a certain amount of closetedness.' Then a thought which had circled around the back of my head, making only the odd middle-of-the-night appearance in my conscious thoughts, came to the forefront again. 'Are you gay, Flynn?'

He spilled his tea. 'No!' Some mopping went on and he had to go in and fetch one of the bar tea towels. 'What on earth made you think that?'

Lots of things. You've never made one suggestive remark to me, after all that sitting in a parked car, chatting. You've never mentioned a girlfriend, past or present. You don't seem to want to talk about why you joined our club either.

'Oh, nothing. Just wondered.'

Those dark eyes, half-hidden behind the gold-rimmed glasses, looked at me very seriously for a moment. 'Because I haven't tried it on with you?'

I felt myself going pink and started slurping at my tea to give me something to do with my face. 'Nnnn,' I garbled, swilling liquid.

He smiled, and shook his head. 'You're either really cocky or...' Now the look became focused and he leaned forward across the makeshift table, which was really a bit of board resting on two chairs. Leaned in really close until he was almost nose to nose with me. 'Was that the sort of man you're used to?' he asked softly.

But I'd learned my lesson from the snotting session. Letting anything out meant letting *everything* out, and I wasn't going through that again. He knew about my mistakes with Dex and he knew about my family, that was enough. 'Nnnn,' I said again, still to my tea. Those 'men I thought were just being friendly until they got me alone in a car or their flat or down an alleyway' were not his business. My constantly mistaking casual sex for love, availability for affection, was not his business.

The fact that I was still learning to like myself sober, was not his business.

Flynn shook his head. 'I don't know who I should feel sorriest for,' he said, dabbing at the front of his shirt where spilled tea was forming a stain the exact shape of the York ring road. 'You or me.'

'Why would you feel sorry for either of us?' I put my mug down on the 'table'. 'We're both doing all right. You've got this,' I waved to indicate the building, 'and I'm hanging in there. Paying my bills, just about. Thanks for employing me, by the way. Any chance of a few more shifts? I could do with a few quid; I want to redecorate the bathroom.'

'Oy, I'm not *made* of money.' He smiled and then the smile faded and left him with that older look, lines around his eyes and mouth. 'No, I'm not,' he said again, but almost as though I wasn't meant to hear. Then a headshake and another smile. 'Right. If you want another shift, you can do tonight if you like. I don't think we'll be busy but I've got some paperwork to catch up on, so you can man the bar while I go behind the scenes, and it means I won't need to do it tomorrow.'

I stood up and picked up the tea mugs. 'Yes, thank you,' I said, but I was wondering. Why was Flynn so avoidant about talking about himself? He knew more about me and my situation than almost anyone apart from Demi, and she hadn't been in contact since I'd messaged her to say I'd lost my job. Probably too busy living in Peterborough, I thought, and tried to keep the sourness out of my head. The more time I spent with Flynn and the rest of the club, the more I realised that Demi and I hadn't really been friends. Not proper friends. We'd worked at the same place and we'd socialised occasionally, that was all, but I hadn't trusted her with my background. She didn't know about my parents and the weird, twisted way they'd brought up my brother and me. She knew about Dex, and some of his more extreme behaviour, but not about the way he'd made me feel. We'd talked about men in general, and I'd sometimes hinted at the fact that I wasn't completely happy with him, but she'd seemed to think of my life as something like *EastEnders*. Something to make her own life seem normal and happy in comparison.

But the Heartbreak Club all had problems. Life had been pretty shit for all of us, in one way or another, and that bound us together in a way that other people, with their shiny relationships and gorgeous partners, wouldn't understand.

Except for Flynn. I left the bar and went back to my flat, leaving him to sort out something with the computer. Flynn was the outlier. He didn't seem to have been particularly cut up about not having a great Valentine's Day. He was part of the club more by default and by always being there. So why *was* he there? I did, for one brief and skin-tightening moment of horror, wonder whether he'd been recruited by Dex to keep an eye on me, to make sure I wasn't seeing anyone else, but I quickly dismissed that idea. Flynn simply wasn't a Dexter sort of person. He didn't have enough tattoos, for a start, and he only swore occasionally, like when he dropped a full bottle on the tiled floor. He didn't leer, he didn't letch. He wasn't like Dexter.

And then, as I put the key in the lock and let myself into the tiny flat and smelled the damp and the washing drying on the radiators, I thought, *I must have been desperate...*

So, when Monday rolled around and I saw the group making their way in ones and twos into the bar, I felt I had to say something.

'Look.' I waited until we'd all sat down. 'I've had a revelation.'

'Go on.' Margot settled her bag on the floor. She'd been remarkably quiet on the group chat this week, I thought. The rest of us – minus Annie of course – had all been busily plotting our Thursday, when finding out where Eddie was going had been our entire topic of conversation. Annie was on the *other* group chat, offering Wren recipes for home-made chicken goujons and talking about curtains.

I had been quietly gleeful that I was in any group chats at all.

'I've realised that it's all low self-esteem,' I said to the expectant faces.

'What is?' Fraser had taken the bowl of peanuts that Flynn had brought over and was shovelling them into his mouth with an open palm. 'Bloody starving,' he said. 'Minnie's all about the protein and the macros and that. She gave me a *list*, and you know something? Starbars weren't on there *at all*.' He chewed frantically for a moment. 'I'm supposed to eat steak,' he said mournfully. 'Steak! I can't afford steak. Can't afford much meat at all. I've even started looking at our Leah's rabbit in a funny way.'

'I only went for Dexter because I have such low self-esteem.' I interrupted the frenetic mastication.

'Well, that was obvious to anyone with a pulse,' Margot said rather brusquely. 'Nobody with any sense of discernment goes for that kind of man.'

I stared at her. 'Well, you could have told *me*!'

Wren patted my arm. 'Margot doesn't mean to be rude,' she said gently. '*Do* you, Margot?'

To my surprise, Margot dipped her head and fussed with her bag, avoiding my eye. 'No, no I don't, I'm sorry, Fee,' she said, and I nearly fell off my chair with astonishment. Margot? Apologising? Was this a remake of *Invasion of the Body Snatchers*?

Then I looked over at Fraser gobbling peanuts and spraying half-eaten ones across the table, and had a word with myself.

'I forget that others haven't had the extensive therapy that I've been fortunate enough to undergo,' Margot went on. 'Self-knowledge is so valuable.' She sounded much more like herself now.

'And we've all had moments like that, haven't we?' Wren went on. 'After all, it took me a lot of self-analysis to realise that Jordan and I were two very different people and just weren't suited to one another.' She gave a rueful little smile. 'That I'm probably a bit too high-maintenance for someone like her.'

'You are *not* high-maintenance.' Margot continued to surprise me. 'You simply have good standards. I've realised – through the therapy that I mentioned – how important it is for us women to have high standards. I have come to realise that, throughout my life, I have sought out men who have been emotionally unavailable, perhaps to protect myself. Even Bruce – otherwise wonderful though he was – couldn't invest emotionally. That lack of emotional investment meant that I never wanted to be vulnerable with him, hence the death of my desire for intimacy. I have decided from now on I shall only seek out men who are capable of empathy and who have reached a well-developed stage of emotional literacy. Keep your high standards, Wren, we should *never* compromise.'

Now it was Wren's turn to contemplate the flooring in the bar. 'Thank you,' she said, almost as though she didn't want to be heard.

Flynn had finished serving the men at the far end – it was poker night again tonight – and came floating over with a peanut top-up. 'What are we talking about?' he said, pulling up his usual chair.

'Fee's self-esteem.' Fraser sprayed peanuts liberally across the table. Annie handed him a wet wipe.

'And Eddie,' I put in hastily, before I could receive more words of wisdom on the subject of my lack of inner resilience. 'We're thinking about where he might be going on Thursday.'

There was a gulping kind of silence and I realised that we *had* been thinking about that, but only on the group chat that Annie wasn't involved in. Fortunately, she didn't seem to notice, or she put this down to me simply saying the first thing I thought of to distract everyone.

'He still hasn't said anything to me.' She put the wet wipes back in her bag. 'Not a word. I was a bit naughty actually...'

I felt my face freeze. I wondered if anyone else had had the 'stockings and suspenders' image again.

'What did you do?' Margot had regained her composure. Over on my side of the table, Flynn and Fraser were fighting a silent war for possession of the peanuts.

'I said that it might be nice if he took a day off soon.' Annie's expression was one of sad mischief. 'Now the weather's getting better. I said we could go for a drive to the beach, Scarborough or Whitby. Eat some chips and walk along the seafront. We used to do that a lot, when we were dating,' she added, now even more sadly.

'And what did he say?'

Annie sighed. 'He said they were really busy at work with some big orders, and he wouldn't be able to take any time off before the summer.' She sighed again. 'I was so tempted to tell him that I knew he'd booked a day off and ask him if it was meant to be a surprise for me.' A suspicion of tears gleamed at the corners of her eyes. 'But I was too afraid of the answer.'

'Oh.'

I opened my mouth to mention that I'd tried to find out who owned the house we'd seen him go into the other week, then remembered that Annie knew nothing about any of that, so I shouldn't be telling her that searching the electoral register hadn't got me any results and that unless I paid money, the Land Registry wasn't going to let me have anything either. All I had found out was that other similar houses on that road had recently sold for upwards of a million quid. I didn't think that finding out that Eddie was seeing someone with that kind of money would help her at all.

'I know you said he's joined a gym and lost weight,' Wren carefully asked Annie, 'but apart from that – I mean, if you join a gym you *should* lose weight...' We all avoided looking at Fraser, whose weight-loss programme looked set to be ambushed by ten tonnes of KP's finest. 'Are there any other signs that he's having an affair? Because he could be doing something else with his mysterious days off. Maybe he's joined a club? I mean, we're here... where does Eddie think you are tonight? I'm presuming you haven't told him you've joined a club for people disappointed in love?'

'He thinks I'm learning Portuguese.' Annie sounded rather proud of herself. 'Lessons once a week, on a Monday.'

'Isn't he going to wonder when you can't *speak* Portuguese?' Fraser took time off from his munching to ask. 'Like, if you ends up on holiday in Tenerife and you can't speak the language? What?' He added, as we all stared at him.

'They speak Spanish in Tenerife.' Flynn grappled for another handful of peanuts.

'Do they? Oh well, you'll probably be all right then.'

Everyone else ignored him.

'Like I said, he's bought himself some new clothes too,' Annie added. 'Nothing fancy, but it always used to take me threatening to throw his old stuff in the bin to get Eddie to buy new trousers.'

'But if he's lost weight,' I said, 'he will need new clothes, won't he?'

Everyone made 'that's right' noises.

'And then there's the phone calls and the emails.' Annie almost seemed upset at my, perfectly reasonable I thought, observation. 'If it was *just* the gym and the clothes, I'd think he was on a health kick. We see so much of it on TV, telling you not to eat this and not to eat that and I know he worries about his health. But he's been getting these phone calls, usually in the morning...' Her face crumpled under her 'sensible' haircut. 'And he takes the phone out into the garden to talk. He's got himself a new email address too – we normally share the same one, it's only for Amazon orders and suchlike. But the other day he was on the laptop and I saw... I couldn't tell what it was, but it wasn't his usual email account. So he's talking to someone and emailing someone and he's keeping it hidden from me.'

'Have you tried checking his mileage?' I asked.

Five pairs of eyes swivelled my way.

'Mileage?' Margot said, very carefully, widening her eyes in my direction and saying as clearly as if she'd shouted in my ear, *We're not supposed to know anything about Eddie's movements, she doesn't know we're following him!*

I ignored them. 'I saw it on some website or another. You make a note of his mileage in the car, then ask some casual questions about his day. If he says he was at work all day and his mileage is way out, you've got evidence.'

Annie looked down at her drink. 'But that would mean I didn't trust him,' she said sadly.

'But you *don't* trust him!'

'It's not that I don't trust him...' Annie looked conflicted. 'Oh, I don't know. Part of me thinks Eddie would never – you know, have an affair. Not my Eddie! He's been as reliable as... as this table, for forty years, not so much as a sniff of another woman on the horizon. All right, I know he had a bit of a "thing" for Kirsty Wark, but, let's face it, she's not going to throw everything over to move to Yorkshire for a pork products admin manager, is she?'

None of us expressed any opinions as to Ms Wark's predilection for bacon and its producers, so Annie went on. 'He's not the most demonstrative of men, but it's been flowers every Valentine's

Day and he always picks me out something nice for my birthday and Christmas. But since January, he's been a bit, well, *distant* is the best way I can put it. And, of course, like I said, he forgot Valentine's Day, and...' She pulled out a tissue and dabbed at her eyes, '...first time in forty years,' she muttered indistinctly from behind it.

After everyone had gone and we'd wiped the detritus of Fraser and the peanuts off the table, Flynn and I lounged behind the bar.

'Do *you* think he's having an affair? Eddie, I mean, not Fraser,' I asked him.

Flynn made a dismissive movement and picked up some empty glasses to put back on the racking. 'I hate to say it, but it's hard to see what else it could be.'

'I wonder what Annie will do?'

'Three choices. She'll pretend it never happened and carry on, turning a blind eye to her husband living a double life; she'll let him know that she knows and he'll pretend to stop seeing the other woman while living a double life and he'll just be more careful; she'll kick him out, get divorced and live a brilliant life solo. She might get a dachshund and a blonde bob. Or a wine bar.'

I looked at him. 'Does that mean you...?'

We were disturbed by a party of ten, staying apparently in one of the holiday cottages up on the moor and desperate for wine. They kept us busy for the evening, asking questions about the locality and what there was to do on wet March evenings. I didn't have time to ask Flynn anything about his somewhat cryptic statement, and he was in a hurry to clean down and close up after the group had left.

I went home and showered, then lay in bed, thinking. My phone was pinging with messages from the others, arranging a timetable for following Eddie on Thursday, but, apart from indicating that I was up for it, I muted the messages.

There was only one reason that Flynn would suggest that Annie could open a wine bar. I absolutely could *not* see quiet, always rather sad, Annie cheerily serving Sauvignon to smartly suited businessmen or inventing cocktails to entice the hen party crowd.

He'd been cheated on. He'd run away to open a wine bar.

Flynn, who always seemed so 'together', so composed. But now I came to think of it, there was a tinge of dark humour about him, as though he rode the edge of sharp pain. Flynn, with his careful appearance, always well turned out but not showy, as though he didn't want to be seen. Plus his careful avoidance of even the most oblique hint of anything flirty towards me. No reason he *should* find me attractive, obviously, but my main experience of men was that they couldn't be alone with a woman for more than three minutes without making a boob joke or turning an innocent remark into an excuse for a dirty laugh. Fraser was a case in point.

Flynn was different. Now I came to think of it, he radiated hurt. I made a note to ask him about it. Then I turned over and went to sleep.

11

I was dreaming. I was in a car, going over speed bumps which made everything rattle. Thump. Thump.

Then my nerves sparked me awake, kicking my brain into action like a battery connection. Or acid pouring through my body.

'Let me IN!'

Dexter. Drunk, by the sound of it, or coked up, shouting on the threshold and hitting the door with a fist. I froze. My phone was across the room on the side by the TV, where I'd left it so I didn't keep getting disturbed by the messages buzzing back and forth from the group. If I got up to fetch it, he'd hear me.

I hoped downstairs were calling the police again, but the silence from the flat below made me think they might not be there. So I just sat, again, with the covers pulled to my neck, and listened.

Dexter wasn't being as outright loud as last time. Less of the yelling and more direct force. I could see the door shuddering as he thumped against it. The whole of the rest of the world seemed to have gone silent, as though there were only me and Dexter still alive, and the door was cracking around the hinges and the lock with the force he was putting into his attack.

Eventually I called out. I was afraid that the door wouldn't withstand too much more of his concentrated attention, and he obviously knew I was here, when last time he'd turned up he'd not known I was in. 'What do you want, Dexter?'

It wasn't enough. It didn't encompass all the things I *really* wanted to say to him, like how dare he keep turning up when he'd been the one to end things, and why did he think I'd still be waiting for him? Because hadn't I always waited before? Hadn't I always let him in before? He was only repeating his usual behaviour – he'd left me alone long enough for me to have felt punished and desperate and now he was coming back to reclaim his property. He'd done it before and I could hardly blame him for thinking that I'd behave as I'd always done; it was *me* that had changed, after all.

At least he'd stopped whacking the door.

'I needs to use the bathroom.' A wheedling, whining tone. It was drugs, then. Drunk, Dexter was overtly aggressive. On coke, he thought he was God's gift and could talk his way into and out of anything. 'Aw, let me in, babe! I just wants to talk to you, to see you!'

'We're over, Dex.' I tried to keep calm, although my heart was beating fast enough to make me feel sick. I crept out of the bed, trying not to make any sound – if he thought I was coming to unlock the door, he'd make even more noise. 'You finished with me, remember? You were going back to Leeds to someone called Henty?' Who, if I remembered the swift, final conversation in front of *Our Flag Means Death*, had bigger tits than me and was always up for sex.

What on *earth* had I ever seen in Dexter? Apart from my rock-bottom self-esteem telling me that any man was better than none, and his lazy entitled behaviour feeling familiar. A sudden crash of realisation on the back of my neck felt like a bucket of cold water. I'd been dating my *brother*, or someone so much like him that they could have been mental twins.

'You and me, babe, it's always you and me!' Dexter was still on with the persuasive tone. It probably meant that Henty, whoever she was, had thrown him out and he'd run out of friends to sofa-surf with.

'No, no it isn't,' I said, seizing my phone. What should I do? Ring the police? They'd come, but it might take a while. Dexter could smash the flat up in the time it would take them to get here. He could, a little thought entered my head reluctantly, like a mouse tiptoeing through a cat show, kill me.

The last message had been from the Heartbreak Club's group chat, so I pressed reply.

> Dexter is outside my door. I think he's going to smash it down.

As though to reinforce my fears, Dex resumed his onslaught on the door. It was cheap and badly hung, there was a street door to the entryway that was supposed to be kept locked at all times, but the flat above mine was empty and being redecorated, so the necessity of tradesmen coming in and out meant that the lock had been disabled by the landlord. It had never mattered before, in this quiet little North Yorkshire backwater, where the worst you could expect was a few teenagers sitting in the passage furtively vaping and a shout of 'get out of it, you little buggers!' was enough to send them scampering home.

We hadn't expected to have to keep out a Dexter. The door hadn't been constructed to keep out a Dexter. It hadn't, truthfully, been constructed to keep out more than the most cursory attempt at burglary. It locked, but the wood was old and the hinges didn't seem to have been replaced since the rooms had been storage for the chemist's shop the building had once been. The rent was so cheap that I'd always supposed that the doors weren't the required fireproof ones that rental properties were legally supposed to have. Nobody complained because nobody could afford to move.

Fireproofness had never been tested. Dexter-proofness was being tested to the max right now, as he redoubled his attack. The wood splintered around the hinges.

My phone pinged.

> Are you all right? Are you safe?

That was Wren.

I answered honestly, my fingers shaking.

> I don't know.

I tried reason. 'Go away, Dex. Come back tomorrow, we can talk about this later.'

I should have known. Drug binges and Dexter were not amenable to sensible suggestions or being talked down. He was fired up and I had rejected him, as he saw it, by not opening the door. I'd never said no to Dexter before, mostly because I hadn't dared, and my lack of self-assertion had led him to believe that I was a pushover.

'I told you, *darling*, I needs the bathroom!'

And here we were. Middle of the night silence everywhere, and a man breaking down my door.

With my heart pounding so fast that my stomach ricocheted with every beat, I dialled 999.

'What's your emergency?'

'My boyfriend – my *ex*-boyfriend is trying...'

The door exploded into splinters and Dexter reached over me and took the phone. 'It's fine, a misunderstanding, that's all,' he said and disconnected the call. The door lay in shattered ruins around the flat, giving the lie to his words. I could only hope that they'd try and trace my call, but Dex had sounded so cool, so reasonable, and if it was a busy night then I might have to wait until everywhere else went quiet before I got some passing officers coming by to check up on me.

Looking at Dexter, it might be too late by then. In fact, the next three minutes might be too late, judging by the way he was bunching his muscles and staring around the flat as though in search of some 'other man' that he was no doubt convinced was behind my not letting him in. That I had someone else, in his mind, would be the only possible reason for my not welcoming him back with open arms. No woman could function without a man, in Dexter's eyes.

'So then,' he said, conversationally. 'Who're you fucking now?'

I could hardly speak. My jaw had clenched itself but was somehow managing to chatter away against my teeth. 'Nobody. Honestly, there's nobody, Dexter.' Conciliatory, as I'd learned to be when he was in one of these rages.

Behind him, the open doorway beckoned. The front door, open to the street. If I could just get out...

I could hear my phone pinging messages, but it was where Dexter had thrown it down after cutting off my police call. I didn't dare go and pick it up.

'So, how've you been?' He leaned against the wall. If I could move him further into the flat... and if my legs would cooperate, because right now they would hardly bear my weight.

'I thought you said you needed the bathroom?' If he went in

there, then I could be out before he finished. But his bladder appeared to no longer be the main cause of concern.

'Yeah, it can wait.' He'd folded his arms and was watching me out of bloodshot eyes. 'Came to see how you're doing.'

'I'm good.' My cheeks were wobbling with my attempts to get my mouth under control. 'How are you?'

Like a dinner party conversation. Like a polite meeting in the street, while we stood with the wreckage of my door scattered around the carpet, Dexter casual as ever and me standing in my pyjamas, exposed and horribly, dreadfully afraid.

'Oh, you know.' He walked further into the flat, his eyes moving from side to side, on the hunt for any evidence of another man. 'Decided I'd give you another chance.'

As he came closer, I moved to one side. If he would only leave the doorway clear...

As he reached out to touch me, I ducked under his arm and dived for the stairs, feeling the sharp wood of the shredded door slicing into my bare feet as I went over it. Down the narrow staircase, banging my knuckles against the wall as I went, with Dexter swearing and coming behind me, until I hesitated at the bottom. Where to go? My neighbours' doorway was dark and quiet, they weren't there, there was no refuge with them.

I ran out into the night, pattering little bloody footprints on the pavement as Dex hurled himself through the doorway into the street.

'Fucking slag! Don't you try running!'

But running was all I had and I fled into the middle of the road, feeling the chill of the night biting at me through my flimsy pyjamas and the sting of gravel on my ruined feet. If he caught me – if he caught me now, I was dead and I knew it. Dexter full of cocaine wouldn't care about how much trouble he'd be in, he'd kill me where I stood and then run. He could be clear and away before anyone found what was left of me.

'Fee!'

I almost didn't react to my name, I was so frozen with fear. But I jerked my head up to see Flynn standing in the side entry to the wine bar, wearing a striped dressing gown, incongruous in this terror-filled night.

'Come here, come to me. Quickly!'

Dexter was almost on me now. He'd hesitated in the street, scanning for people, scanning for vehicles. He'd retained enough of his faculties, clearly, to not want witnesses. When he saw Flynn, he roared.

'That's the bastard, isn't it?'

As quick as a ghost, Flynn wrapped a gowned arm around me and scooped me into the passageway around the back of the wine bar, slamming and locking the gate behind us.

'Is that Dexter?'

I *wanted* to quip that, no, I had a veritable army of insanely jealous men on Class A drugs who spent their leisure time being surly at me, but I couldn't speak. Literally could not get a word out. I just nodded.

'Okay. Okay, it's all right, I've got you.' Flynn hugged me tight against him. The shivers started and we heard the sound of Dexter trying to climb over the gate and get into the yard. 'Come on, inside. The police are, hopefully, on their way, but it might take them a while. The police are coming!' he finished by shouting at the lumpen shapes that were Dexter's knuckles, gripping the top of the gate.

A car swept into the end of the road, headlights fierce, and Dexter dropped back to earth, swearing copiously.

'I... I can't...' was all I could get out, shuddering like an earthquake zone.

Feet, running. Lights. A loud shout and the sound of something heavy falling, then voices. Voices I recognised.

'Flynn? We're here, it's us.'

Wren. Wren was speaking from the other side of the bolted gate, sounding calm and assured.

'You sit there. Okay?' Flynn guided me to the little chairs we'd sat on before and carefully placed me so all I had to do was bend my legs, then he went over and unlocked the gate. I could see through and out into the street beyond, where Dexter was flat on his face on the road's surface, being sat on firmly by Fraser. Margot appeared to be reading him the riot act.

Fraser saw me looking and gave me an enormous grin and a thumbs up. Dexter tried to wriggle underneath him, but Fraser pushed on the back of his head until he went quiet. Wren came into the yard.

'Fee! Are you all right?'

I *wanted* to say that yes, of course I was. But my feet were bleeding, I was cold in my pyjamas and the wooden surface of this seat was damp. I tried to speak, but all I could get out was a kind of half-swallowed howl.

'She's here, Margot, she's all right,' Wren called back over her shoulder, peeling off her jacket and putting it around me. Margot glanced up, nodded and then went back to speaking to Dexter, who had gone very still. Flynn was out there too now, with his stripy dressing gown flapping, and looking a little bit like an escaped patient from an institution.

I saw him bend close to Dexter's head and show him something on his phone screen, holding it out at arm's length, strangely confrontational. He was speaking but I couldn't hear what he said, though it was clearly something that made Dexter strain under Fraser's incapacitating solidity, then freeze as though he'd just been given bad news.

Flynn tucked his phone away, nodded once and came back into the yard. 'The police will be here shortly,' he said.

'Take Fee inside,' Margot said. 'We're in control out here.'

'I got him!' Fraser added cheerily, as though he were reclining on a sun lounger rather than my ex-boyfriend. 'You'll be all right now, Feebs.'

'Your poor feet.' Wren looked down at my bleeding soles. 'We'd better get those cleaned up.'

I couldn't stand either. It was ridiculous. I wanted to say how ridiculous it was, but the words wouldn't come; they were smothered by the tears that had started falling, prevented from forming by my mouth twisting around the sobs. Wren put her arm around me and Flynn took my hand and between them they managed to lead me in through the side door and into the wine bar, where Flynn fetched two chairs down off a table and sat down beside me.

'I'm going to help Margot,' Wren said, looking from me to Flynn and back again. 'Look after her, Flynn.'

'Absolutely,' he said, pushing up the sleeves of the dressing gown and keeping hold of my hand. His presence so close and warm was reassuring, and now I was indoors I felt safer and the tears began to dry up, leaving me hiccupping and still in possession of a mouth that wouldn't cooperate.

'Would you like a brandy?' Flynn asked, staring around the bottles on their racks. 'Supposed to be good for shock.'

I thought about it. Alcohol, warming me, scaffolding me from the inside. Fake courage. I shook my head. 'I wouldn't mind a cup of tea,' I managed to get out and Flynn laughed, an odd bark of a laugh.

'Well done,' he said. 'Fee, I'm going to leave you here a moment and put the kettle on upstairs. Will you be all right?

Margot, Wren and Fraser are there outside and acting as a human shield so that piece of filth can't get up and come after you again.'

'I'll be fine.' I nearly said that I had no 'worse' to descend to, so this was going to be as good as it got for a while.

'Okay.' Flynn dithered. 'I don't want to leave you.'

'I need tea.' My voice sounded a bit more normal now. 'And probably some Dettol or something.'

We looked at the trail of bloody footprints on the tiled floor, where I'd walked in from outside.

'Tea and Dettol, yep.' Flynn moved to the door again. 'Actually, not sure I've got any Dettol. Not really much call for it in the barkeeping trade. I might have some antiseptic cream or something, will that do?'

'That,' I said, my voice gaining in strength with every word, 'will do nicely.'

12

The police arrived about half an hour later, at the same time as Annie, accompanied surprisingly by Eddie.

'This is my husband, Eddie,' she introduced him and we all had to pretend that we'd never set eyes on him before and nod and murmur hello.

Fraser, showing an intelligence that outer appearances belied, especially outer appearances that were wearing a Bugs Bunny pyjama set and slippers, said, 'Oh, I know you, I sees you in the mornings at the gym!'

'Oh, yes.' Eddie looked a little embarrassed about that. Almost as though he didn't want anyone to know about the gym thing.

'We came as soon as we could,' Annie went on. 'Eddie had to get the car out, you see.'

The police interviewed me and told me they'd arrested Dexter. However, since he hadn't actually attacked me, all they were going to be able to get him for was threatening behaviour, and the likelihood was that he would be out and about within the week, and did I have anywhere else to go, particularly since my front door was now missing?

'She can come here,' Flynn said confidently.

'Are you sure, sir? We can't guarantee that the individual won't try again.' One of the policemen looked worried at the proposition. He had no doubt met people like Dexter before. 'His sort usually do,' he added. 'I'd take out an injunction, if I were you,' he said to me.

'He'd only break it.' I sipped at my tea. 'Dexter doesn't really care.'

'I don't think he'll be back.' Flynn still sounded confident. Beyond him, in the wine bar, Margot, Wren and Annie twittered a dubious dawn chorus. Fraser and Eddie were talking about treadmills and comparing weight loss and inches gained.

'I admire your positivity, sir.' The police radios crackled and they set off with Dexter in the car, bound for paperwork and frustrating attempts to get him to admit to having done wrong.

'How are you all here?' I'd stopped shivering now. In fact, draped in a blanket from upstairs and drinking my third mug of tea, I was slightly too warm. I suspected that Flynn had turned the heating up. I'd given Wren back her jacket too, although there had been something about the slight trace of perfume on the collar that had made me want to keep it. It felt maternal, and that was a first for me. 'What happened?'

'Wren has been staying over at my house,' Margot started.

'I can't bear to be in the flat. It reminds me of Jordan,' Wren said. 'It's just so quiet at night, and I was worried I might give in and text her.'

'So, when you messaged, we went over and picked up Fraser and got here as fast as we could,' Margot finished.

'We were later because Eddie had to get the car out,' Annie said again. Unless Eddie had the car garaged in Tierra del Fuego this didn't really mean anything, but she was obviously desperate for me to understand that her delay wasn't from lack of intent.

'And when we got here and saw that man trying to climb the gate, we knew who he must be. Fraser was most impressive, I have to say.'

At the mention of his name, Fraser looked over. 'He were trying to run,' he said proudly. 'I got him.'

'Most impressive,' Margot repeated.

I looked around at the club. Margot was wearing what looked like yoga gear: lovely flowing trousers and a zip-up top. Wren was in leggings and a T-shirt with her jacket over both. Fraser's Bugs Bunny was crumpled as though he'd been asleep, and Annie had a nightie on under a big coat. Tears began to trickle from the corners of my eyes again. They'd come. They'd heard I was in distress, and they'd all come.

'Thank you.' I could only get a whisper out again, but this time it was emotion rather than terror stopping the words.

Wren gave me a quick hug. 'We're glad we got here when we did,' she said. 'He was trying to climb over the gate. He only started to run when we put the headlights on him, and I dread to think what might have happened otherwise.'

'Hey.' Flynn, who had been standing silently behind the bar, joined in now. 'I can fight.'

'He was *enormous*,' Wren said dubiously. 'Fraser had to sit on him.'

'All right, I can't fight very well, but I could have hit him with a chair or something.'

I looked around the wine bar. Its acres of glass windows looked suddenly vulnerable and I felt very exposed in here. 'If he's been on the coke, Dexter doesn't stop,' I said sadly. 'It's like he's impervious or something. You could probably shoot him and it would take an hour for the message he was dead to get to his brain.'

'Ah.' Flynn gave me a grin. 'But he's gone for now, so let's not go armed for the time being, all right?'

Behind me, Annie yawned, and Eddie put a protective arm around her. 'I ought to take the little lady home,' he said. 'She would come out to make sure everything was all right.' He gave Annie a fond look. 'The silly sausage,' he said.

'I was worried for Fee,' Annie said. 'Margot was certain that something might happen to her.'

I winced at my sore feet, now covered in some suspicious yellow cream that Flynn had found in his bathroom cabinet and smelling slightly of lavender. I'd had to borrow a pair of socks to stop me sliding straight out of the door when I stood up, so I was now resplendent in my own pyjamas, which had inexplicable streaks of blood up both legs, an enormous pair of football socks of Flynn's and a fluffy blanket with a picture of a kitten on. I looked like a triumphant last-minute goal scorer after a particularly savage match in the Arctic Cats' Home.

'Something did happen,' I said, words still filtered through tears. 'Dexter.'

'You're still in shock,' Margot asserted. 'We'll go now and let you get some sleep. Flynn, you'll look after her?'

I saw Flynn give a sharp nod as though this matter had never been in doubt.

Margot lowered her voice now, although it wasn't really necessary; Eddie was guiding Annie carefully out of the bar with Fraser trotting alongside, wittering on about his month's membership almost being up. 'Will you be all right for...' she lowered her voice still further and I had to lean forward to hear her, '...*the Thursday thing*?' An emphatic jerk of her head towards the door followed her words, as though I might not have grasped her meaning.

'I'll be fine.' I sounded a lot firmer than I felt. 'But...'

Wren hurtled in. 'We ought to go, Fee, if you're sure you're all right.'

'Yes, yes, of course.' Margot jingled her car keys. 'Well. We look forward to hearing from you during Thursday. And we'll see you next Monday, of course.'

And they were all gone, leaving Flynn and me still in the bar.

'Come on.' He put a solicitous arm around my shoulders. 'I've got a spare room and I'll tuck you up, then go over to your place and make it secure.'

I ought to have protested. I ought to have maintained that I would be fine in my own flat; Dexter had been arrested, which would give us a day or so's grace before he started anything else, and I could put a curtain over the doorway in the meantime. But I didn't. All my strength seemed to have ebbed away, seeping out of me with the blood that my slashed feet had left. I just wanted to be helped into a warm bed and not to think about anything for a few hours, so I let Flynn guide me upstairs as though I were an elderly invalid, and I fell into the bed he offered and unconsciousness.

* * *

Flynn let me spend the next couple of days upstairs. The flat was bigger than I'd imagined, with two bedrooms, a large living room, a storage area and a wonderful kitchen and bathroom that looked as though they'd been newly installed.

Walking was painful, so I tottered about using the furniture to bear my weight. By the time Flynn came up for lunch on Wednesday, I'd reached the point of being able to stand without seeping and I made sandwiches.

'What do we do when he comes back?' I said.

'Who?'

'Dexter. I know him, Flynn. The club showed him up. *I* showed him up. He won't like that and he won't rest until he's made me suffer.' That awful flash of thought that I'd had the night Dex had broken his way in – *he's like my brother*. 'I know men like him.'

Flynn regarded me carefully from over a toasted cheese sandwich. 'You really do have a pretty shit family,' he said, as though he knew exactly what I was thinking. But then, I had gone into some detail about my parents and their somewhat sideways approach to bringing up children, which mostly seemed to involve pitting them against one another and siding with the boy until the girl was a broken shadow with no conviction in herself.

'Yes, that has occurred to me once or twice.' I made a rueful face. 'But it was my normal. I didn't know any other way of being and I'm only gradually making my way out from it. I thought that's what men are *like*,' I finished.

Flynn pointed at himself. 'Me too?'

'You were different. You weren't trying to pick me up, for a start.'

'And you thought I was gay. And, before you go down that line again, I'm not responsible for the flat. I got interior designers in.'

'Stop it.' He made me laugh, that's what it was. That was why Flynn was so different to every other man I'd ever known. He didn't mind looking silly, he didn't mind poking fun at himself. Most other males of my acquaintance would have drowned themselves off Flamborough Head rather than reveal any weaknesses or vulnerability. Flynn didn't seem to mind looking a bit daft now and then. 'You are the most together man I've ever met. I'm having trouble adjusting.'

He jerked his head sideways, negating my opinion, but then I was very used to men doing that too. 'Not always. I am not altogether the vision of combined manliness and emotional intelligence that you see before you right now. Sometimes I can be very, very stupid indeed. Incidentally, Eddie and Annie? He didn't really behave like a man in the throes of an affair the other night, did he?'

I stopped chewing. 'Are you trying to hint to me that you had an affair? Is this the subtlety I've heard so much about but rarely seen demonstrated in the male – particularly when Fraser is about?'

Flynn finished his sandwich and put the plate down. 'Er, no. I think you might be hearing my attempt to change the subject and conflating two very different things.'

'But why change the subject? You know all about the club, all about what happened to us, why are you so coy about your own love life?'

He got up, brushing crumbs off his lap onto the – beautiful and very obviously expensively restored – oak floorboards. 'I'm not coy. I just don't think any of it is relevant, that's all.'

I wondered what he'd do if I asked. But I wouldn't ask, *couldn't* ask. I'd been trained out of trying to get sensible answers a long time ago: parents who pretended not to hear anything unless it was my brother asking if he could have fifty quid to go out with his mates, and a brother who seemed to believe I'd been put on this earth purely for his amusement.

No *wonder* I let myself get used by people like Dex. No wonder I made shallow, casual friends like Demi, who had really only included me in her life because I was convenient and available. I wondered why it had taken me so long to come to these conclusions, and then realised that I hadn't come to them by myself, the Heartbreak Club had prodded me in that general direction.

'Annie and Eddie,' Flynn went on, pulling me back into the moment. He probably thought I'd been quiet for too long. Maybe he even thought I'd been wondering about him. 'She clearly adores him and he really seems to love her too. I must admit all that "little lady" stuff made me want to sit him down in front of some feminist literature, but if it works for them...'

'I suppose...' I said slowly, running with his desire to change the subject, 'that it's possible to have an affair and still be in love with your wife?'

'They don't have children, do they?'

'No. Annie skates over that subject a bit, which makes me gather that they both wanted them but it never happened.'

'So maybe he's got a secret family somewhere? Maybe he met someone else to do the "children" thing with? And he's leading a double life but this is the first time that Annie has had suspicions?'

I stared at Flynn. 'That's an odd conclusion to come to.'

'Too much daytime TV.' He waved airily. 'Anyway, now I've met him, somehow I can't quite see Eddie as a babe-magnet. He even *looks* like an administration manager in the pork products industry.'

'Someone might find that absolutely riveting. Plus, women go for all types of men. Dexter is a case in point.'

Flynn sighed. 'I cannot believe you found that attractive. He looks like the stereotype of a drunken street fighter. Not at all the sort of man I would have thought you'd go for.'

I stood up now and instantly got stabbed in the feet by the pain of a thousand small cuts. 'Ow.' I hobbled a few steps.

'Are you going to be all right tomorrow? For Operation Follow Eddie?'

The topic had changed again. I was getting used to this from Flynn. 'Try and stop me, I'm looking forward to it. Well, no, not looking forward, that sounds awful, as though I'm really gleeful about catching him out; I'm only happy that we might be able to get some answers for Annie. Even getting some photos of him with another woman might help her throw him out. Or confront him, at least.'

'Do you think she will?' Flynn didn't seem keen to return to talking about my taste in men, for which I was grateful. 'I think she'll keep quiet and just live with it. She seems to be so besotted with him, she'd forgive him anything.'

'But at least she'd know what he was up to,' I said, toddling slowly across to the kitchen with my plate. 'So she would be in a position of power. It's the not knowing that's eating her up. If she decides never to mention it to him, at least she knows what he's up to.'

'It will be out of our hands anyway.' Flynn had come into the kitchen behind me. 'Up to her what she does with the information we get. You go and sit down again, I'll tidy this up, you need to rest your feet.'

His concern made that unaccustomed sensation creep over me again. The same sort of 'something bursting inside' that I'd experienced when the club made me feel included; the feeling that had reduced me to tears when they'd all turned out to make sure I was all right when they knew Dexter had appeared. As though something gentle was hatching under my heart. With it came the tears again.

'Oh, blimey, sorry! I didn't mean to... but you're still in shock, I should think. Do the feet hurt?'

'No,' I said, trying not to cry but failing. 'It's not that. It's you being nice to me. *People* being nice to me.'

Flynn hunted around until he found some kitchen roll and handed me a couple of pieces. 'People must have been nice to you before, though? You've not gone through life being totally reviled.'

'Of course not.' I spluttered a snotty laugh. 'But it's always been an impersonal niceness, if you see what I mean. Teachers were nice, my grandma was nice. Maybe nice is the wrong word, maybe it's considerate that I'm trying to say. Nobody has ever really considered my feelings about anything before you and the club. I'm a bit overwhelmed.'

He shook his head slowly. 'Then it's precisely time that you were out of that situation,' he said. 'I'm glad you found the club. Or they found you. Or we all found each other.'

'Me too.' I snorted.

We stood for a moment or two longer. Me leaning against the door of the fridge, holding tissue, Flynn standing with one hand on the open cupboard door. From outside came the sound of cars parking, people chatting, the little town going about its business and it all felt a very long way away, suddenly. Flynn dropped his head and his glasses slid down his nose to make him look like a short-sighted Cousin Itt. 'I'm glad I found you.'

He reached out a hand and awkwardly patted the top of my arm, as though it were a small dog. Then he whirled away again to head downstairs to ready the bar for opening and left me standing open mouthed.

Well. Flynn. *Flynn.*

Just like that, I realised I was very, very fond of him. I'd been confused into thinking he was simply one of the club by the fact that he was so different to the other men I'd known. It had never crossed my mind that he could be – more. Slowly I inched my way downstairs after him, having to negotiate some of the steeper sections on my behind to avoid having to put all my weight onto one raw foot.

'Flynn?' He wasn't in the bar. He wasn't in the office either. I found him in the toilets, rubbing a brush under a rim in a manner for which the word *desultory* was hardly inconsequential enough. When he heard me come in, he straightened away from the bowl, rubber gloves flapping and the toilet brush dripping off-puttingly from one hand.

'Ah,' he said. 'You must be recovering. I hoped I might have a little bit longer to compose myself before I had to face you.'

'You said...'

'Yes, Fee, I'm well aware of what I said.' He went to push his glasses further up his nose, realised he was wearing rubber gloves, and performed a movement with his upper arm to sweep them into the correct position. The brush dripped again.

'Did you mean...?' I couldn't seem to get a complete sentence out.

Now Flynn came in close. 'Well, I thought in terms of heavy hints, I was doing a pretty good job.'

'But Dexter...' No, it was no good. I'd got all the beginnings going on but the endings were eluding me.

'Dexter has been well and truly warned off.'

We were standing almost nose to nose in the toilet cubicle. Half of me wanted Flynn to put his arms around me and kiss me, but the half that was very aware of the rubber gloves and brush element was keeping a wary distance.

'He won't stay warned off.'

'He will.' Flynn sounded so definite that I knew it was more than wishful thinking.

'How do you know?' I looked at him hopefully. I so wanted it to be true, that Dex would leave me alone for evermore, that Flynn and I might have a *something*, whatever this feeling of potential might lead to.

Flynn looked down again and his glasses slid to the end of his nose once more. 'Do you think that you and I... I mean, could you ever... Do you...?'

I moved in close. Closer still, until we were touching. Raised my head until I could look into his black eyes and feel his breath on my cheek. 'I think we could,' I said.

As his mouth moved into a lazy smile, I kissed it off him. After a moment of fumbling, the gloves and toilet brush crashed to the floor and his hands were in my hair, holding me steady as he kissed me back until we were breathless and potential was colliding firmly with actuality.

Eventually we drew apart and I took in a huge lungful of the scent of domestic toilet cleaner, which was filling the air. 'Well,' I said.

'Not just well but pretty bloody amazingly fine, I'd say.' Flynn shook his hair back. 'And maybe now we should talk.'

Talking had not been the verb that I'd had in mind, not with him looking so dishevelled and sexily overheated, but I'd go with it. 'What about?'

'Let's go and sit in the bar. Would you like a glass of wine?' He was watching me.

'No thanks. I want to know what we're talking about.'

We shuffled awkwardly out of the toilets and through to the cleaner air of the bar, where we pulled our chairs around the club's usual table, and Flynn took out his phone. 'This is what I showed Dexter.'

It was a photo. Flynn, with shorter hair and looking smart in a business suit, next to a man I vaguely recognised. The man had his arm around Flynn's shoulders and a broad smile on his face.

'That's...'

'That's me. Yes. Last year, in Oz, right after we'd won an award for the rooftop bar I was managing.'

'That man, that's Andrew Mays-Harrison, isn't it?' An entrepreneur, a TV pundit on *The Apprentice*, sometime Dragon on *Dragon's Den*. Businessman, football club owner, sponsor of an F2 team, general public moneybags. Made Alan Sugar look as though he was scrabbling about down the back of the sofa for 50p's.

'Mmm.' Flynn put his phone away. 'He's my dad.'

I jumped to my feet unwisely fast and felt the stabbing of those thousands of splinter cuts anew. 'What? Bugger, ow!'

'And I told Dexter that if he came near you in future, I'd bring the whole of my dad's security detail to bear on him and he'd be lucky if he ever saw daylight again. He'd actually be lucky if he ever saw anything other than the bottom of a deep river, and nobody would know where he'd gone.' Flynn cleared his throat. 'A little bit hyperbolic, I have to admit, and Dad's not quite as much of a gangster as I made him out to be, but the end result would be the same.'

I stared at him. 'But that's...' The ends of my sentences had clearly wandered off again.

'I apologise for not telling you this before,' Flynn went on, leaning his elbows on the table. 'But I had to be certain that you didn't already know this. About who I am, I mean.'

'What the hell difference would it make?'

'Ah, you sweet innocent.' He gave me a grin that was almost pure mischief. A small proportion, though, seemed wary. 'Margot recognised me. Her husband and my dad were on some kind of committee together, apparently, so she'd met me before, a long time ago. I didn't remember. We meet a lot of people.'

'She didn't say anything to me.' I still felt winded by his revelation. Why had I never asked his surname? Why had I gone on assuming that he was just a barman?

'No.' Now Flynn looked serious. 'I had to know that you thought we might have a shot together before I said anything to you. I needed to be sure...' He stopped and became very interested in the floor underneath our table. 'I needed to be sure that you wanted *me*,' he said, slightly muffled by his own collar.

'As opposed to? Henry Cavill? He wasn't here snogging me in a toilet though.'

'As opposed to wanting an "in" on Dad's corporation. I've got a bit of precedent for women who – well, let's say that I wasn't the main reason they wanted to be with me.' He was still talking to the floor.

'And that's why you left Australia?' The winded feeling had turned to a vague prickliness, almost like the onset of a faint. As though the world had suddenly become unreal.

'Mmm. Two in a row. Second one wanted to move in with me, and I was just starting to clear the ground for that to happen, finding us a bigger place to live in one of the suburbs...' Flynn looked up at me now. 'In Australia, there's a common law agreement. If you live together for two years then split up, it's the same thing as a marriage split: you divide property and finances and all that. Luckily I found out in time – she already had a boyfriend. She was using me, going to wait out the two years and then take me for financial support and a share of the property.'

'Oh, Flynn,' I said softly. Although his words were matter of fact, there was a creasing around his eyes and a tightening of his mouth that said he'd cared, and finding out that he was being used had hit him hard.

'Yeah, they were in it together, her and her boyfriend. She was going to set him up in his own business with the money she took off me. Marry him and leave me in the dust.'

Despite our recent close encounter, I felt strange touching him, but I put my hand on his arm. 'That must have been hard.'

'My mum died when I was fifteen,' he said.

'Right. I have no idea why that should have any relevance to this, but I'll go with it.' I kept my hand on his sleeve and he put his over the top.

'After she... died, me and Dad... we only had each other. He taught me all about business but he kind of left out the mum stuff. The bits about how you deal with women. So, I'm an idiot sometimes.'

We sat, while the spring sunshine sloped its way up the road towards the pub, pausing only to glance in at our windows. 'I don't think you're an idiot,' I said quietly.

'Back then, it genuinely never occurred to me that someone might try to use me for money,' he went on, but at least he was talking to me now, rather than the floorboards. 'Dad's always been a wealthy man, so it's my normal. It just doesn't feature in my thinking.'

I wondered what he thought about me, with the fishy staircase to my flat and the three crowded rooms. My hand fell away from his.

'So, I needed to know that you weren't looking for an easy road to money,' Flynn went on. Then, 'I'm sorry. I don't mean to insinuate that you ever would. But Tamar did a bit of a number on me, I'm afraid. It's made me – nervous.'

'That's why you didn't have a Valentine's date?' My words came out a bit tight. 'Because you think everyone's in it for your money?'

'Or access to Dad. You'd be amazed how many people want an introduction as soon as they find out who I am.' Flynn's eyes dropped away from mine and he slumped forward, cupping his face in his hands. 'I just want to be *me*,' he said, a little indistinctly.

'But you're not above using your dad to threaten bully boys?' I tried to lighten him up a bit. The implications of all this were beginning to dawn on me but I couldn't look at them now. Flynn was anxious, that much was obvious, and I didn't want long silences to fill with his doubts.

'He deserved it. And, by the way, I meant every word of it. If

Dexter shows his face around here again, I shall be on the phone to some *very* unpleasant people, who could teach him a thing or two about throwing weight around.' He gave me a slightly watery grin. 'I've got cameras, you know. Dad won't set up any kind of enterprise without the full security gear in place. I told him it was ridiculous in a place this size, where you have to worry more about a wandering bullock than terrorism, but it looks as though he may have had a point.'

I couldn't help it. I started to laugh. The whole thing was utterly absurd. Flynn, lovely dark Flynn with his desire to clean everything he saw and his way with a hundred and one cocktails, was actually the son of a business mogul. It was ridiculous. Although, thinking about it, I had been very incurious about the whole 'dad made this place over to me' and 'managing a bar in Melbourne'. They were hardly the sort of thing that the local farming fraternity could throw into conversation.

Maybe it was me who was the idiot here.

'Dad gave me the third degree,' Flynn went on, getting up to arrange glasses behind the bar. 'After Tamar. I thought it was a bit late, and I could have done with all that before Oz, but never mind, he gave me all the warnings eventually. Make sure a girl wants me for who I am, not what I'm going to inherit. Make sure she's not got some firm plans in place for how to spend anything she gets from me. Make sure she's – well, make sure she's *nice*.'

I stayed sitting on my chair, behind the table. It felt good and solid, because the world had gone unreal again.

'And you are, I think,' Flynn went on, reshelving some flutes up on the high shelf – we didn't have a lot of champagne drinking going on in here. 'You've had a rough time. A rough *life*.'

'I don't need rescuing, Flynn,' I said carefully. I didn't want to put him off totally, but I didn't want to feel like a soggy kitten in a snowstorm. 'I'll be fine when I get my feet back under me. I've got

somewhere to live and a job – thanks again for that, by the way –
and I will get by. Oh, and the feet thing wasn't a pun, I only
meant, once I get a new front door and some full-time work.' I
waggled a foot under the table. Thick socks padded the worst of
the injuries and they were healing.

'I don't want to save you.' He was keeping his back to me, as
though he knew that my pride had been wounded and wanted to
look as though this was a casual chat. 'I really don't. I like you a
lot, Fee.' Now he turned around and his expression was urgent
and somehow very focused. 'You're lovely. You bumbled into the
club, mostly I think because you were too drunk to go anywhere
else, and you're helping people through things. You haven't asked
for any help yourself. Oh, and I've already had a new door fitted
on your place, so you don't need to worry about that.'

'I'm not helping anyone, am I?' This was puzzling. Was he
sure he'd got the right person?

'You don't take any shit from Margot; she actually listens to
you. You're kind to Fraser, who's a plonker, and you're driving us
around keeping an eye on Eddie. You're kind to me. You included
me in the club, and you didn't have to.'

I thought back to that first meeting. The dark man behind the
bar who'd caught my eye, listening in. 'I couldn't not. You practically had us bugged.'

'But you could have just treated me like the bloke who served
the drinks. And you didn't.' A glass slipped from his hand and
broke with a punctuating tinkle on the floor. 'Bugger. You're a nice
person, Fee. And that's what I need: someone real, someone nice.
Someone good.'

'Someone who isn't haunted by a six-foot skinhead who wants
to beat up anyone who talks to them?'

'He won't be back. The cameras would give me a head's up –
we've got facial recognition programmed in, he'd be spotted

before he got within ten metres and the bells would go off. One phone call and he's toast. Dad plays golf with the chief constable,' Flynn added, smoothly.

'I thought that was just something people said in detective dramas. Do chief constables really play golf?'

Flynn shrugged, throwing his hands wide. 'This one does. And I'm pretty certain that your Dexter's feet wouldn't touch the ground if he tried anything round here.'

'Wow.' The sense of unreality was back. 'Facial recognition?'

'Oh, we've got all the tech. Dad insists.' Flynn vanished behind the bar and sounds of dedicated sweeping reached me. 'He's a bit of a fan of all the new stuff. You should see his house, the whole place runs itself from his phone. I think his house-keeper gets a bit annoyed, mind you. It must be surreal, going into rooms to turn things on and off only to find they're doing it themselves in front of you.' He popped back up again and grinned broadly. 'You'll love it. I'll take you up there soon, he'll want to meet you.'

'To vet me,' I said. 'I'd better be able to walk properly by then.'

'Ah, you're his type. Down to earth, sensible. He's always telling me to find a sensible girl, someone who isn't afraid she'll break a nail if she makes a sandwich.'

There was nothing I could say. Nothing. Although I did enter-tain a brief moment of imagining how my brother would react on finding that his sister was with the son of a multimillionaire and being glad I'd blocked his phone number years ago. Mum and Dad would try to guilt me into keeping him in the style to which he would very much like to become accustomed, and that was not going to happen.

'You go back up, get yourself fit for tomorrow morning,' Flynn said cheerily, as though he was unaware that he'd just rewritten my future.

'No, it's all right. I need to occupy my mind,' I said. 'This has been a bit of a shock, and I ought to get myself a bit more mobile anyway.'

He looked at me critically. There it was again, that tight focus that hinted at the fact that he was so much more than a bartender; while it didn't exactly shout about the sheer amount of backing he had, it certainly suggested that this was a man who'd had a good deal of expensive education and was much more intelligent than he appeared. It was a look that understood.

'If you're sure...' he started.

'I am. Most of the healing is done. As long as I don't dance the samba in the next twenty-four hours, I'll be fine.'

'Great. Because I didn't finish those toilets. I was distracted.' An enormous grin. 'Off you go, now.'

My return of his look was a lot less focused and a lot more vitriolic. 'Bastard.'

'Yep.'

So, I went to scrub the loos.

13

At twenty past five on Thursday morning, we were parked at the bottom of Annie's cul-de-sac of bungalows on the outskirts of Pickering. It was dark, and the streetlights were making all three of us look blue-toned and sickly.

'Why are we here so early?' Fraser whined, for about the tenth time.

'Because we don't know that he'll go to the gym this morning,' Flynn explained again, for about the eleventh time. 'He might pretend to go early and head off somewhere else. He's got all day, after all.'

Lights had gone on inside their house. They illuminated the carefully mown lawn, which had clearly had its first cut of the season, and a flower bed for which *tended* was the only word that applied. Some unwisely early bedding plants had been put out in rows which looked as though geometrical instruments had been used in the scheme, and outlined by white-painted stones.

'Minnie says he's anal,' Fraser observed, and both Flynn and I turned to the back seat in choreographed unison. 'You know, like obsessed with order?'

'I think she might be right,' I said, faintly relieved. 'Which makes this whole "having an affair" thing even weirder.'

'You and Minnie?' Flynn turned even further around, so that he could properly see Fraser. 'You an item?'

'God, no!' Fraser shuddered. 'She's got a bloke. He'd cream me. He's ten foot tall or something, played prop for the Leeds Rhinos. It's a rugby team,' he added when I frowned. 'She's great though, Minnie.' He seemed to go off into a little daydream for a while. 'She says we should start up in business together.'

Flynn almost corkscrewed himself into the seat and I swivelled back around again. 'What sort of business?'

'Well, it's like, I've made such good progress and everything, and she wants to set up by herself as a private instructor and her bloke says he'd put up some cash, and she asked me if I'd take some qualifications and be a trainer. For people who start out as real fat bastards and don't know how to exercise. To, like, encourage them and everything.'

'But you've only been going for a month,' I said weakly.

'Yeah, but I go every day. Nearly every day. Five days a week. And that's dedication, Minnie says, and she reckons I could inspire other people to turn their lives around.'

Flynn and I locked eyes. Our mutual doubt was almost solid. 'But you only went every day because we've been checking up on Eddie.' Flynn sounded almost as weak as I had.

'But I'm going to keep on! Minnie got me a year's membership, cut price cos I'm on benefits. She's going to train me up and I'm going to be an inspiration. She says.' Fraser almost glowed with achievement. 'So I'm going to go later. On the bus.'

'Good on you.' Flynn sounded as though he meant it. Although, to be honest, Fraser's new sense of purpose seemed to have been the best thing that could have happened. Well, he'd stopped wearing *Star Wars* T-shirts, anyway.

'Look, this might be Eddie.' I nudged Flynn as I saw a strip of light beam out across the manicured lawn, indicating an opened door, then the light went out and a figure stepped into the dark. 'Annie must still be asleep.'

Eddie was wearing his work clothes, but apparently over the top of ordinary things, because he looked bulkily overdressed. He turned once to look back at the house, then walked over to the garage and, under cover of the dark and a quite frankly hugely overwrought pergola, began taking off the top layer. Under his work suit he was wearing a polo shirt and chinos. He opened the garage door, flipped open his boot and carefully placed his work things in there, closed it again, and then got in to reverse the car out.

Flynn, Fraser and I crouched down. We were almost opposite the house and, as Eddie had met us all now, didn't want to be spotted by him, although we needn't have worried. He pulled out tidily, checked all his mirrors and, tweaking the driver's mirror into a more central position, he drove off down the road.

'Quick!' said Fraser, unnecessarily. 'We don't want to lose him!'

Losing Eddie at six in the morning on the almost deserted roads around Pickering would have been a near impossibility. Being spotted by him was far more likely, so we had to hang back quite a way as he drove five miles under each speed limit out towards the dual carriageway that led to York.

'Bugger me, he's a slow bastard, isn't he?' Formula 1 Fraser commented.

'Probably doesn't want to get pulled over,' I suggested. 'Hard to explain to Annie how he came to get a speeding ticket miles from where he's supposed to be.'

'Or he's anal,' added Flynn, as Eddie carefully indicated, on a road deserted apart from him and us, to go straight on around a roundabout. 'Drop back a bit, Fee, he's going to spot us.'

'But we know where he's going – to that place in... Oh.'

Instead of turning into York to head for the house we'd seen him visit before, Eddie stayed on the main road. We all exchanged another look.

'I hope he's not going too far,' Flynn said. 'I've got a delivery coming at twelve.'

'He'll have to be back by half past five this afternoon.' I dropped back a little way and a Mini got between us and Eddie, so we could relax. 'He hasn't told Annie he's taken the day off, remember? So he has to pretend to have been at work.'

'Oh, so that's why he'd got his suit on! In case she woke up and saw him leaving.' Fraser slapped his forehead. 'Thought that was weird.'

In the most well-mannered and careful car chase ever, we pursued Eddie to the motorway and down to Doncaster where he turned off.

Fraser was asleep in the back, head lolling. Even so, I didn't want to raise any personal matters, so Flynn and I travelled on in silence, with Flynn looking out to watch the dawn break over the grey hills and me concentrating on the rolling tarmac ahead. There was more traffic now as we approached the cities, more people on their way to early shifts or home from all-nighters, and the reluctant sun peered from the regular clumps of cloud to illuminate us all.

'Where the hell is he *going*?' Flynn shifted as Eddie indicated scrupulously and pulled off the motorway. The exit led to an out-of-town retail park, dominated by a large chain hotel and conference centre. 'Even the shops aren't open yet.'

Eddie seemed to know exactly where he was going. He parked his car, precisely centred in the space as usual, and got out. He stretched, locked the car and then set out for the hotel, looking purposeful.

I parked behind a lorry to conceal us from view and we watched as Eddie strode into the reception area. I saw him talk to the receptionist, who gave him something and then pointed to the stairs.

'He's checking in!' Flynn announced so loudly that Fraser woke up with a snort. 'It bloody *is* another woman! He's meeting someone!'

'I'm not certain,' I said, slowly. 'It didn't look like a key card. To me, it looked more like a lanyard.'

'Wha'?' Fraser sat up and wiped the back of his hand over his mouth, where he'd been noticeably drooling.

'I don't think he's here to meet anyone. I think he's here for a conference. Or a talk or some kind of get-together, anyway.'

We all stared for a moment at the corporate hotel. It did not look like the kind of place anyone would head to for a romantic tryst, certainly. It definitely *did* look like somewhere that might host a pork by-products seminar. It looked a little as though it had been *built* from pork by-products as it glowed pinkly under the rising sun, rimed by the last glimmers of frost. It actually resembled a giant bacon rasher, but I didn't like to say so. It seemed unnecessarily whimsical.

'But why the hell take a day off to go to a work meeting? And why not tell Annie?' Fraser scrubbed a hand through his hair now.

'Only one way to find out.' Flynn opened the car door and a shot of cold morning air enlivened us all. 'We have to follow him.'

I hung back. 'What if he recognises us?'

'The place will be busy, we can hide in the crowd. If he does see us, we can say we're here for... ummm... wild sex away from home.'

I looked at Fraser, who was wearing a tracksuit, had his hair on end and the remnants of his sleep-dribble on his chin. 'What, we're having a threesome?'

Fraser brightened. 'I'm up for it.' Then, catching sight of Flynn's face, 'Er, pretending, I mean. Not for real. Honest.'

We trotted across the car park, weaving our way between other arrivals. It was approaching eight o'clock and the hotel seemed to specialise in breakfast meetings or at least very early starters, because the reception area was busy.

'No sign of him,' Fraser reported, hiding unnecessarily behind a potted palm while Flynn and I scanned the area.

'Maybe he's having breakfast.' I nodded towards the hotel restaurant, which was filling up with people in suits. There was a cadre of brightly dressed women too, who wafted down the stairs and across the reception area, all chattering together, and through the restaurant doors.

'Breakfast?' Fraser asked, hopefully. 'Could do with a fry-up. Er, if nobody tells Minnie.'

'He's in there.' I dodged out into the crowd, mingled with the colourful women for a second under cover of their shawls and capes, and back to the men. 'Sitting by himself eating muesli, it looks like.'

'So, not a room.' Flynn frowned. 'Okay. My turn.'

Confidently, as though he owned the place – which, a tiny stab of memory told me, he might well do, or his father, at least – Flynn approached the receptionist on duty, a very well-groomed lady behind a computer screen. I watched him stride over to the desk smiling, and felt a momentary doubt follow that memory thrust. Flynn. Lean and dark and with that slightly diffident air that made him fade into the background. I wondered if he'd learned that from being around his father, who, if I remembered rightly, was practically mobile foreground. Could he and I ever...?

I was nothing, a struggling nobody and he was – well, he was Flynn.

Then I remembered his unhappiness, his confessions about picking the wrong woman, his insecurity in his own judgement. Flynn might be from a wealthy background, he might have all the advantages, but really he was just a bloke. A rather nicer bloke than the ones I usually associated with, admittedly, but, at base, just a bloke.

We had as good a chance as anyone else.

'Right.' Flynn bundled Fraser and I backwards until we were concealed in a little seating area behind a screen, obviously meant for businessmen to sit with their laptops between meetings. 'She can't tell me where he's booked, obviously.'

Fraser frowned.

'GDPR,' Flynn explained.

'What, like Russia?'

'Data protection. But she did tell me that there's a few talks, meetings and conferences going on here today, and that Eddie is most likely booked onto one of those. They all start at nine.'

All three of us looked across at the restaurant. Eddie was still there, drinking something that looked like a green smoothie. He was taking this 'healthy eating' thing as seriously as Fraser, I thought, looking at another table where a couple were working their way through a plate of eggs, beans and toast, and feeling my stomach give a little wriggle of hunger. The air smelled of coffee too, which didn't help.

'What are they?' I asked.

Flynn took out a piece of paper. 'Right. So, Meeting Room One is something to do with fashion design, Meeting Room Two is medical, Meeting Room Three is overseas sales, and the Hobson Suite, whatever that is, is a local arts committee meeting.' He looked at us. 'So, take your pick.'

We looked at the printed sheet.

'Can we have breakfast?' Fraser rubbed his stomach. 'I'm starving here.'

'In a minute,' I replied, as distractedly as though Fraser were an annoying child we'd brought along.

'Well, I need a wee then.' Fraser headed for the toilets and Flynn sighed.

'Why did we bring him?'

'Because we can't leave him at home alone, it's not kind.'

We both grinned. 'And he's all right, is Fraser,' Flynn said and winked at me. 'I don't suppose any of these meetings are under-cover pork products.' He bent back to the page.

'What else does Eddie *do*?' I wracked my brain for anything that Annie may have mentioned. 'He does the garden. He goes to the gym. None of those things are covered here either.' A distant memory jangled. 'But she did say that he was buying a lot of new clothes...'

'Fashion design?' Flynn said, with disbelief dripping from every syllable. 'You think?'

I shrugged. 'Could be. Perhaps our Eddie is a thwarted Ozwald Boateng.'

We stared at one another. Each of us was clearly writing Eddie an alternate history in another life. 'Bit of a step from just buying new clothes though.' Flynn clearly couldn't reconcile Alternate Eddie with the one we had actually met.

'True.'

Fraser wandered over. 'He's gone,' he said. 'Can we go in the restaurant now? If I don't get at least some coffee and a sausage sarnie, I'm going to be ill.'

Flynn jumped up. 'Bugger! I was going to follow him and see which meeting he went into, and we've missed him.'

I patted his hand. 'We're not professionals. It's not our fault.'

'Okay. So, we have to wait for him to come out.' Flynn looked worried. 'My delivery comes at twelve. Damn, I'll have to put that off.'

'We could go round all the meeting rooms and pretend to have walked into the wrong one?' I suggested. 'See which one he's in. And if he's with anyone,' I added.

'That's me.' Fraser straightened his back. 'I'm born to walk into rooms I'm not wanted in. You should have seen our Chloe's face when I walked in on her and...'

'Good man,' Flynn interrupted. 'Well volunteered. We'll be right behind you.'

'But can we have breakfast first?' Fraser wheedled. 'Might not have the strength otherwise. Might not make it up the stairs.'

So, we all went and had breakfast. Eddie was, as Fraser pointed out, in here somewhere. All we had to do was find him, and it would be easier if we were full of bacon and egg, plus we had to give him time to get settled.

Once we were all refuelled, we set off.

'Let's start at Meeting Room One and work our way round,' Flynn suggested, as we walked confidently up the stairs – 'The secret is to look as though you belong here,' he advised – and found the first meeting. 'Designers' Guild of Britain,' it said on a temporary sign tacked to the door.

Fraser opened the door cautiously and slithered in. He was there for a couple of minutes, then slithered back out again, if anyone as robust as Fraser could be said to slither.

'Nope,' he said, definitively. 'There's loads of women and blokes in very tight trousers, though. It was all about colour, and scarlet will be "in" in 2028, apparently.' He nodded wisely. 'Which is great. It's a good colour. Covers up the stains.'

'But no Eddie?' I asked.

'Nope,' he said again. 'Unless he were hiding behind one of the skinny blokes.'

'All right.' Flynn led the way down the carpeted corridor. 'Oh. This is Meeting Room Three. Meeting Room Two must be on the other side. Let's try in here. This ought to be...' He took out the now much-folded piece of paper. 'Overseas sales. It doesn't say sales of what, though.'

Fraser again opened the door a crack and inserted himself into the room.

'I was sure he'd be in design,' I said sadly.

Within seconds, Fraser was back out again, holding a leaflet. 'Someone tried to sell me a chalet in Lloret De Mar,' he said, looking shell-shocked. 'Honest, do I *look* like someone who can afford a chalet in Lloret De Mar? Where is Lloret De Mar, anyway?'

'Spain,' Flynn said. 'No Eddie?'

'Hard to tell. Lots of people moving around, but I couldn't see him.'

I tapped my finger against Flynn's printout. 'If it's something like timeshare, and Eddie's looking at buying a place... could be. Annie did say he watches *Escape to the Country*.'

'All right. We'll keep an eye on Room Three when they come out,' Flynn said. 'Look, Meeting Room Two is over here. What was that?'

I looked at the paper. 'Medical. Is it worth bothering? Eddie's not exactly a paramedic wannabe, is he?'

'Ought to check,' Fraser said. 'You never know.'

'All right, on you go.'

Flynn and I stood shoulder to shoulder at the door as Fraser went in. As we jostled against one another, Flynn looked down at me and winked again. Behind those glasses, his eyes were full of laughter. 'What the hell are we doing?' he whispered. 'Playing Columbo?'

'We've come all this way,' I whispered back. 'We might as well...'

From the other side of the door came a sudden thump, then the sound of a lot of people becoming agitated. Flynn and I looked at one another, then threw the door open.

Fraser was lying on the floor, a few metres into a large room. About twenty people were sitting around a table, and a woman was standing at the front of the room, obviously showing slides on a screen which had been erected on a smaller table. On the screen was a *very* large image of something that looked like a joint of beef, under the enormous headline:

Gangrenous Limbs

Three of the seated people had got up and were attending to Fraser, who was moaning slightly as he came round.

Eddie was sitting at the front of the room, staring.

'What's going on?' the lady at the front with the laptop clicker looked baffled.

'I think I fainted,' Fraser said in a distant tone from the floor. 'That's *horrible*.' He waved a hand at the slide, without looking up at it.

'You'll be all right,' said one of the men who'd assisted him to start sitting up. 'Take it steady. Try not to think about what you saw. God knows, we all are.'

'Can you turn it off, please?' said another man. 'It is a bit... well.'

'But that's the *point*,' said Laptop Lady, looking from the enormous picture, which I could now see was a rotting limb, to Fraser and then to her audience.

'I know. But let's get this bloke out of here first, all right?'

Gently they got Fraser, pale and wobbly, to his feet. Eddie was staring at the three of us with an expression that indicated he expected a UFO to come and beam us all up any second.

'Er,' he said.

'But... who are these people?' Laptop Lady looked as though she was on the verge of tears.

'I think...' Eddie said slowly, 'that it's my wife's Portuguese evening class.'

Now we'd attracted the attention of everyone in the room. Someone laughed.

'Why on *earth* would your wife's Portuguese evening class be crashing our lecture?' This was a man sitting sideways on his chair.

'I'm not entirely sure,' Eddie said, now looking as though the UFO couldn't come quickly enough. 'It's very strange.'

The screen at the front went blank. 'I think,' said Laptop Lady, still looking shaken, 'that we'll have a ten-minute break for coffee.'

Fraser, holding on to chair backs and tabletops, inched his way over to Flynn and me. Eddie was coming too, creeping his way between his fellow lecture attendees and the chairs as though he didn't really want to see us at all and hoped we'd turn out to be figments of a custard tart-inspired imagination.

'I think we might have some explaining to do,' Flynn said, his voice low.

'That's all right, so has Eddie,' I replied. 'Are you all right, Fraser?'

Fraser shuddered and, hand-over-hand, made his way towards the door. 'Nobody,' he said heavily, 'should be surprised by gangrene after a fry-up.'

The crowd trickled out, some throwing us puzzled looks as

they went, until it was only Flynn, Eddie and me in the room, with Fraser in the doorway taking deep breaths. We all looked at one another, nobody knowing quite where to start.

At last Eddie spoke. 'Did Annie put you up to this? Does she know?'

'She thinks you're having an affair,' I said. 'And no, she doesn't know we're here.'

'An *affair*?' Eddie sat down suddenly on one of the plastic chairs. 'Good Lord. Really?'

'We're not really a Portuguese evening class,' Flynn said. 'We're the Monday Night Heartbreak Club. Formerly the Disappointed Valentines' Club. Which, I think, says it all, really.'

'Vengeance Squad.' Fraser, sounding a little pathetic, was sticking to his guns. We ignored him.

'Dis...?' Eddie looked down at his knees. 'I bought her flowers,' he said sullenly.

'The day *after*,' I chimed in. 'You forgot for the first time in forty years.'

'And you've lost weight.'

'And bought new clothes.'

'And then there's the gym,' Flynn finished. 'Plus taking days off and not telling her. An affair was a logical conclusion to draw.'

'Bloody right,' put in Fraser, still avoiding coming back into the room.

'And you went to that place in York,' I said.

'You mean you've been *following*...? Oh.' Eddie glanced over at Fraser. 'The gym. You've been watching me.'

Eddie looked as though his world had vibrated underneath him and shaken him to a different location, one where he was lost. He put his head in his hands and groaned faintly.

'So, what's it all about?' I asked. 'And I warn you, we're on

Annie's side here, so we won't be keeping any dirty little secrets you might have.'

'Oh.' Eddie slumped even further. Not as dramatically as Fraser had evidently done, but he leaned forward until he was staring at his knees. 'Oh.'

'And why are you at a medical convention?' Flynn asked. 'Being shown dreadful pictures of limbs?'

Eddie took a deep breath but kept his eyes downcast. 'All right,' he said. 'I'll tell you. But you mustn't tell Annie. I'll tell her myself, but I need to do it in my own way and my own time. I need to think how best to phrase it.'

Visions of *incredibly* kinky sex swam before my eyes again for a second. Flynn nudged me and when I looked at him, he nodded towards Eddie. Clearly questioning the accused was my job today.

'Eddie,' I said as gently as I could manage. 'You'll feel better if you just tell us.'

'All right. But not here.' Eddie tried to raise his head. 'I can't face them now. Can we go downstairs?'

'I need a milkshake,' came Fraser's voice from the doorway. 'Can you buy me a milkshake?'

'I told you we should have left him at home,' Flynn observed.

'I've had a shock.'

'Right. Downstairs. We can have this discussion over a pot of tea,' I said.

'And a milkshake,' came Fraser's input.

'And a milkshake for the four-year-old.'

We followed Eddie as, with footsteps that scraped the nylon carpet with their reluctance, we all trooped downstairs.

14

'I love Annie,' Eddie began when we'd settled ourselves at a nice corner table with a large pot of tea and Fraser was making obscene noises with the straw in his milkshake. 'You have to understand that. Forgetting Valentine's Day was... an aberration.'

I poured three cups and tried not to think how ridiculous it was to be drinking tea while someone confessed to... to whatever it was Eddie was confessing to. I *really* hoped that there wasn't going to be anything kinky involved, it would ruin my appreciation of a good cup of Yorkshire Tea forever.

'I've been distracted,' Eddie went on.

'By someone?' I asked, genteelly adding a touch of milk and passing the sugar. If royalty ever had to discuss sexual profligacy, I thought, they'd do it like this.

'No. At least, not in that way.' Eddie took a huge breath. 'I get medical check-ups through work,' he went on. 'We get private healthcare as one of the perks of management, and I got my pre-sixty MOT at the beginning of the New Year. It showed...' He breathed heavily again. 'It showed that I was starting to develop diabetes.'

Things suddenly began to make sense, and Eddie seemed relieved to be able to talk, because there was no stopping him now. 'Well, I don't want to have to inject myself and take tablets and look at everything I eat! The nurse said that I might be able to reverse it if I lost weight and started doing exercise. So, I did.'

'Why didn't you just *say*?' Flynn asked.

'Look, Annie worries. She's a worrier. She'd be forever checking that I hadn't put sugar in my tea and she'd be weighing my supper and fretting over everything I ate. And she's got plans, you know, for when I retire. How could I tell her that I might not *get* to retire? How could I say that I was ill?'

'So, you...?' I prompted.

'I joined the gym, I started dieting. Yes, I lost weight and bought new clothes, but not because I met someone else – because I love my wife and don't want to die!' Eddie almost hissed the words. 'I *had* to buy new clothes because my old ones didn't fit any more.'

'The place in York?' I'd begun to feel a bit stupid. It was all horribly obvious, once you knew. 'Where a woman met you?'

'She's a diabetes nurse. I go once a month. It's a private diabetes clinic; they do my weight and my bloods and my sugars and run through how it's all going. I've reversed the onset,' he added proudly. 'Just have to keep an eye on it all now.'

'So, what's this about?' Flynn waved a hand at the hotel. The restaurant was filling up again, obviously some of the other meetings were having their mid-session break. 'Taking time off. Coming to hotels. In Doncaster.'

Eddie flushed and dropped his head again. His bald spot glowed. 'We're a support group. We have... incentive meetings. Talks, medical information, that kind of thing. They show us what can happen if diabetes gets bad – that's today's talk. We discuss diet and what works best, we talk about foods that are good and foods that are bad.' He raised his head now. 'Lean pork is very good, you know.'

'But *Doncaster*,' Flynn went on. 'Why here? Surely they must have these talks closer to home? In York?'

'Well, yes.' Eddie's head went down again. 'But I worried that Annie or one of her friends might see me going in. So, I joined the support group that was a bit further away. Oh, it's not every week or anything, I've only been to a couple of meetings, but it helps.' He looked at Fraser, who was licking the end of his straw. 'They can be quite graphic, as you saw.'

'How come you forgot Valentine's?' Fraser put in.

'I'd found out that I'd got a condition that might, if I didn't do something, kill me before I could get to retire. Annie wants to go on cruises,' Eddie said, slightly forlornly, as though Annie's plans for his retirement were objectives that absolutely must *not* be thwarted. 'I was distracted and I forgot the date.'

'You need to tell her, Eddie.' I bent forward over the table to bring my face closer to his. 'Because what she's imagining' – I didn't add that we'd *all* been imagining Eddie and a scantily clad, much younger woman and lots of frisky sex – 'is much worse than having to monitor your diet and keep your weight down. And that's not fair.'

Eddie sighed. 'I know.' He looked at the three of us, sleep deprived and a little bit rumpled. 'Are you *really* a club for heart-broken people? Did Annie honestly join something like that? It's not the sort of thing she usually does, when she's worried, she normally just crochets something.'

'She was lonely,' I said. 'We were all lonely. She's only got you and she thought she was losing you, so she wanted to find other people who understood how she felt.' Like we all did, I added silently. We'd all wanted company in our misery. Now – I glanced at Flynn, who was drinking his tea with his hands wrapped around the cup – I felt a lot less lonely. 'After all, *you* joined a group to help you. Why wouldn't she?'

'Oh.' Eddie's head went down again. 'I was trying to protect her,' he said glumly. 'It didn't work, did it?'

'I'm sure she'll forgive you. When you tell her the truth.'

There was a moment's more tea drinking. 'I will,' Eddie said. 'Thank you. She ought to know.'

'Everything will be better if you tell her,' I went on. 'You won't have to sneak out of the house or take days off any more.'

'She's going to read all the books.' Eddie still sounded mournful. 'She's going to end up knowing more about diabetes than I do. And I've been to these things,' he added, looking around the hotel.

'It might be for the best. And... can you not mention us?'

'Oh, Lord, no!' Eddie looked alarmed. 'No, I don't want her to know that you've been investigating me. I'll tell her the truth tonight. I promise.'

'Lovely.' Fraser stood up. 'Can we go now?'

There didn't really seem much more to say. Eddie clearly felt ashamed of himself for letting his wife down, and we were collectively horrified that we'd followed him to Doncaster to find out he was just trying to avoid getting ill. Somehow a showdown in a hotel room with a naked woman clasping sheets to her chest and protesting that she didn't know he was married would have been more satisfying.

But this was better. Definitely better. We all agreed as much on the way home, while Flynn was checking the status of his delivery and Fraser was messaging Margot to let her know the outcome. Eddie not wanting to appear vulnerable to Annie and not wanting to let her down, while managing to let her down by forgetting her usual Valentine's flowers, was the best possible outcome. She wouldn't have to decide whether to forgive a cheating husband and live with the uncertainty of not knowing whether he'd do it again. Yes. Much better.

'So, what's next?' Flynn and I went up to the flat over the wine bar. He went up two steps at a time while I was still limping. 'Do we reconcile Margot and Bruce? Find Wren someone who wants to treat her like a princess? What do we do for an encore?'

'I think we live happily ever after, don't we?' I looked out of the window. At the back, the flat looked out across the little yard and over the jumble of roofs, a tangled medieval building pattern of random houses and gardens that stretched to the edge of the moors. 'In whatever form that takes.'

Flynn came over and looked out with me. 'I'd like it to be with you,' he said quietly. 'I think we can make a go of it.'

I turned around and he was right there. 'Do you? I'm not much of a catch. I have a brother I hate and parents who think that everyone should love him as much as they do.'

He reached out almost dreamily and touched my hair. 'I lost my mother when I was fifteen,' he said. 'That kind of complicates one's thinking about family.'

I moved closer. All my skin wanted to be close to Flynn right now. 'We can see how it goes,' I said softly.

'I think that sounds like a bloody good idea.'

The kiss was better than the one in the toilet. This one involved no rubber gloves or toilet brush, which meant that Flynn had both hands free, and we made use of all our hands until we reached the point where bed seemed more appropriate. His room was closer and we tumbled together onto the soft path indicated by sheets and duvet until we reached a common destination, out of breath but happy with the view.

'Wow.' Flynn still had his glasses on, which was a miracle. 'That was... exciting.'

'Evidently.' I blew my hair out of my eyes. 'I'm glad I wasn't a disappointment.'

'You,' he kissed my shoulder, 'could never be a disappointment, Fee.'

'Perhaps you'd like to pop round and tell my parents that.'

From outside there came the sound of a large vehicle rumbling to a halt at the kerb and Flynn jumped up. 'Hell, that's the delivery!'

He then carried out a rather strange performance, where half of him leaped out of the bed and the other half tried to stay in, while he grasped at various things, some of them me. 'I don't want to leave you like this. But – the delivery...'

'It's fine.' I laughed. 'Go and sort the bottles.'

'But it feels... wrong.'

'We'll have plenty more opportunities for this.' I pushed at his hand. 'Just go.'

Flynn stood beside the bed for a moment, gorgeously naked and sexy. 'Work isn't more important than you,' he said. 'I want you to know that.'

'Because?' I had to shake my hair out of my eyes now. There had been a degree of heat that had stuck it down.

'Dad – he's a bit of a workaholic. I know it made things difficult for Mum, and I don't want to be like that.'

'Flynn, your dad is a multimillionaire. You don't get that without putting the hours in.'

Downstairs, the lorry beeped its horn.

'I know. I just want you to know that I'm not like that. I work, yes, but other things have to be important too.'

'Is this because of Eddie?' I struggled myself up in the bed. The mattress was soft and wanted me to stay.

'Kind of. I think so.'

The delivery driver leaned on the horn now.

'Go. Get that sorted. I'll limp slowly down and help you.' I pushed him again.

'I just wanted...'

'Yes, I know.'

At my obvious insistence, Flynn pulled on his trousers and T-shirt and went off downstairs, leaving me to lie back against the pillows and make a face at myself. Flynn's consideration made me smile. His obvious prowess in bed wasn't off-putting, either. He clearly had issues with his father – well, that was to be expected; you couldn't be the son of someone who seemed to pop up on each continent starting a new business every fortnight without there being repercussions.

Flynn worked hard. I'd seen him behind the bar, and running this place wasn't a job for the faint-hearted either. But he didn't want to be his father. He *wasn't* his father, about which I, at least, was glad. His father was a craggy-faced bloke with an abrupt air, or at least that was how he came over on TV, and neither of those things appealed. Plus, he didn't want me to think he was a workaholic. Good.

I lay a while longer, listening to Flynn outside chatting to the delivery driver, and looked around his bedroom. There was artwork on the walls, which made a change from my place, where the only things on the walls were the stains from dinners that Dexter had thrown. When I realised that the artworks were probably originals and that the paint on the walls probably cost more than my monthly rent, I had to get up and go and help with the delivery.

I could take the change in standards. I would just have to take it slowly, that was all.

Margot erupted through the wine bar door on Monday, early, out of breath and evidently over-excited.

'Tell me *everything*,' she said.

'I have told you everything.' I wiped down the bar. Our phones had almost blown up with the number of messages that had flown to and fro. Only Annie had been noticeably quiet.

'Oh.' Margot calmed down. 'I rather hoped there would be more.'

Behind her, Wren and Fraser came in. They'd obviously all travelled together again.

'It's two people's lives, Margot,' Wren said gently. 'I keep telling you.'

'I *know*.' Margot sat down at her usual place. 'But all those hours of watching Eddie and following him – it doesn't seem *enough*, somehow, to find out that he's simply managing his diabetes.'

'I think it will be enough for Annie,' I said. 'It's quite a lot to come to terms with. She's been planning for a wonderful retire-ment and lots of travelling and all that, and there will be complications that come from having to watch Eddie's diet and everything.'

'But she don't have to worry no more,' Fraser put in, hanging hopefully over the bar in case Flynn might have some peanuts. 'He's not shagging someone else.'

'Exactly.' Wren sat down too now, next to Margot. 'It was the best possible outcome, really.'

'I like this club.' Fraser gave up hope on the peanut front. 'When I joined, when my friend Scousie told me I ought to join, I thought women were like this weird bunch. Like, all they wanted was to sit at home putting make-up on and watching *Loose Women*, waiting for a man to earn some money and come back and shag them.'

We all stared at him. 'Did you actually *know* any women at all?' Wren asked, slightly faintly.

'Well, yeah. My sister, my mum. Our Chloe, our Leah. Lots of women.'

'And how many of them are sitting around waiting for a man?'

Fraser yanked out his chair with a good deal of noise, and collapsed onto it. 'They're different. They've had blokes and had kids. The blokes have gone off, and my sister's bloke died, so they have to work and stuff. Only my sister's inside now, from doing the wrong stuff.' Unconcerned, he sipped at his wine.

'But your opinion has changed?' Wren still sounded taken aback.

'None of you lot are like that, are you? You're women but you're like proper people. You do stuff, like blokes.'

We sat in silent astonishment for a moment, before Flynn said, 'Your mate Scousie, does he get out much, at all?'

'He's got a girlfriend,' Fraser said, slightly defensively. 'I mean, he's never met her or anything, but only because she lives in Alabama, otherwise he definitely would have done by now.'

The door opened and Annie came in. To our surprise, Eddie was with her, looking a wee bit downtrodden.

'I've got some news,' Annie said.

'*Bom dia*,' Eddie said, keeping to the 'Portuguese evening class' fantasy.

We chorused '*bom dia*' back, even Fraser, who I was fairly sure thought it meant 'let's blow up wildlife'.

'And what is your news, Annie?' Margot said, sounding as though she were reading from a script.

'Yes, do tell us,' we all chimed in, likewise all quoting from a Miss Marple adaptation.

Annie came over and Eddie pulled her chair out for her, waited for her to settle herself and then pushed it in again. He leaned against the bar, trying to avoid looking at any of us.

'Eddie's told me everything,' Annie said. We all shuffled our feet. 'It wasn't an affair at all, it was making sure that he didn't tip over into active diabetes! Aren't I a big silly? Fancy ever thinking that my Eddie would do a thing like that!'

There was much scripted-sounding laughter. None of us could look at any of the others, and Eddie was now carefully scrutinising the arrangement of glasses behind the bar. Eventually I said, 'Oh, that is good news, Annie,' and flashed the quickest of questioning looks at Eddie, who shook his head very slightly. It looked as though we were off the hook.

'Yes, it's funny really, he came home from work today and sat me down, said he had something to tell me and that he really joined the gym and changed his diet because he'd been diagnosed as pre-diabetic! Those days he took off were to have checks and things – but he hadn't wanted to worry me, the daft ha'p'orth.'

Good. So Eddie had told Annie everything. I wondered how long it would have taken him if we hadn't called him out.

'So, I might not be coming to the Portuguese lessons again very often,' Annie said. 'I need to research his condition. To make sure that I know what he can and can't eat, keep his weight under control, all that sort of thing.'

I was about to say that we didn't need to keep the fiction of the Portuguese class any more, that Eddie already knew what we really were, but decided not to. How much Eddie told her about why he had finally come clean was up to him, so she still thought that *he* still thought this was nothing more than a foreign language evening class. That was fine. Everyone saved face, all down the line.

'But I would like to stay in touch,' Annie went on. 'Make sure that you all have your happy endings, like I've had mine. Er, I mean, when you go on those holidays you're planning. And we've talked about so much other than holidays in Portugal, haven't we?' she added quickly.

I felt, rather than saw, Flynn look at me.

'I'm all right,' Fraser said. 'I've lost two stone and I'm going into business with Minnie, training people who've never lifted more than a sandwich. After I gets back from, er, that place I'm going to in the summer.' He finished, with a slight touch of geographical desperation.

'Bruce has agreed to all my revised pre-divorce terms,' Margot said. 'Personally, I think he'd agree to anything if it means he's free to get out and have sex with someone.'

Annie shook her head. 'I didn't mean like that,' she said sadly. 'I don't want you to be lonely any more.' An arch look. 'After all, that's what was behind us all joining the Portuguese speaking class, wasn't it? Loneliness?'

Margot looked awkward. Fraser just beamed. 'Ah, there's *loads* of women up the gym,' he said happily. 'I'll be fine.'

'Anyway.' Annie stood up and Eddie pulled her chair out for

her. 'I thought I'd pop in and tell you, stop you worrying. We're off out now. We're going to the pictures, aren't we, Eddie?'

Eddie, who was still clearly atoning for having upset Annie, nodded dismally. 'Going to see a rom com,' he said, in the tones of a person who is off to the funeral of a loved one.

The pair of them left, Eddie's hand on Annie's shoulder, steering her out of the bar and down onto the street. Flynn let out a huge sigh. 'Thank goodness,' he said. 'I've no idea what the Portuguese is for goodbye.'

Wren dabbed at her eyes. 'Is this the club splitting up?' Her voice was a bit wobbly. 'I mean, are we over?'

'Not if we don't want to be.' Margot patted Wren's shoulder. 'We can still support one another.'

'Are we still heartbroken? Should we change the club name again?'

'Vengeance Squad,' Fraser muttered.

Flynn briefly leaned his weight against me and I glanced up to see him raising his eyebrows. I smiled. He was right, with his silent question. The club didn't seem to be needed any more except by Margot and Wren.

'How's the divorce going?' I asked, hoping that Margot was going to now report a hunky male solicitor dealing with her paperwork and a new lusty desire for rampant sex. I'd quietly mused about Bruce and come to the conclusion that there must have been something about either his appearance or performance that had so completely put Margot off sex with him. I had high hopes for her discovering a wild and kinky mojo and running off to Biarritz with a professional paraglider or something.

'Very smoothly,' Margot replied, fumbling in her handbag. 'Bruce is prepared now to relinquish the cabin in the Highlands in return for my not chasing half of his pension. I would really miss that cabin, it's gorgeously located and I decided I just couldn't hand it over. Let me show you.'

She pulled out her phone and scrolled. Wren looked interested, Fraser looked agog.

'What, like a log cabin?' he asked, leaning forward. 'Like on *Seven Brides for Seven Brothers*?' We stared at him. 'My mum likes old musicals.'

'Well, yes, I suppose so.' Margot had found the right album. 'Look.'

She flashed her photos. It was less of a cabin and more of a high-end bungalow, with a hot tub and small plunge pool, set in carefully landscaped acres with mountains forming a picturesque backdrop. I could see why she would have been sorry to relinquish it.

'Who's the bloke?' Flynn asked, when scrolling revealed some pictures of a man leaning against a bicycle, obviously recently returned from pedalling his way around Auchtermuchty or similar.

'Oh, that's Bruce,' Margot said airily.

I rewrote my view of her marriage. Bruce was far from being the hideous and dishevelled creature of my imaginings. The pictures showed a tall and tanned man with lots of hair and a beaming white smile. The cycling gear didn't leave much to the imagination either. Bruce had clearly not been off-putting in the physical department.

'Nice you get to keep the place now,' I said, slightly weakly and fighting the urge to fan myself.

'Oh yes. I'm going to head up there in a couple of weeks, for a break.' Margot seemed to be saying this for a reason which I couldn't grasp. The sentence sounded as though it had had an expected ending amputated at the last minute. She stopped and then apparently realised that more was needed, because she went on. 'Before the midges get started. They can be a real problem, during the season.'

Fraser leaned back. 'Swanky,' he said.

'It's very comfortable. Perfect for couples.' Again, those words seemed to hold a secret meaning, but as nobody reacted, I decided I was just feeling a little bit sensitive. Having Flynn sitting next to me could well have accounted for that. 'In fact, I've joined a dating app.' Margot sounded almost defiant. 'For high achievers, it's very exclusive.'

A moment more of phone scrolling and she held the screen up again. 'I've been chatting with Alexander, Imran, Michael and Willhelm,' Margot went on. 'They are all very lovely and very keen to meet.'

'They could be scammers.' Fraser stared at the photos on Margot's phone. 'Are there even that many good-looking rich blokes in the world?'

I gave Flynn a sideways look and smiled to myself. 'Apparently so,' I said.

'Well, you be careful.'

The incongruity of Fraser giving dating advice clearly stunned even Margot and she tucked her phone away again.

With that, the meeting broke up. I hobbled my still slightly sore way back behind the bar to serve the Monday night men – who had returned to poker again tonight – and to stand and think.

Could I have a future with Flynn? Would Annie and Eddie live happily ever after? I had to suppose that forty years of what seemed to have been a blissfully happy marriage was not going to be rocked to the core by his keeping a health scare from her. Annie would probably just become a little bit more preoccupied with Eddie's diet; at least it would give her a new hobby. Eddie really did seem to love her. A happy ending. Wasn't that what we all wanted?

Fraser looked set to make himself a new life too. I wiped the bar in a desultory way, listening to Flynn loading the glass washer out at the back. Surely if even *Fraser* could have a brand-new future, then I could allow that I might too? Despite the fact that, on paper, Flynn and I had very little in common, we got on well, liked each other and laughed a lot – would that be enough?

I wiped the bar again and watched the poker players for a while. This place, this tiny wine bar in this little corner of York-shire, was hardly going to make enough profit for Flynn to be happy, surely? While he seemed reassuringly free of his father's workaholic genes, would this be enough to keep him engaged and busy? The occasional hen party, wandering businessmen, locals who wanted something other than pub life and a gradually dissolving club for sad people weren't going to bother the Inland Revenue into fits of examining our turnover, and I'd seen Flynn pulling faces at the spreadsheets on the computer. No, I couldn't see him staying here forever, and where would that leave me?

The last poker player bid me goodnight and I locked the door behind them, turning the retro metal door sign to CLOSED. I could take this for now, I thought, looking out across the road at the empty windows of my flat. I hadn't ended my lease, hadn't wanted to bank too much on Flynn letting me stay on here, so it was still mine. If everything ended, if Flynn decided to move on and that I had been a temporary, if pleasurable, blip, I'd always have the flat to go back to. Hopefully Dexter had been warned off sufficiently never to come back, and I could find another job some-where. There were supermarkets and shops that needed staff.

For now, though, this was great. I made a mental note to intro-duce Flynn to my family sooner rather than later, so that they would know that, even if temporarily, I'd had something in my life that had been worth it. I wanted to show him off, that was it. To show them that I wasn't the little loser, the also-ran to my exalted brother, and that I was making myself that good life that they'd always thought would be beyond me.

After that, I never needed to see them again.

16

The next Saturday, therefore, we went to York to 'pop in' on my family.

Flynn drove us for the first time. To my surprise, he had a car, new but not flash, and he drove like someone more used to the wide roads of Australia, with occasional muted swearing at potholes. When we arrived my parents were, to even more of my surprise, polite – they even made my brother get up from his usual position, lounging along the sofa, so that Flynn could sit down. They made us both a cup of tea and smiled their way through introductions.

Maybe they had changed, I thought, as I drank my tea. Or maybe I had been mistaken in how I had remembered family life? I began to feel better, relaxing a little as I listened to Flynn telling them about the wine bar, about using it as a place for clubs to meet. Perhaps this little house, which smelled of my brother's trainers mouldering in the corner and my mother's vicious attempts to hoover the pattern off the carpet twice a day, actually *could* be a refuge for me. My old bedroom was still as I'd left it, as though my parents were waiting for me to give up trying to live independently and come back, and it was beginning to look as though, should Flynn and I not work out, I could.

My brother would still be a work-shy misogynistic bully, of course, but one day he would move out. Surely. He was thirty-five; sooner or later his girlfriends would get tired of being taken back to be greeted by our mum in a dressing gown, asking if they wanted a coffee. Surely. Tired of being woken by a knock on his bedroom door and told that breakfast was on a tray on the landing. *Surely*.

I left Flynn telling my father about the different kinds of wine he stocked and how he favoured Australian origin. I had no idea why Dad was even listening to this, he hadn't drunk anything but Tennent's during my entire lifetime, but perhaps this was another symbol of change. I'd done the right thing, I told myself as I nipped upstairs to the all-too familiar bathroom. Leaving home, getting away, had shown them that I was an actual person rather than the general secretary for my brother, as they had treated me before.

Pride made me look fondly at the pink bathroom suite and green washbasin – my brother had broken the original matching one in a fit of temper one day and Dad had sourced a cheap replacement. I was making a go of my life. I wasn't falling into the role that had been prepared for me, and they were accepting my moving on.

I dried my hands on the thin hand towel. Yes, I *should* come back more often. Mum was looking put-upon and worn, my brother and Dad had always been a bit keen to sit down and put their feet up and never consider that maybe *she* would like to rest sometimes too. Maybe I could pop back for the odd weekend and give her a hand. If I could deal with Dexter, I could certainly face up to my brother who, apparently, still didn't have a job and was 'thinking of going travelling', which meant going on the train to

Bristol to sponge off his old mates down there, if Mum would give him the train fare. He, at least, would never change. Why would he when he was cosseted and treated like a little prince and congratulated just for taking off his shoes before he put his feet on the sofa?

My mother thought 'double standards' were a size of bedsheet.

The stairs were thickly carpeted, so nobody in the kitchen heard me coming back down. But I could hear them. Mum and Dad and brother, all gathered in there, having a hushed conversation.

'I reckons she's rented him,' my brother announced confidently. 'Pay-by-the-hour type thing.'

'He's certainly too nice for her,' Mum said. There was a clinking of cups. 'Well, he'll see through her soon enough. He seems an intelligent lad, she won't be able to keep up looking clever for long.'

'She's got make-up on, did you see?' my brother said smugly. 'Trying to pretty herself up.'

'I have no idea what she's done to her hair,' continued Mum, whose hair was still in the coy 'Princess Di' that she'd had since 1981, according to the photographs. 'Why is she trying to change how she looks? I mean, it's obvious to anyone with any sense that she...'

I hit the bottom step at the same time as my heart hit my stomach. *How could I have been so stupid?* The impulse to gouge a strip from the tidy wallpaper almost overcame me and I had to curl my fingers into my palms to stop myself. Of course they hadn't changed. I was still the useless one, who should stay at home and pay bills that my parents couldn't manage because they gave all their money to my golden, do-nothing-wrong brother. I should exist to serve, to do as I was told.

That training had led me to Dexter, who had been the best I thought I could get.

'Come on, Flynn.' I opened the living room door and surprised him looking at the collection of family photographs on the vigorously polished shelving above the TV. 'We need to go.'

He nodded and we left without saying goodbye. It wouldn't matter, my family would spend another hour dissecting my visit; telling one another how I'd never had any manners or decency and how I probably had to get my paid-for 'boyfriend' back before his time was up. They'd get enough mileage from their happy annihilation of my character to keep them busy for weeks.

Neither Flynn nor I said much on the drive back. He was still swearing quietly about the state of the rural roads and I was thinking, hard: trying to beat down the memories of my childhood and adolescence in a household where I had been 'the girl' and, as such, liable for helping my mother in her attempts to martyr herself to the cause of masculinity.

Staying in at weekends to do the laundry, while my brother went out with his leering friends. Watching whatever he chose on the TV, because his opinion counted, while mine didn't. Getting a holiday job in a café, starting at six, while my brother lay in every morning. Lying awake while he and his current girlfriend made enough noise in their room to make the neighbours bang on the walls, and my parents' tolerant 'boys will be boys' comments if anyone dared say anything.

It had been like the Dursleys and Harry Potter, only without the magic.

'Well.' Flynn drove the car around to the garages at the back of the wine bar. I'd never noticed these before. They were the old stables from when the building had been a pub, somewhere to put the horses on market day or to stall the beasts that had pulled the delivery dray. Now they were full of boxes of glasses.

And Flynn's car, obviously. 'A lot of things make sense to me now.'

'Mmm?' As we got out of the car, I was still lost in remembering one particularly savage summer, when my brother had encouraged his friends to follow me around town, heckling and trying to corner me in out-of-the-way places. I'd been reduced to tears, hiding in the toilets in Browns until they gave up, when I'd run home to be told that I was late back and wouldn't be allowed out again for the rest of the week. The memory of that cold fear of not knowing what might happen next, of having to get away fast, had made Dexter's brand of unthinking cruelty feel predictable and a known quantity.

'You know they don't have a single photograph of you up on the wall?' Flynn went on, almost casually. 'Loads of your brother, some of your parents, some of them together. None of you.'

'I'm not photogenic,' I said absently, repeating what I'd always been told. 'They don't have any good pictures of me.'

'Fee.' Flynn sounded so solemn then that I had to look at him. He put both hands on my shoulders. 'You are lovely. Your family, on the other hand... are not.'

There it was again, that cold shutter coming down when I thought of my childhood. The knowing in my rational mind that it had been unfair, warped. And yet the pull to the familiar, wanting so badly to be needed and loved that I would do anything asked of me to feel that I belonged. 'My parents prefer my brother, that's all.' I tried to sound breezy. 'He was born very premature and they weren't sure he would live, so it's only natural that they...'

'No, it isn't.' Flynn sounded almost angry, and Flynn didn't seem to have any real anger in him on a day-to-day basis. 'There is nothing natural about any of it. Blimey, I thought my dad was quite hands-off with me, when really his only life advice was to do a business degree and steer clear of women who know I'm, well, okay for money, but your family is next level. They make Dad look as though he wanted a spreadsheet of my movements.'

He shifted and brought his face closer to mine. There was a suspicious gleam in his eyes. 'Your life has been so shit, it's a miracle that you are even slightly normal,' he said. 'I wondered how someone as intelligent and aware as you could have entertained someone like Dexter for more than five minutes, but now I can see. You were taught that was all you deserved.'

'I know it really,' I said, watching his gaze travel over my face. 'I do know. That's why I came away. I wanted to escape but I didn't really know how. Hence...' I waved a hand, meant to indicate my flat but really taking in this little cobbled yard and the padlocked doors, 'Dexter.'

'Oh, Fee.' Flynn kissed me now, a kiss that was softer than his usual kisses, something that felt like the promise of summer after a winter's chill. 'Fee.'

'The club was so good for me,' I went on. 'Not being alone. Being able to do something to help Annie. I even...' I stopped, unsure of whether this was the right time or the right place, but Flynn's expression encouraged me. 'I've even thought of training to be a private investigator,' I said in a speedy burst. 'I've looked it up, there are courses and all sorts of qualifications you can take. It would be good to have a proper job, something that's me, if you see what I mean. And,' I went on with a renewed enthusiasm because he hadn't laughed, 'I think I might be *good* at it. I've never had something to be good at before, but all that following Eddie and the planning and deciding what to do next... I know it sounds horrible because it was Annie's life we were poking about in, but I *enjoyed* it. I've never really had anything I enjoyed before.'

Flynn took a couple of steps back. Now he was looking at me differently, head slightly to one side, as though there was something new about me that he'd never noticed before. 'That would be amazing,' he said slowly.

'I need to... to not be someone who just gets sucked into things,' I went on. A little flame of enthusiasm had lit from the spark of the idea and Flynn's not shooting it down. 'I love working in the wine bar, of course, and it was so good of you to offer me the job. But I'm doing it because it's *there*, if you see what I mean. Like the call-centre job – I only went for that because I was desperate and I saw the advert online. It wasn't as though it was something I've always wanted to do. But being an investigator – I think I could be *good* at that, and being good at something hasn't happened to me that often.'

Flynn smiled. He had a slow smile that seemed to inch across his face a little at a time, starting in his eyes and then spreading down to his mouth. It was very attractive. 'Yes,' he said slowly again. 'I can see that.'

'And I think I'm born to blend into the background. There's nothing about me that stands out; I'm so ordinary that I'm almost invisible,' I went on.

'I think we might still need to do some work on your self-esteem. You are very far from ordinary and invisible, Fee.'

'Maybe,' I said slowly, the idea crystallising in my head as I said the words, as though they were ice, helping my thoughts to set. 'Maybe I *need* to be ordinary. It will mean that everything I've learned throughout my life – all the blending in and trying to be what everyone wants of me – will be *useful*. After all, I could hardly follow Eddie, or anyone else really, if I had purple hair and was so beautiful that I stopped traffic, could I?'

Flynn laughed. It really did make him step out of *his* ordinary bracket; it made his dark eyes glow behind his glasses and his mouth pleated upwards in a way that highlighted the generally pleasing shape of his entire face. I had another of those moments where I felt a sudden knowledge of inclusion in the human race. Flynn liked me. Margot, Wren, Annie and Fraser liked me. I wasn't the apparent monster that I'd been brought up to think I was: the stupid, unsexy, ugly and unlovable person that Dexter had always yelled at me that I was, that my *parents* had tried to convince me I was.

People liked me. People *listened* to me.

'I think you could do anything you set your mind to,' Flynn said, turning to open the back door to the bar. 'I've never met anyone as determined as you.'

He often complimented me in bed, and sometimes when I learned a particularly tricky cocktail recipe, but this was the first time the compliment had felt personal. It was the first time in my life that I'd ever had a moment's pride in myself.

'Thank you,' I said quietly, and meant it for more than the words he'd said.

17

Monday, club night, rolled around again.

Fraser was late. He messaged to say that he was coming straight from the gym on the bus rather than grabbing a lift with Margot.

'He's really taking this whole "getting fit" thing seriously, isn't he?' Wren said, sipping her orange juice. She'd taken Annie's usual seat, I noticed. Clearly we supposed Annie had now moved on to other things; maybe she'd really take up Portuguese evening classes. She still messaged us, though, the group chat was filled with breathless and rather strangely punctuated tales of redecoration and holiday bookings. Her emojis were prolific and not always up with current usage – she used the purple aubergine whenever she mentioned Eddie's love of her lamb moussaka, for example, which was off-putting for those of us who'd enjoyed moussaka up to this point. But it was Annie, and she was so clearly enjoying her renewed security in her marriage that none of us liked to tell her what it meant to anyone under the age of thirty when she sent doughnut and cucumber emojis side by side.

'Fraser was looking for a purpose,' Margot said confidently, laying her phone on the table and squaring her handbag on the floor under her chair. 'He was never going to find a girlfriend living the way he did, and now he at least stands a chance. He and Minnie seem really keen on starting classes for people who are total beginners, and I think he will be extremely good at it.'

Margot seemed to have softened a lot since the club started too, I thought, helping Flynn bring a couple of bowls of crisps and peanuts to the table. It seemed safe enough, with Fraser not here yet.

'Do you think he can keep it up?' I asked casually, clearly having caught the spirit of Annie's unintended double entendres.

'Fraser is showing a single-minded dedication to an idea that has, I must admit, surprised me,' she replied. 'I have to say that I have learned a lot from Fraser about not judging a book by its rather tatty and somewhat juvenile cover.' She gave an unexpected smile and I noticed that she was wearing a lot less make-up than she had at our earlier meetings. Margot seemed to have loosened her stays a little. I wondered if one of the dating app men was responsible.

'Fraser's cute,' Wren said, and we turned to her with such speed that whiplash was a possibility. 'Oh, not like *that*,' she added. 'Sorry to disappoint anyone but I'm still not attracted to men.'

Margot coughed as though this had broken a train of thought. I wondered if she had been quietly trying to set Wren up with Fraser behind the scenes. If Wren had been straight then it would have been an obvious tidy ending for our club, and Wren and Fraser could, I had to admit, have made a nice couple. Her desire to be looked after and, as she said herself, 'treated like a princess', would fit right in with Fraser's still slightly outdated beliefs about women and traditional roles.

Bugger. I wondered if a purely platonic household might be possible, Fraser looking after Wren, and her washing his gym kit and cooking for him. The spectre of the big purple aubergine swam before my eyes and I shook my head.

'I meant that he's very simple and straightforward,' Wren went on. 'There's no beating about the bush with Fraser.'

Oh God, those emojis and entendres were going to haunt me forever. Margot coughed again and I wondered whether she was thinking the same as I was.

'He's kind and he's got no "side" to him,' Wren went on. 'What you see is what you get with Fraser and I think he will make someone a wonderful boyfriend. But not me,' she added, dashing my slowly rising hopes for a friendly household.

Thankfully for those of us who were straining credulity at this point, Fraser himself clattered through the door carrying his rolled-up towel, as ever, which he flung on the bar as he collapsed into a chair.

'Bugger me,' he said succinctly. 'Minnie's had me lifting. Anyone got a horse they want turned over, I'm your man. Oh good, peanuts are out.' He took a double handful scoop of the recently arrived nuts and threw them into his mouth with the eagerness of a man in a desert arriving at a waterhole.

Margot was averting her eyes.

'Slow down, mate,' Flynn said cheerily. 'There's only another five hundred bags in the storeroom and I don't want to run out this early in the week.'

'Sorry.' Fraser sprayed the table with partly masticated nuts. 'Bloody starving. Been in the gym all day with Min, filling in forms for personal trainer courses. I'm not great at the writing, what with my dyslexia, so Min has to do them for me.' He looked around at us. 'What we talking about, then?'

In the face of the peanut-spray, the hint of body odour and

Fraser's general Fraser-ness, nobody seemed to feel able to say, *How nice you are and how you'll easily find a girlfriend.* Fraser was definitely one of those people that you can think fondly of when they're not present, but whose reality gives you second and third thoughts.

'Annie,' I said. 'Now she's got her happy valentine after all.'

'Oh yeah. And you're shagging Flynn, and I've got the gym – just got to set these two up and we can all die happy.' Fraser waved a salty finger at Margot and Wren, who stared blankly at him. I absolutely did *not* say what I'd been thinking about Wren and him setting up home together. Nobody should have that kind of idea put in their heads.

Flynn dropped his head and was trying not to smile. Margot kicked over her handbag and had to bend down under the table to pick it back up again and I felt my entire face go so hot that the peanuts were in for another roasting.

'What?' Fraser stared around us again. 'Am I not supposed to know that these two are banging? Bloody hellfire, it's like a f—it's like a romantic novel in here some days, with them gazing in each other's eyes and trailing hands and all. My Mum reads Mills & Boon books,' he ended proudly. 'Out loud.'

'And we are all very happy for you.' Margot glared at him.

'I wants you to get married,' Fraser went on, completely unabashed and covered in peanut crumbs. 'I loves a good wedding. Great food and I gets to throw some shapes on the dance floor.'

'I think we might be a way off that yet,' Flynn said faintly. 'But it's an idea.'

Two men came in through the door at that point and Flynn had to get up to serve them, which was good for my blood pressure and the tone of the conversation. I told the club about my idea of becoming a private investigator, which they all approved heartily, and Wren said that she'd followed Margot's example and joined a dating agency.

'Honestly, it's fairly slim pickings on there on the gay side,' she said. 'But I thought it was worth a try. I can't live alone for the rest of my life and I don't much like cats. It's been lovely staying with you, Margot, and thank you so much for putting me up, but I can't keep you from your own love life forever by being the gooseberry in the living room!'

'How're you getting on on that site then?' Fraser nudged Margot in a particularly 'matey' way. 'Anything worth shagging? Anything you're *actually* shagging?'

Margot got bubbles from her tonic water up her nose and started a coughing fit at that point, which made her go very red and her eyes started to water. Fraser clapped her on the back so hard that she kicked her handbag over again.

'I have *contacted* one or two very nice gentlemen,' Margot finally managed. 'They all seem very keen to meet. I've not found the time to arrange an actual date yet.'

'So no shagging yet then,' Fraser said cheerfully. 'Join the club. Oh, not this club, I mean the one where there's no shagging. The shagging one's reserved for these two.' He gave Flynn and me a look that crinkled at the edges with envy.

Margot stared into the final remaining bubbles of her drink. 'They all seem a little *too* keen,' she said. I wasn't quite sure what tone her voice held. It sounded a little wistful. 'It makes one slightly suspicious of their eagerness, so I am taking my time. Choosing wisely, you know.'

'You are so right,' Wren chimed in. 'I don't want to fall into another relationship like I had with Jordan. This time round I want to take my time, be friends first; Jordan and I got serious very quickly and I think that was my mistake.'

Over at the bar, Flynn was in conversation with the two men, who had bought a glass of wine each and were drinking quickly, a sports bag on the bar between them. He saw me look over and winked, then mouthed *two minutes* at me. I didn't know why. He was working, it wasn't as though he'd excused himself to wander the high street, accosting women. I smiled back.

Outside, the night was leaning in through the windows as though pulled in by the light. I watched Flynn bid the two men good evening as they drained their wine glasses and hurried off to whatever business summoned them. Flynn headed off towards the back room, possibly to fetch more glasses, and I had one of those moments where I felt as though I were existing in the closing titles of a film. Everyone was happy. I had a gorgeous boyfriend and the hope of a new life. Summer was coming, slowly this far north, but definitely advancing on us, as evidenced by the recent crop of hanging baskets and new planting around roundabouts and road verges. My family had been shown that I could have a wonderful future and was far from the loser status that had been attributed to me almost as soon as I was born. They might think I had to rent it by the hour, but it was still more future than they had, stuck in that little house, re-enacting the rituals they'd been set in forever. I had Flynn and I was free.

Any minute now, the titles would roll, the screen would be bathed in a golden glow and we'd all hasten off to our new futures, I thought, leaning back with a satisfied sigh and watching Wren mopping Margot down with a handful of tissues while Fraser carried on eating peanuts as though we were about to whip the bowl out from under his hand. I half-noticed that the men who'd left in such a hurry had put their sports bag on the floor and forgotten it, and the thought of them having to turn around and come back made me smile. More haste, less speed, I thought, lifting my glass of juice to finish it.

And then the bomb went off.

18

Of course, I didn't know it was a bomb. At first it was just a noise, as though a car had driven straight into the windows of the wine bar, a tremendous roaring and crashing. Then there was something that felt as though the air around me had hardened and was forcing me backwards to the floor. All the while, the noise was still going on and all I was really aware of was being cut by everything flying around me, much as I flew around everything else until I hit the rear wall and landed hard enough for my breathing to stop.

Then I didn't know what happened. The loudness was followed by an incredible softness, as though something had popped in front of me. No sound at all, nothing to see but blackness and an awful smell, chemicals and alcohol and dust that seemed to swirl into my nose and down to my chest until I was coughing and retching around a pain that made my ribs snag onto my lungs.

I stayed where I was and gradually sensation started to come back. First to arrive was sight. Pinpricks of light swam from the blackness and coalesced into shapes, swinging and dancing until I felt sick. Then came hearing, slowly, slowly building credible sound out of the receding silence. Finally, touch returned, all sensation at once, so that I could feel a bruising kind of numbness everywhere and an oddly sharp something sticking into my cheek. I was breathing, but every breath came out with a moan accompaniment.

Then I heard the screaming, alarms ringing, something cracking and voices. Lots of voices, shouting. Emergency lighting came on, bathing the whole scene in a sickly green glow that made it look like the inside of a spaceship that has had to make a hurried landing in a swamp. Someone was crying but my ears still weren't operating properly and I couldn't triangulate where any of the sounds were coming from.

'Wha'?' my mouth said, the word coming out with blood.

I was down on the floor, the wreckage of the table barricading me against the wall, and broken glass scattered over everything like a parody of snow.

'Wha'?' my mouth said again.

And there was Flynn, upright but with his shirt torn to tatters and blood pouring down his face, kicking his way towards me through the rubble. In the nauseous lighting he looked like the Incredible Hulk, bathed in the green glow. 'Fee!' I knew he was shouting but my hearing was still muffling everything, so it sounded as though he was calling from a very long way off. 'Fee!'

People were staggering to their feet or sliding themselves up the furniture to sit. I saw Fraser, a heroic trail of blood running from his hairline down the side of his face, moving some splintered wood off a body which lay huddled in the centre of the floor. It was Wren, that calm part of my mind that was watching everything going on from a hidden place, told me. Wren, unmoving and small.

More movement. Margot, with her linen shirt and wide-legged linen trousers ripped and wrenched around her body like a hurricane in Boden, was dragging herself across the floor towards Fraser and his attempts to rouse Wren.

'Wren!' That shout got through my cotton-wool hearing. It was a cry of pure anguished desolation. 'Wren!' Margot crawled over the smashed chairs, reaching out. She grabbed a handful of Fraser and tried to pull herself past him.

'Don't move.' Flynn had found me now. I was distantly aware that he was wiping my face with something soft, but, like sound, touch was coming in at one remove. 'Lie very still.'

I wanted to say that I couldn't do anything else right now, what with having half a table on top of me, but there wasn't enough breath in my lungs for me to speak with. I was having to concentrate on using what air came in simply to keep me ticking over.

'Leave her,' Fraser said to Margot, almost grappling with her to prevent her from lifting Wren up. 'I don't think she's still with us.'

'No!' This was a howl, a cry so desperate that I found I was fighting the vagueness that threatened to overcome me to keep watching. 'No, Wren, come on, you can't die like this! What happened, does anyone know what happened?' Margot was on her feet now, spinning around, alternating between trying to get past Fraser and also trying to catch the eye of anyone else who was upright.

The bar had been largely empty. Just the Heartbreak Club, the poker players and the two men who'd had the hurried glass of wine. But they'd gone before all this happened, hadn't they? Had they? My mind was full of the blackness still. Who was here? What was going on?

More alarms, which turned into sirens and blue flashing

lights accompanying them. 'Help is coming,' Flynn said gently. 'Hang in there.'

He sounded very concerned and I wasn't sure why. I was fine, only breathless, and that was no surprise given the dust and the smoke and the fact that everything to which feeling was returning hurt and ached.

'Bastards! Bastards. I wonder if they were... where they came from. Trying to get to Dad...? Stupid! Stupid! I should have – I dunno, what could I have done here, better security measures?' Flynn was talking to himself, or it could have been to me but I wasn't up to answering. 'I should have been on my guard. Dad was right about needing security protection. At least they'll be on camera, they won't get far. Just have to lock down the footage.' He was speaking fast, in a half whisper. It sounded as though he was trying to distract himself from what was going on right now by trying to work out what had happened.

His eyes were all I could see, black as night, and there was a cut across the bridge of his nose where his glasses must have been. They were gone now. Everything recognisable was gone. When I could focus past Flynn's face, I could see that the windows had blown out, leaving huge blank spaces, and the bar was a tangle of splintered wood and upended bottles like some weird barricade from *Mad Max*. The wine bar, previously so orderly and cosy, now looked like a post-apocalyptic speakeasy.

Flynn dabbed at my face again. 'Shit! Shit. It won't stop bleeding.'

I couldn't feel myself bleeding, everything was numb, apart from the sharp pain in my cheek and the ache of my ribs. I managed to stretch out a hand, feeble and floppy, and touch the side of his face where he was bleeding too.

'Wha'?' I said again.

'Those two who came in for a glass of wine, they had a bag.

I... Stupid! Stupid... I didn't think twice about it. They must have left it on the floor and set a timer, then made a dash for it. I never thought I'd be important enough to try to take out,' Flynn said, with a brave attempt at a humorous tone.

Over in the middle of the floor, Wren moaned. Margot fell down on her knees so quickly that it looked as though she was collapsing. 'Oh my God. Oh, Wren, my love, are you all right?'

Fraser slumped to the floor again to allow Margot to wrap her arms around Wren. I knew I should be thinking something about this vignette playing out in front of me, but my brain was too scrambled. When Wren began to sob, and Margot sat on the floor, drawing her close, stroking her hair gently and murmuring to her, all I could think was, 'Oh.'

'Bugger me,' Fraser said. 'You two as well? I feel left out. Anyone round here want a shag?'

'Not just now, thanks.' A paramedic, his uniform all highlights from the blue lights outside, stepped in through the wreckage. 'But maybe later, you never know your luck.'

More uniformed people were coming in now, police and fire as well as the ambulance crews; the wine bar was more full of people than I'd ever seen it before. A shame, I thought dreamily, that all the bottles had broken or we could have made a fortune.

Flynn was gently moved to one side. 'She's...' he began.

'Yep, we can see.' Calm faces, without blood, loomed in front of me. 'Hello, love, can you tell me your name?'

''S' Fee.'

'Right then, Fee, my love, I think we're going to have to carry you out. Wait there a moment.'

Others were swirling around Wren and Margot down on the floor. A policeman drew Flynn to one side and I saw them move to the far end of what was left of the bar. Fraser was being helped to his feet again by the paramedic who had been first in. Two people in dark firefighter uniforms were discussing something over near the door. I kept seeing things in brief flashes between blinks, as though each scene were separately staged. Tattered clothing. The shimmer of glass. A random playing card, the ace of spades, sliding bent-cornered along the bar. The top row of bottles, untouched.

I *wanted* to think about what Flynn said had happened. Had someone been sent to blow up the bar because of who his father was? I supposed that famous rich people must live under a constant level of threat and Flynn would be included in that, but it did seem rather extreme – or maybe that was why his father insisted on high security and all the latest gadgets. Was that what I wanted? To live with Flynn, all the time knowing that someone might, at any point, try to get to his father through him? But these thoughts, too, came through treacle, felt unimportant.

'We just need to get this bleeding stopped,' said the paramedic, beckoning over a colleague. I had no idea why everyone kept on about bleeding. *Everyone* was bleeding, Flynn still had blood sliding down the side of his face, I could see him occasionally swiping at it with his hand as he spoke to the police. Fraser's hair was matted with blood. Only Margot and Wren seemed to have escaped the sanguinary effects, but they were both looking battered and confused, sitting on the floor with their arms around each other while another paramedic tried to talk to them.

'Are you allergic to anything that you know of?' the paramedic asked me, so randomly that I almost laughed but didn't have the breath. His tone was calm and measured, as though we were meeting at a party, rather than in these circumstances.

'Guinea... pigs,' I forced out, remembering coming out in a rash after having tea with a schoolfriend and playing with her pets. Mum had sent me straight to my room when I got home in case I had something infectious, because she didn't want my brother to catch it. I'd itched all night, but it had gone, eventually.

'We'll try not to expose you to any, then.' There was a mask coming down over my face but I pushed it away with the floppy hand. The other arm didn't seem to be attached to me any more; at least, it wasn't obeying commands. 'Where... Flynn...?'

'I'm here.' He was too, right beside me, standing over me like an avenging angel all in black.

'Come... with...' I panted.

'Of course.' He grasped my feebly flapping hand.

'We're going to have to take everyone,' the paramedic said, still unnaturally cheerful. 'I hope we've got enough space.'

The mask dropped back over my face and everything went completely black.

19

I lost myself for a while.

There were voices and lights and questions, all of which swirled in a background that moved and had changed every time I forced my eyes open. My lids wouldn't stay apart though, and I'd find myself drifting away from the noise into a comfortable sea of blackness, where I bobbed about dreamlessly for a while, only to come back and repeat the performance.

Eventually I found my eyes staying open for longer and longer and at last I could focus on my surroundings. On the wall in front of me was a huge clock, the minute hand jerking every so often to a new position, although at present, time meant nothing and it all seemed very random. When I moved my head, the pillow underneath it crackled. Another half-turn and I could see a drip stand with lines running down to disappear under the edge of a sheet, and Flynn. He was crumpled into a small chair, glasses askew, asleep.

'Flynn?' My mouth was so very dry that the words came out cracked, but he jerked awake, sliding upright in the chair and righting his glasses as though it was a subconscious motion.

'Fee? You're awake.'

'Apparently,' I chipped out. 'Water. Please.'

Flynn fetched a glass from a side table. There was a straw in it. I didn't like the look of that straw. It had all the appearance of incapability about it. What was wrong with an ordinary glass? 'Here. Have a little, go carefully.'

That first taste of water was fabulous, even though it was flavoured with antiseptic and at a temperature that suggested it had been drunk once already. 'Hate to say this,' I said, when he'd returned the glass to its shelf. 'But where am I? And what happened?' The words came out in little puffs. I was still as breathless as if I'd run a mile.

My eyes had got used to the white walls and the drip stand now, and I could look properly at Flynn. He had a narrow line of stitches along one cheek, stark against his skin, which was very pale.

'What the hell *happened*?' I repeated, shock getting hold of me again. 'Is everyone all right?'

I grabbed at the tattered remnants of memory: loud noise and things flying about, blood and pain and a strange numbness, *Margot and Wren...*

Flynn took a deep breath. 'Everyone is recovering,' he said. 'More or less. It was a bomb, Fee. Those guys who came in that night with the bag, they left an explosive device. An amateur, home-built one the investigators think, not much more than a timer, a detonator and lots of messy black powder. But effective, obviously.'

'Why? Why would anyone do that?' I looked thirstily at the glass of water again and Flynn refilled it. 'And *that night*? How long have I been here?'

'A week.'

'A *week*!' I jerked my head up off the pillow and something somewhere went beep. A quick mental audit told me that my back hurt, my legs were tingling as though I had ants running under my skin, and the upper left quadrant of my body didn't seem to be there.

Flynn held the glass carefully up to my face again. 'I think – the police think it was something to do with Dad,' he said. 'Couldn't see what I'd done to upset anyone, but Dad can be a bit abrasive sometimes and they thought some business rival might have wanted to make a point.'

I shook my head, which took some coordinating. 'Have you got the film from the cameras?'

'I've sent a copy to the police. They're hunting those two men down. That explosion was the biggest thing they've had to deal with in months, so they're being quite enthusiastic about it.'

There was a moment's silence. In the background, I could hear voices outside in the corridor, someone laughing distantly. Cars passed outside a window I couldn't see out of, set high in the wall as though this were some kind of prison. 'So, how bad is it?' I asked eventually, when Flynn obviously wasn't going to say anything else.

He swallowed and I saw his eyes travel over my face, flick to my left shoulder, then come back again to their resting position, staring at his hand on the edge of my bedsheet. 'The doctors need to...'

'Flynn. I want *you* to tell me.'

'All right.' He gave me a small smile. 'Not as bad as it could have been, and not as bad as they first thought, actually.'

'I'm alive, that's pretty good going from where I'm standing. Lying, I mean.' My heart was solid in my chest. 'Look, just tell me.'

'Fee, you understand that nothing is definite? They've got great treatments now and we can afford the best...'

'Flynn.'

'Right. You've lost the use of your left arm and hand, and your face – well, you aren't going to be able to disappear in a crowd, put it that way. But,' he added hastily, as I struggled to lift the left hand that felt as though it wasn't there, 'plastic surgery is brilliant these days and your arm might well recover, they aren't sure about the extent of the nerve damage. You've also got three broken ribs, a shattered cheekbone and your eyebrow-shaping bill isn't going to be troubling you again for quite a while.'

I blinked. My legs tingled. 'Can I walk?'

Flynn had obviously decided not to prevaricate any longer. 'You will be able to. There was spinal cord trauma, and the doctors were a bit dubious, but they think you should get full use of your legs back eventually. You might have a bit of a limp, that's all.'

I sighed. 'I knew being a private detective was a pipe dream. Unless I can operate in crowds entirely made up of people who look like Igor – is it that bad?'

'No. No, not at all.'

'You're lying.'

He sighed. 'Sorry. I'm not very good at it, am I? And I'm going to have you moved to a private rehab unit. You'll get the best care that money can buy.'

Everything was crumbling. That bright, shiny new future that I had thought I was walking into – well, limping into, now, was falling apart in front of me. Cautiously, I lifted the hand that would obey me, and it came up, trailing wires, clips and drips, and touched my face rather harder than I'd intended.

'Ow.'

'No need to slap yourself. It wasn't your fault.' Flynn grinned at me and I realised that at least *this* part of my life seemed to be steady. 'Hold on, there's a mirror here.'

I didn't recognise myself. My face was swollen and bruised, there were lines of stitches criss-crossing the whole of the left side and half my scalp was bare.

'You were closest to the blast,' Flynn said, trying to sound neutral. 'But nobody looks good, if that's any consolation.'

You do, I thought. *You might have stitches and a cut that makes you look as though you've had an amateur nose job, but you still look fabulous. Though that might be because you're actually here, which I notice is a state that my family don't seem to have entered.*

At that moment, there was a tap on the door and Margot put her head around. 'Is she...?'

'She's awake,' and the tone of relief in Flynn's voice told me all I needed to know about that state of tension he'd been living in for the past week.

Margot's head withdrew and there was a moment of hissed conversation in the corridor. Then it popped back again. 'Is she up to visitors?'

'You can ask me directly, Margot,' I said, managing to get some strength into the words. 'I'm injured, not mute.'

Another withdrawal, another conversation. After a few moments, the door opened fully and Margot, Wren and Fraser trooped in, looking a little chastised.

'It's Monday,' Wren said. She and Margot were holding hands, I noticed.

'Can't miss a Monday meeting,' Fraser said jovially, glanced over at me and winced. 'Bugger me. You look like you went through the mincer.'

Margot glared at him, although her glare had lost some of its previous power. She seemed to have softened around the edges; the power hairstyle had given way to something more casual and she was wearing the yoga outfit that she'd worn the night the club came to rescue me from Dexter. It made her look younger and happier, or maybe that was Wren's proximity. She did, however, have some technicolour bruising across her forehead that made her look like a mobile sunset.

Wren herself looked cheerful and bubbly and less birdlike than she had, despite a swollen lip. 'So, we thought we'd all come over and see how you were doing,' she went on, ignoring Fraser, who was bobbing about like a tethered balloon.

'And Annie says to get well soon. She's going to pop in when Eddie gets the car out,' Fraser added.

We all looked at each other. 'It's in the garage,' Flynn said. 'Why does she make it sound as though they have to go and rope it in like a wild horse?'

We all shrugged. Well, the others shrugged, I managed a one-sided motion that set the machines beeping again. It reminded me of why we were here. 'Have you got access to the security film?' I asked Flynn.

'I can source it via my phone.'

'Ooh, get you, Mr Mission Impossible!' Fraser bounced over and sat on the edge of my bed next to Flynn.

'Ow, you're sitting on my drip.'

'Sorry.' He moved a couple of centimetres. 'Let's have a look then. I want to see the big explosion.'

'Fraser!'

'Sorry, Margot, but I does. I was practically a hero, and it's the nearest I'm ever going to get to being a hero.' Fraser looked a little crestfallen. 'But Minnie was right impressed when I told her. I had to have clips put in,' he added to me. 'Look,' and he lifted his hair to show a line of tiny clips that kept his scalp together. 'It's like hair extensions, only skin.'

'Fraser, you are revolting,' Margot said firmly. 'But it would be nice to see the film, Flynn. Have you watched it?'

'Endlessly.' Flynn was scrolling on his phone. 'I've even

shown it to Dad, but we don't recognise the goons. He's in the middle of some takeover in the Middle East somewhere, we thought this might be rivals wanting to put him off. Ah, here it is.'

The film was from a camera above the bar, with a wide-angled lens. I watched our group arrive, saw Margot and Flynn put the peanuts out, everyone moving jerkily like in a ridiculous 1920s silent film.

'I'm playing it back at twice normal speed,' Flynn explained. 'To get to the good bits.'

'I look good,' Fraser said wonderingly. 'Wow.'

He'd arrived pantingly through the door and thrown himself upon the peanuts.

'You look like an industrial digger,' Margot observed.

'Margot!'

'Sorry, Wren.' Margot gave Wren a small, secret smile. They were still hand in hand and nobody was commenting, so I decided to keep quiet too. 'Sorry, Fraser.'

'Nah. I were hungry. And Minnie says nuts are good.'

We all crowded in close around Flynn's phone screen to watch. At least, everyone else crowded and he was holding the phone almost under my nose, so we were all bundled together. Nobody, apart from Fraser, had remarked on how bad I looked, or my injuries, and I guessed that the group chat had been kept fully up to date with my progress. Maybe they'd already visited when I'd been out of things? The thought of Fraser looming by my bed when I wasn't conscious made me pull a small face.

'Here.' Flynn tapped the screen. 'This is where they come in.'

We watched the door open, and Flynn changed the timer to show everything happening at normal speed. Two men came in and stood by the bar, putting the bag between them.

'I should have noticed the bag,' Flynn said sadly. 'But it's so ordinary.'

The pair moved, talking to Flynn on the screen, and I jerked.

'Fee?' Wren looked sideways at me around Margot. 'Are you all right?'

'I know them.' My voice sounded as cracked as it had when I had first woken up.

'You *know* them?' Margot peered more closely at the screen now.

'Yes. Well, I sort of do. I recognise them, anyway. I didn't really look at them that night, they had their backs to me and I was too busy...' No. I couldn't tell everyone that I was too busy being smug about my new future. 'That one, the tall one, he's called Axe, although I very much doubt it's his real name, and the other one is always in the background. He deals drugs, he lives in Leeds...' I moved my head on the pillow. 'His name is... No, I can't remember. But I've met them both. With Dexter.'

Flynn let the phone drop. '*Dexter*? You mean, your ex did this?' He gestured at the screen.

'Looks like it.' My voice was small. 'Sorry.'

'Not your fault,' Flynn said sternly. 'At all. But I need to call the police and tell them.'

He went out and left the remaining four of us looking sheepishly at each other. 'I'm sorry,' I said again. 'I didn't realise he'd go that far.'

'Look.' Wren sat down beside Fraser, poking him until he moved towards the end of the bed and she could sit next to me. 'You can't take responsibility for your ex's actions. You didn't force him to be a jealous, possessive, thuggish bastard, did you?'

I moved my head on the pillow again. It wouldn't quite shake, I couldn't get it far enough over to the left, so it was more of a one-sided flop. 'I honestly thought he'd just forget about me. I should have remembered that Dexter is...'

'A sad, pathetic excuse for a psycho?'

'Yes, thank you, Fraser. I should have remembered that Dexter doesn't like being shown up and Flynn showed him up good and proper. He wouldn't have come round, he'd been well warned off, so he sent his mates. I wonder if they knew what was in the bag?'

'If they didn't, they got out of there pretty sharpish,' Fraser said, finding the bowl of fruit that someone – Flynn, most likely – had placed beside my bed, and peeling a banana.

'True.' Wren smiled. She and Margot locked eyes for a moment and then both turned away in a movement so similar that it looked synchronised. 'And one good thing did come of the explosion, Fee.'

Margot took over. 'I would never have – well, I wouldn't have come out if I hadn't been so terrified for Wren,' she said. 'I knew I had... *feelings*, but I wasn't sure and I was too scared to say anything.' She gave a soft smile towards Wren. 'Especially with all that talk about dating sites. I really didn't think you'd noticed me at all.'

'We had a long conversation in that ambulance, didn't we?' Wren almost giggled now. 'There were quite a lot of admissions going on. I'd fancied Margot right from the first time we met, but I didn't think that she felt the same way, until that dreadful night.'

'I would have thought it was fairly obvious,' Margot went on. 'Inviting you to stay? Making your favourite meals?'

'I thought you were just being nice. Helping me get over Jordan.'

'I didn't altogether realise what I was doing, I suppose. Not at first.'

'Yeah, yeah, lovely. So far, so Thelma and Louise,' Fraser burst in. 'Can we get back to what those two pricks were doing in the bar? You can drive the car off the cliff later.'

We all stared at him. 'Thelma and Louise weren't gay,' I said eventually.

'Bloody were. I've seen that film about four hundred times.' Fraser ate another banana. 'It's our Chloe's favourite. I can do all the lines too, if you want.'

'Probably not necessary.'

Fraser, the unintentional film subtext critic, started on the grapes. 'So, you reckon your ex wanted to smash up Flynn's place?'

'I think so,' I said. 'We were collateral damage. He had no way of knowing we'd be in there that night; he must have just wanted to get at Flynn for daring to take me away from him. That's how he sees it,' I finished quickly, in case anyone thought I'd been two-timing Dex with Flynn. 'I was his property, because that's how he thinks of women. He was probably delighted to find out that I was badly injured.'

'Prick,' said Fraser, dribbling grape juice and ignoring the fact that he wasn't exactly squeaky-clean in the female disenfranchisement stakes.

At that point, Annie came in, flustered and ruffled. 'Eddie's just parking the car,' she said. 'Dreadful parking facilities here, aren't they? Anyway.' She plopped a paper bag of grapes onto my bedside table and Fraser started on those too. 'How are you feeling? I saw Flynn in the corridor on the phone. Is everything all right?'

There was a moment of busy conversation as we all tried to tell the story, but the mixing of perspectives meant that it was jumbled and probably didn't enlighten Annie as much as she'd hoped.

'Someone deliberately tried to kill you?' She looked aghast, her eyes travelling over my drip stands. 'How dreadful.'

'I'll be fine.' I tried to smile bravely but the stitches wouldn't allow it.

All of a sudden Annie's face seemed to melt. Tears flowed

down her cheeks and her mouth writhed. 'Oh dear. It's *all* so dreadful!' she said again, pulling a large handkerchief from the sleeve of today's cardigan. 'When I heard... well... Eddie had to take me to the doctor, I was that distressed.'

Margot patted Annie's hand, the one that wasn't mopping her face with the enormous hankie. 'Everyone is all right, Annie,' she said soothingly. 'We're all still here.'

'I didn't realise...' Annie sobbed on. '...just how fond I've got of all of you. I thought it was just meetings, somewhere to offload how worried I was about Eddie, but listening to you all being so... *brave*.' She sniffed and blew her noise. 'It made me realise that we're less a club and more like a little family.' A wavering smile broke through beneath the mopping and she straightened herself a little, the cardigan flapping around her shoulders. 'Aren't we?'

There was a thin chorus of agreement from the others and I felt a momentary jolt in my chest. *Found family*. Wasn't that the phrase? Although my actual family might be less than satisfactory, why shouldn't I make myself a new one with people I actually cared about?

I joined in with the general concurrence. Even Fraser had slowed down his grape ingestion to nod thoughtfully.

'I got a great family,' he said slowly. 'But not what you might call *supportive*. Our Chloe laughed at me doing my stretches the other day.' He chewed, ruminatively. 'The cow,' he added. 'I got to get out of there.'

'I never had children,' Annie continued. Her voice was a little lower now, as though the words weren't really meant to be heard. 'We did try, but... well, never mind. That was all a long time ago. And for all the societies and hobbies I'm part of, there's nobody who's ever really taken an interest in my life. You all listened to me. You made me feel like I mattered.'

Now there was a silence, only slightly mitigated by the somewhat industrial sound of Fraser eating my grapes.

'It can be hard.' Margot spoke now and her voice was similarly low. Confidential. 'When you try to conceive and nothing seems to happen. Everyone else is popping out little ones as if they don't even think about it, even people who don't seem to want them.' She patted Annie again, but this time it looked as though there was a weight of understanding in her touch. 'I've seen too many of the end results of unwanted and unloved children turning to crime as a cry for help.'

More silence. More mastication noises. Then Fraser said, through a mouthful, 'Bugger me, we're here to cheer Feebs up, not depress the whole lot of us. Anyone want a grape?'

Flynn came back into the room, looked sideways at Fraser eating all the fruit and handed me the phone. 'It's the police,' he said. 'They'll come and talk to you when you're out of here and feeling better, but right now they need everything you've got on those two that came into the bar, and what happened with you and Dexter.'

I took his phone. 'And I shall be delighted to tell them.'

Everyone else started to talk about holidays and the atmosphere lightened a good deal, for which I was grateful, but they ate all my grapes, for which I wasn't.

* * *

What I could tell the police wasn't enough, of course.

We had the security footage, we had everything I knew about Dexter and his 'friends'. The police were grateful and tried to sound encouraging and positive, but it wasn't *enough*. All I had was one fake name and the knowledge that they were connected to Dexter, who lied as easily and regularly as he drew breath.

Despite the police's assurances that everything was being done, I knew that everyone concerned would have gone to ground and would be busy laying alibis as fast as they could. Some film, however good quality, of two people who probably wouldn't look anything like the participants by the time they'd cut their hair, grown beards and moved to Carlisle, wasn't going to do any good. Plus, it didn't include Dexter, and unless his mates were prepared to drop him in it, he would get away with this.

Surprised at my jaw-clenching desire to see punishment for Dexter, I wondered why I had suddenly become so keen for retribution. I'd let him get away with everything he'd done to me so far: the criminal damage, assault, coercive control... He'd used me and mistreated me and I'd been afraid of him, but fear didn't explain why I'd kept letting him back in. Had he really been all I thought I was worth?

I lay back on the hospital pillows, still unable to sit up unaided, and wondered about my life choices that had led me here. If I hadn't looked Dexter's way, if I'd never gone home with him that evening, if I'd never let him into my life – I wouldn't be here now, looking at an existence so completely altered.

The smell of disinfectant, that awful boiled-air smell that hospitals have, made my nose itch, and with all the drips and clips, it took some effort to get my working hand up to my face to scratch it. Then I stared at my arm for a bit, because it was that or watching the clock with its oddly erratic tick, painfully marking the interminable passing of seconds while I lay here.

How long would Flynn put up with me now? I couldn't even help in the bar if I was going to have to limp slowly everywhere and couldn't lift a box with one hand. He seemed solid so far, but that was probably shock. What the hell was I going to *do*?

A few sparse tears squeezed from the corners of my eyes made me feel a little better. If this was rock-bottom, then it could have been a lot worse; I was still alive, all my friends were still alive. Maybe it was going to prove impossible to get Dexter to face up to what he'd done and be punished; his associates were still being hunted by the police – a scenario which gave me a frisson of pleasure – but he couldn't stay underground for long. Dexter had so far barged his way through life feeling untouchable, actually *being* untouchable, apart from brief arrests and detainments, because everyone was too scared of him to give any evidence against him. Now, I realised, that it didn't matter any more what he thought of me. I wasn't afraid any longer. The second he put his head above the parapet, I was going to bring him down.

If he never did, of course, if he kept his distance and stayed away from me, that would be a victory of sorts too. Not as satisfying as seeing him imprisoned for what he'd tried to do, but I'd be free. Or would I? Was I going to spend the rest of my life attempting to look over my shoulder in case Dexter decided that now was the time to show me what happened to those who tried to get away?

20

Most of the big stuff had to wait until I was out of hospital. Flynn wanted me moved to a private rehab unit – he showed me the pictures. It was a lovely old country house with grounds, where I could be wheeled happily about in the sunshine and have daily physiotherapy in the large pool or totter around the well-padded rooms with their careful artwork. Like a ninety-year-old in a care home. Looked after, but out of the way.

I refused to go. Flynn clearly thought I was mad, but he didn't push the point. He smiled ruefully and said, 'I suppose you're going to want to come home then?' We moved into my flat, the wine bar being basically rubble and unsafe floors, and he paid to have a temporary stairlift fitted up the fishy stairs.

'Two weeks! It's only been two weeks!' Flynn said, slightly exasperated, when I refused the stairlift as well and insisted on making my slow and painful way up to the flat on my own legs.

'If I don't do it, I'll never do it,' I puffed, having to go up like an elderly lady with gammy hips, one step at a time. Plus, I couldn't use my left arm to hold on to the handrail, so I lurched around with my good hand. It took twenty minutes to get to the first floor and Flynn had made two cups of tea and a sandwich by the time I got there.

'Well, I'm glad you did. The club are meeting here tonight, and Fraser, apparently, has News.' Flynn was the only person who could look me in the eye when I smiled. Everyone else averted their gaze and sort of shuddered, but that was fine, I was used to it. My entire adolescence had been like that, growing up with my brother. Things would improve. Things *were* improving. My parents had even come to visit me in hospital once. 'I want to know what that is.'

'I don't know whether to be optimistic or overcome with dread.' I hauled myself over the threshold and stood panting inside the door, hanging on to the new, reinforced door frame that Flynn had had fitted to go with the new door he'd put on, after Dexter had battered his way through the old one.

The club had visited me, separately and together, almost every day. Eddie had, apparently, managed to get the car out on several occasions and Annie had come bearing pots of chrysanthemums and copies of *Woman's Weekly* and made small talk about her neighbours, while Eddie and I had tried to avoid one another's eye and winced every time Doncaster was mentioned in her passing conversation. Margot and Wren were planning a trip up to the Scottish cabin together for a romantic break. Their happiness was a joy to see and helped my recovery quite a lot.

Fraser was – well, Fraser. But he had never turned up without a bar of Cadbury's Dairy Milk – most of which he'd eat himself during the visit, but the thought was there – and had happily told me that I looked like shit and his stitches were healing faster than mine.

Flynn very carefully didn't say anything as I collapsed now, slowly but gasping, onto the sofa. He brought one of the cups of tea over and placed it neatly on a side table I'd never seen before.

'You... made up the sofa,' I said, trying to keep my breathing even and not sound as though I'd exhausted myself coming up the stairs.

'Yes. It's nice to have somewhere to sit.' Flynn wouldn't look at me, which made me feel worse than I had after my ascent of the staircase. I knew I was a bit sweaty and the whole 'hospital ambience' was sticking to me as closely as my hastily donned jumper, but was I really so dreadful to look at? 'I've been turning it back into a bed at night, don't worry. I did buy a new mattress though; that one you'd been sleeping on had a big dip in the middle.'

'Yes, I know.' He still sounded – odd. 'Flynn, what's up?' I decided to face it head on. 'If you're having second thoughts about...' I waved a hand, because I couldn't bring myself to say the words *you, us, this place, our relationship*, '...things, please tell me.' Mentally I'd resigned myself to losing him already. He was too nice, too decent, too, well, *rich* for someone like me. And now I didn't even have looks to fall back on, with my scarred face and my dragging walk. I didn't deserve Flynn on any level, and I'd stiffened my backbone and worked on my 'sympathetic, hurt yet stoic' expression, for when he told me, all the time I'd been in the hospital.

Flynn almost jumped. 'What? No! Oh, I'm so sorry, Fee, I never wanted you to think that!' The glasses got a shove up his nose and he sat down beside me, making me rock as his weight caused the sofa bed to lurch dramatically to one side.

He took my hand, hot and damp as it was, and linked his fingers through mine. 'You... you're my *friend*. First and foremost, you're my friend. Whatever else we've got here, if this is love or lust – or some other thing that we haven't defined yet – at base what it comes down to is *friendship*.'

I looked at him and thought that love and lust weren't too bad from where I was... well, rather lopsidedly sitting. But he was right. Our relationship had come from friendship, the same friendship as I had with Annie, Margot, Wren and, yes, even Fraser too. Although I didn't want to wrap myself around any of them and hold them close through the night, it didn't make our friendships any less valid.

'I've been so wary, after Australia,' Flynn went on, looking down at my hand as though it were the prime exhibit in a museum of body parts. 'It hit me hard. Being used for your money isn't nice.' Now he glanced up at my face, as though he expected me to understand.

'Flynn, if you're wanting me to sympathise, I'm sorry. I've never had a bean. Nobody has ever wanted me for my money and contacts, unless they've fancied my brother to a lunatic level and wanted me to introduce them.' I took a breath. 'Actually, anyone fancying my brother is already well on their way to lunacy and I wish them all the happiness in the world, there.'

He grinned, and it was a Flynn-grin, eyes glittering and his face relaxed. He shook my hand lightly. 'Don't be bloody daft. It's more that you didn't know who I was for a long time. You got to know *me*, the me that's underneath all the stuff about my dad and having a business empire and all that. You liked *me*. Er' – he looked deeply into my eyes – 'you *did* like me, didn't you? For a while back at the beginning, it was rather hard to tell.'

'I thought you were a student doing bar work in the evenings,' I confessed.

'Oh. I don't know whether to be flattered or horrified.' Another shake of my hand. 'What I really mean is, we were friends before you knew I had a dad who is trying to be Britain's answer to Elon Musk, without the dodgy political leanings. It's not all about the money for you. I never thought I'd let anyone get close to me again. And yet, here you are.'

'I couldn't move away if I tried.' I gave a small smile. 'I'd fall down the stairs, for a start.'

He laughed and his glasses slid again. 'You're very different, is what I mean. You turned down the rehab. It looked like an expensive hotel with specialist equipment that might have helped you back onto your feet faster, and you turned it down.'

I felt the twist inside. It had cost me a lot to turn the offer down. Part of me had looked through the brochure and thought how wonderful it would be to feel cared for. Food delivered to your room, top-class medical attention, a personalised exercise programme – it would have been wonderful. But I would have felt like an embarrassment, tucked away and invisible. Plus, my parents would have laughed themselves stupid at me getting top-notch treatment, and my brother would probably have visited just to call me horrible names and try to get me to extract money from Flynn so he could buy another car he couldn't drive.

No. Here was where I belonged.

'I've got something to show you,' Flynn said later. 'I've been trying to think how to bring it up and I can't come up with anything tactful or non-prejudicial, so I thought I'd show you and let you make your own mind up.'

'Mmm?' I'd been dozing, feeling uncannily close to the granny-in-the-care-home that I'd worried I'd become if I went to the rehab facility. Something about the change of air between hospital and the flat, plus the exertion of getting up the stairs, had made me ridiculously tired.

'It's... I didn't want to worry you and it's probably nothing, but...'

I sighed. 'Show me, Flynn.'

'Are you sure you're up to it?' He was fussing about with his phone, opening it and closing it again, putting it down on top of the cupboard and then picking it up.

'As I don't know what *it* is, I really can't pass judgement.' I wriggled my way up to sitting properly. My wonky leg wouldn't push off the floor properly and I performed a strangely sideways sort of flop, using my elbow to correct myself. Having a body that was uncooperative was taking some getting used to.

'Okay. Here, look.' Now he had his phone open on the app which played recordings from his security cameras. 'I set this one up in your hallway when I came over to fit the new door, after your charming ex kicked the old one down.'

'Oh.' How did I feel about that? 'You didn't tell me you'd put cameras around the place.' Violated? Spied on? But I'd not been back here after that night, had I? A warmth came over me when I remembered how caring Flynn had been, giving me somewhere to stay and, eventually, half of his bed.

'Not around the place. Just covering your door. I thought I'd warned him off sufficiently but I couldn't be quite sure, and I didn't know that we... that you and I were going to... that you wouldn't be coming back here,' he finished, looking a bit pink around the ears. 'I wanted to make certain you'd be safe. Hence the security door I had put on, too.'

I'd noticed that as I limped in. The big, heavy door that had replaced my old flimsy front door and hung there in the rein-forced frame like a Dwayne Johnson ornament. Nobody was going to kick that down, without the strength of Arnold Schwarzenegger.

'You didn't have to,' I said, sounding slightly sulky, even to myself.

'I know,' Flynn said brightly. 'But I thought it might be a good idea and I was right. Look.' He held his phone screen up in front of me.

The recording was surprisingly good quality. It showed the patch of hallway right outside my door, at night, from the low-level lighting. 'You're not going to win any Oscars for this one,' I said, pushing the phone down.

'Keep watching.' He lifted the screen again.

Now the recording showed a distant light source, my downstairs neighbours, I thought, opening and closing the front door. Grainy darkness reigned on. Then, after a few moments, a shape materialised out of the blackness. Someone, wearing dark clothing, a hoodie it seemed, had come up the stairs and was standing in front of the new door, glancing from side to side.

'That's Dex,' I breathed.

'He keeps his hood up, so I couldn't tell.' Flynn turned the phone sideways to maximise the screen.

'It's him. I know it is.' A shard of coldness slid between my shoulder blades. 'What is he doing?'

'Looking at the door.' Flynn slid the timer along the bottom to speed up the passing of film time. 'It seems to have taken him by surprise.'

The figure, moving jerkily now in the rapid frame-time, put a hand against the door and seemed to push once or twice. Then it looked all around the door, face still hidden inside the hood; just the tip of a nose and a chin occasionally caught what little light there was. Another push, at the frame now.

'I had a steel reinforcement put in,' Flynn said, smugly. 'He won't get through that without a forklift truck.'

Another moment in which the hooded figure seemed to consider the door. Then a foot came out and smashed against the bottom, in an angle the camera didn't catch. The shape disappeared and then rematerialised, hopping and waving its arms.

'He probably broke a toe.' Flynn's smugness had reached maximum levels. 'That thing is solid.'

'I wonder why he came?' I stared at the footage. Dex, after a few more shoves in the direction of the security door, slithered out of the frame, obviously back down the stairs again. 'Surely he'd worked out I wasn't there.'

'Dunno.' The film ended. 'I thought you ought to see. I wasn't certain who it was – I mean, I had my suspicions, but he kept his face hidden.'

'It's Dexter. I recognise the shape and the way he moves.' I'd often thought Dex moved like a cat, with that springy, cocky kind of walk that cats have when they know they own the garden. It was beginning to dawn on me that he'd moved like a cat which had prey on its mind.

'So, anyway. He came here, and the date on this film is just after the explosion. He must have known you were in hospital then; it was in all the local papers. Dad managed to get it listed as a gas explosion, I didn't think you'd want your business spread over the media.'

'Gas explosion? How very *Harry Potter*,' I said, weakly. I'd never even *thought* about it being reported. It never crossed my mind that there would be any kind of scrutiny as to why a random wine bar in a tiny Yorkshire town might be blown up, but of course there would. Not much else happened around here on a wet night in April. The next item down on the news agenda would be the local car boot sale timings.

Flynn shrugged. 'It was the first thing that came to mind. Anyway. Now you know. He's still out there. Shame the police didn't put this place under surveillance but – well, they're doing their best. Two people that they currently can't find blew up my bar. The bastards,' he ended, the words mild.

'I think I might need another cup of tea,' I said. My body had tried to go to Full Alert status, but with wonky legs and an arm that wouldn't obey me, this had only served to make me feel even more vulnerable. Dexter. Waiting outside my door.

'On it, boss!' Flynn swung over towards the kitchen area, and then came back, his face creasing into lines of worry. 'And I'm saying that purely for comic effect, you understand. There is no way in the world that you are bossy or controlling.'

Now I found I could smile properly. 'Flynn, I know what you meant. You're the most open and honest person I know. Dex was the master of negging and my brother didn't even bother to sugar-coat his contempt. I can spot an insult when it comes wrapped in chocolate, trust me.'

'Phew. I wouldn't want you to think I was anything like those two.'

He went back to tea-making, humming slightly. It was an irritating noise, yet oddly reassuring.

I sat back as the adrenaline from seeing Dex, albeit on a screen, abated. Dexter. He'd come *here*. But I'd been in hospital, and he must have known that. Besides, he hadn't been banging and yelling like he had that last night he'd come and tried to attack me. He'd come silently, trying to work out how to get into the flat.

Before the – well, I couldn't call it an accident, could I? Before the explosion that had given me this notable scar and off-centre walk, I had been reading everything I could about becoming a Private Investigator. The potential of an actual vocation had tingled through my veins in the same way as alcohol used to, giving me *something*. Hope, a future that I couldn't see yet. *Anticipation*. All right, all the alcohol had anticipated was a disturbed night's sleep and a headache in the morning, but the feeling was similar. None of that would come to fruition now, of course; I couldn't run an investigation if I couldn't drive and stood out in a crowd like a bluebottle in a saucer of milk, but the reading had still inspired me. Right now, it felt as though there was an idea knocking at the back of my brain, trying to get my attention.

'Flynn, can I look at that footage again, please?'

'Before or after the tea?'

I looked down at my unresponsive arm, sitting on my lap like a sleeping cat. 'Before, I think, so I don't spill.'

'Here, then.' He dodged across the room and put the phone in front of me. 'Just press – that.' Then he whirled back to attend to the kettle and teabags, like the perfect butler.

I watched the film again. Then again. Simultaneously, that other night replayed on a loop in my mind. *Why had he come? He said to see me, but he'd come back when I wasn't here, desperate to get in. He came in that night, but he'd chased me out and the guys had taken him down and had him arrested. Then Flynn had had the flat secured...*

I watched Dexter kick the door, to the detriment of his footwear and, hopefully, his actual foot. *Think, Fee, think...*

That last time I'd seen him, when he'd kicked his way in, what had he said? It had been something that had made my internal 'that's odd' meter start ticking. Something incongruous, something that hadn't fitted with the Dexter I knew. And all this time my brain had held on to those words, preserved them, because it *knew* they were strange. Those Investigator books had encouraged that sort of thing. 'Anything unusual can be a give-away.' 'Never underestimate your ability to read a "tell".' 'People betray themselves all the time...'

What had he said?

'Go easy on the tea consumption.' Flynn put the mug down in front of me, moving his phone slightly to one side. 'You'll be in the loo all afternoon at this rate.'

I jerked and almost got myself to standing, managing full upright posture by grabbing the side table. 'That was it!'

Flynn stared at me and then at the tea. 'Was it? I used the teabags in the cupboard.'

'No. The bathroom. That was what Dexter said that struck me as odd! When he broke in here that night? The night when the club came to my rescue?' I gave Flynn a grin that was, no doubt, wild-eyed and slightly mad.

'There's no need to ask me, I've got that night engraved behind my eyes like the worst kind of horror film,' Flynn said levelly. 'You leaving a trail of blood, running down the street in your pyjamas with that...' He was groping for a word and I helped him out.

'Violent abuser.' Two words. But they summed Dexter up. 'On a drugs binge.' I added, for clarity.

'Yes. Him. With him chasing you. It was terrifying. *I* was terrified.' He moved in and gave me a sudden hug. 'It could all have gone so wrong.'

'But it didn't. You, the guys – you all saved me.'

Flynn looked wryly at my limp arm. 'Not quite fast enough, though.'

'You weren't to know he'd send his goons in to pay you back. But I thought at the time that it was overkill. All that, blowing up the bar, over *me*?' I copied his ironic expression. 'I mean, I'm great, but I'm not worth all that.'

The embrace deepened until I could feel Flynn's breath against my cheek. 'You are,' he whispered. 'You so are.'

For a few moments I gave in to the hug and allowed myself to feel protected. Important. Worth something. I might not believe it yet, deep down, but Flynn did, and that was what mattered.

'Anyway.' I stepped back, but only a little way because having Flynn hold me was worth any amount of explosive injury. 'I remembered what it was that Dex said that night. He said that he needed to use the bathroom.'

'Seems an odd turn of phrase,' Flynn observed, groping one hand for his own mug.

'Exactly. Dexter never said that. If he needed the loo he'd say something wonderfully poetic like "I want to piss", or "gotta take a shit." None of this "use the bathroom" nonsense. It's been processing, all this time, in my head. Being blown up put it on the back burner a bit, but now I'm starting to wonder – did he cause that explosion to make sure I was out of the way so he could get into the flat? Was it the toilet he needed? Or the actual *bathroom*? Those books I was reading when I thought I really could be a private investigator told me that people tend to say what they *really* mean without knowing it.'

I gave Flynn another wild stare.

'I'll go and...' He moved, but I put my tea-holding hand, the only working one, onto his shoulder to stop him. Tea slopped along his shirt but he didn't remark on it.

'No. I'm going to do this. I've got an idea.' I put the tea down, just too late to save Flynn's shirt, and began my lurch across the floor towards the bathroom door, gripping onto furniture on my way to help me stay upright, although the sheer fizz of adrenaline was almost propelling me towards the ceiling right now.

Flynn watched my progress. 'Anything I can do?'

'There's a hammer in that drawer.' I pointed with an elbow as my hand was holding on to the wall. 'We might need it.' Then the reality of what I needed to do crowded out the buzz of impetuosity. 'And I might need to use you to do the actual mechanics.'

I received a bright smile and he went off to rummage in the Drawer of Stuff, as I continued my inching progress into the bathroom.

I switched on the light and stood and stared around the dingy

little room. At that moment, my downstairs neighbours slammed
their front door and, obedient as ever to cheap landlord issues,
the shower cubicle rocked. The sink was immaculate; Flynn must
have cleaned in here, even the mirror had been wiped. And,
thanks to my earlier mending activities, the floor no longer tipped
and tilted as the loose boards moved.

The loose boards. Moved.

'Quick, Flynn!' My voice cracked under the weight of
certainty.

'Quick as I can! This drawer is a mess... Oh, here it is.' A
second later he appeared in the doorway, in time to see my unpic-
turesque descent to the floor. 'Are you all right? Fee?'

'No, no, that was intentional! Here.' I rolled up the mat that,
despite being little bigger than a bath towel, was large enough to
cover most of the floor. 'Can you lift up these two boards here?'

Flynn stared at me. 'Seriously? We're in the middle of all this
and you want to do some home renovation work?'

I was out of breath. Getting myself down onto the floor
without hitting my head on any of the fixtures had exhausted me.
'Dexter. Bathroom. Loose floor,' was all I could say and I saw the
understanding come into his eyes.

'You think...?'

'Flynn, I *know*. Dexter's never read a book in his life, he's
hardly going to have come over all CIA, is he? Do it.'

With some difficulty, because I'd nailed those boards down
fairly securely in my earnest attempts to improve my surroundings, Flynn lifted the floor. Underneath was a small dark and
dusty space. 'Go on then,' he said, sitting back onto his heels. 'You
check.'

Gritting my teeth and supporting my weight against the side
of the shower, I reached my fingers into the gap. At first there was
nothing, and my eyes pricked with dawning disappointment, but

half a moment of groping more and I touched the edge of what I had known must be down there. There were two of them.

'Two *phones*?' Flynn wrestled with the hammer, clearly unsure as to what to do with it now. 'Why would he have two phones?'

'Two phones, hidden away in the flat of someone that wasn't closely connected with him? He hardly took me out and showed me off, did he?' I'd obviously read far more of the dodgy gangster end of the fiction market than Flynn had. But then his dad had probably had him studying marketing manuals as soon as he started phonics. 'I think there will be a LOT of information that the police will be interested in on here.' I shook the phones. 'He's probably got the squeaky-clean ones somewhere in Leeds for the police to find. These ones he kept here, nice and out of the way. He could take them whenever he wanted to and just pop them back, I wouldn't notice.'

Flynn's mouth twisted as though he were eating grapefruit. 'What a... tosser.'

'Couldn't have put it better myself.' I straightened carefully, sweating and exhausted. 'I think you'd better call the police, Flynn.'

21

'The police will be here in ten minutes,' Flynn said, sometime later. 'I'm glad you made it back in here. It would have been an awkward interview, with you leaning against the bathroom wall.'

He hadn't helped me. He had so clearly wanted to that I'd had to send him out to get some more biscuits.

'I'm going to sit here and be all regal and imperious,' I said, from the seat I'd finally reached. 'Unless they're going to arrest me, in which case they can carry me out in the chair.'

Flynn stopped, mid chew. 'Arrest you? Why would they arrest *you*? You didn't set up the whole bomb thing, did you?' Then, with narrowed eyes, 'You didn't, did you?'

I smiled at him and took the sandwich he'd made me in my wobbly right hand. My face was healing, the cheekbone mending and the stitches had come out, but whenever I smiled, I looked like a badly made-up extra from *Night of the Living Dead*, so I tried not to do it too often.

I stayed, queenly and triumphant, in my chair, hoping that the smell of boiled cod wasn't too noticeable to the sergeant and police constable who turned up later and sat drinking tea on the edge of the sofa, looking at me curiously.

'You wanted to talk to us?' The sergeant, who was young and pretty and kept casting Flynn sidelong glances as he brought biscuits on a tray, asked me. They were clearly baffled as to why they were here.

'Have you got any closer to finding anyone connected to the bomb, yet?' I asked.

The police looked at each other. 'Not really,' the constable said. He was also very young and had a sort of 'scraped clean' look, with very pink, bare skin, as though he didn't shave, he scoured. Neither of them could look at me directly for any length of time. 'Nobody is saying anything. We've got the names of his mates, but no one is talking, just saying it's nothing to do with them.'

'So, Dexter gets away with it.' I took a deep breath. 'All right. Here.' I handed them the two phones.

One of them said a muffled 'bloody hell!' and then it was all a crackling of radio and some hurried phone calls being made. I gave Flynn a sad look.

'I don't know what's going to happen now,' I said. 'But I bloody love you, Flynn.'

He jerked. The L word hadn't been uttered by either of us, neither in passion nor when he'd been carefully helping me in or out of bed. We cared, that was evident and enough, for now. But – I wanted him to know.

'I dunno, we can't get in without the experts.' I was being looked at seriously by the police sergeant, the first time she'd actually focussed on my face. 'But it looks like a good 'un.'

'Fee?'

I sighed. 'In case they think it's anything to do with me, Flynn. I could have been in on it all. After all, I've got the phones.'

'But you *found* those! When you worked out what he'd been doing!'

I gave a one-sided shrug. 'They might not believe that. This is what they call, I believe, a calculated gamble.'

Flynn's expression was fierce now. 'I won't let them take you,' he said, and his voice was low. 'Dad can...'

'Your dad can be kept out of it. Let's see how things pan out.' I raised my eyebrows, although this must have made my scar stretch horribly and I felt like a *Munsters* outtake. 'You can't turn to your father every time things go pear-shaped.'

I got a half grin for that, and the two police officers, who were both still talking on their respective devices, gave one another an eyeball roll.

'No. You're right. I can't say that I want independence on the one hand, and then go running to him to sort stuff out every five minutes, can I?' Flynn looked a bit shamefaced now. 'I need to learn to walk the walk.'

'Don't worry, I can give you lessons,' I said cheerily, because nobody had threatened to arrest me yet and things were looking up. 'Only not in the walking bit. I can show you how to lurch, though, if you like.'

Flynn moved as though he wanted to hug me, eyed the police presence, and resumed his place over by the table.

The sergeant, looking a bit shell-shocked, finally hung up her phone. 'That's... err, we're hoping that's going to provide enough evidence to put a lot of people away.'

'Dexter hid them here to be out of the way,' I said. 'I didn't know, so I couldn't tell anyone. His fingerprints will be all over both phones and they should have everything you need about his drug empire – and I use the word *empire* in a form so loose that it's hanging on the floor. He was using me, not just for sex' – that eyeroll again, I clearly looked as sexually alluring as the fish this place smelled of – 'but as somewhere to hide his evidence. I've just found it,' I added quickly, in case they thought I'd been keeping something from them.

'You've done the right thing.' The constable still looked flabbergasted.

'And you can't think that Fee had anything to do with any of it,' Flynn put in quickly, still obviously worried that I was going to be bundled off into a van.

I waved my working hand at my face and smiled. Clearly the 'stitches and broken bones' look was still working, because everyone shuddered, and Flynn began collecting teacups in a busy way.

'You've been the one reporting him all down the line,' the sergeant said. Then, with admirable honesty, she added, 'I wish we could have put him away sooner for you.'

'If he'd left me alone, I might never have found these.' I pointed to the phones, now in evidence bags on the table. 'They might have stayed under my floorboards forever. Or until Dexter could get in to take them back. Either way, you wouldn't have them. Now – well, if you can connect him and the phones to the explosion and get him on attempted murder... I need never worry about running into him again.'

'I can't believe you put it all together,' Flynn said, when the police had gone away with the phones held at arm's length in their carefully sealed plastic evidence bags, leaving Flynn and me standing on the pavement watching them go. I'd forced myself to bump back down the stairs to see them off, trying my best to look bloodied but unbowed. Now I was out of breath, tired and propped up against the front wall. I'd been given a frame to help with the walking, but I was *buggered* if I was going to use that when anyone was watching.

I did the one-shoulder shrug. 'I'm glad all that reading I did before – well, before all this – came in useful,' I said.

'I rang Dad.'

'Oh, yes?'

'If it comes to... Well, if they try to get you as an accessory... if you need it... we've got the best legal team in the business on our side.'

Now I laughed. I felt the tension in my sewn-up face and didn't care. 'You are a very useful person to know, Flynn Mays-Harrison,' I said, trying not to fall over.

'Sssshh. Not many people know who I am round here. I'm just the guy with the wine bar, trying to make a living.'

We both sadly rotated and looked at what was left of the wine bar. Scaffolding held up the front, sheets of plywood covered the windows. Careful examples of exquisite interior designers' best work now hung through gaps in the walls. 'Oh well.' Flynn sighed. 'At least the insurance will pay out.'

Two passing locals, young men whom I'd seen in the wine bar when they'd been scrubbed and sleek, passed us in their work uniforms of overalls and boots. 'Mornin'!' they chorused, and then looked back over their shoulders at the wreckage of the bar. 'That's rough,' one said, with Yorkshire under-statement.

'You rebuilding?' the other asked.

'I don't know yet.' Flynn returned their looks with bland politeness.

'Not likely to blow up twice though,' the first passer-by observed. 'And it's nice to have somewhere posh to go of an evening.'

With a cheery wave of farewell they continued stomping, heavy-booted, up the hill towards the shops. Flynn sighed heavily.

'They think it was posh,' he said. 'I was trying for ordinary. There's more money in ordinary.'

I looked up and down the street. It was a narrow, workaday Yorkshire market town: pavement, cobbles and a narrow strip of roadway. Plenty of room for a horse and cart to take the coal from the now-defunct railway station at the bottom of the hill up to the Big Houses at the top, where local landowners who'd rented out their farms had lived in four-storey splendour.

Now these were flats, and even the old manor house that loomed at the top of the town had been subdivided into a terrace of three cottages.

'I'm not sure we're ready for posh,' I said.

Flynn sighed again. 'We weren't exactly rammed with trade, were we?' He held out a hand to me. 'Ah well. Maybe Dad was right. Maybe I don't really have a head for business. Perhaps I'm just a born underling.'

'Flynn!' I was surprised by his sudden lack of confidence. Flynn always seemed so self-aware, so certain, that this moment of weakness seemed very unlike him. 'You were doing fine. Until my ex blew the place up, of course.'

We looked again at the tumbled shell of a building. There was a cat sitting up on the scaffolding, washing itself in the spring sunshine, and one of the sheets of hardboard that covered the windows flapped desolately at one corner.

'Ah, I know. I might be getting a bit tired of being in Dad's shadow, that's all,' Flynn said slowly. 'I used to think it was great, being a Mays-Harrison. Ready-made empire to inherit, money to bail me out of unsuccessful enterprises...'

I shivered. 'Don't talk about bail,' I said quietly. 'If Dexter gets out...'

'You think he will?' Dark, earnest eyes behind those glasses which reflected the sunlight searched my face, snagging briefly on the pink scar. 'After everything you've given them? Those phones...'

'When they crack into them, it should put Dexter in the frame for almost every crime committed in Yorkshire for the last ten years,' I admitted. 'I know he wrote stuff down – well, not *wrote* because I'm not sure he can write.'

'Dyslexia?' Flynn nodded. 'Like Fraser.'

'More like, too arrogant to ever go to school. He once told me he'd been involved in crime since he was ten. But he kept stuff. He recorded stuff, he photographed stuff. He always said he was untouchable because of his insurance policy; nobody would dare turn him in because of what he'd got on *them*.'

'And that's what's on those phones?'

'I'm hoping so. If they were decoys, then I am in *so* much trouble. But when I think of that film of him standing outside, trying to work out how to get through the security door...'

'Do you think he'll know what you've done? Will he work it out?'

I shook my head. 'Dexter thinks women are stupid. All we're any good for is looking pretty, tottering in high heels and giving blow jobs. Ah well, I'm still tottering. One out of three isn't bad.'

Flynn smiled now, and it was his old, familiar self-assured and slightly cheeky grin. 'There's always Australia,' he said. 'If Dexter manages to worm his way out of everything, we could take off over there. Plenty of room to hide in Oz.'

'But what would we do out there?' I had to admit it, there was allure to the idea. Big continent, new start, my brother and parents several thousand miles away.

'Dad's got loads of businesses. I could go back to the bar in Melbourne. You could...' Flynn stopped and his eyes slid off my face.

'Yes, my kangaroo-wrestling career has been rather thwarted, hasn't it?' I said, to help him out. 'And anyway, weren't you just saying that you didn't want to work for your dad forever?'

'Was I?' He still wore the grin, but it had slipped sideways and now looked a touch more sardonic than was usual from Flynn. 'Well. Needs must, and all that.'

'Anyway. Dexter is stuffed. When the word gets out that his secret insurance policy has been busted open, practically everyone in the criminal underworld is going to be after him, including Jack the Ripper and whoever stole Shergar. He's more likely to need Australia than we are.'

'That's reassuring.' Casually, Flynn put his arm around my shoulders. I rocked but managed the extra weight rather well. My legs were tingling a bit, but I was absolutely *not* going to mention that.

'Why are we out here?' I said, to distract myself from the fact that I was beginning to buckle at the knees.

'We're expecting a visitor. I thought you'd feel better out here than doing the whole queen thing, sitting in your chair. That's why I didn't stop you coming down to see the police off. Here, you're upright and everything.'

'A visitor?' I couldn't stop myself, I put a hand to my hair to try to tidy it. The sides were still shaved but growing back to a centimetre or so of bristle, while the top had retained its length, but I hadn't been able to wash it properly one-handed and with stitches in my face. In consequence, I looked like a really bad punk. In fact, I thought, with the scar and the limp and the arm that had a brace to keep it straight even though it didn't work, I looked far more like a career criminal even than Dexter.

'Yes. Sorry I didn't mention it before, the police rather drove everything out of my head.' Flynn sounded perfectly relaxed. 'Ah. Here he is.'

'But...' *And* my jeans were halfway down my backside; I'd lost a fair bit of weight in hospital. *And* I'd spilled tea on my shirt; drinking one-handed was taking some getting used to. *And*, with the way my legs were tingling, I was beginning to contemplate using the stairlift, this once.

'Hi, Dad.'

A car pulled up beside us. It was a Bentley, but from there, any resemblance to any car types I could name stopped. My brother or Fraser would probably be able to tell me how much it cost, what upgrades it had had fitted and its top speed, but that was their area of special interest and I didn't care. All I knew was that it was sleek and shiny and being driven by a man I'd seen featured in the *Financial Times*, who looked even craggier and sterner than he did on the TV.

'Hey, Flynn.' Careless of the double yellow lines and the small knot of people collecting on the opposite pavement, Andrew Mays-Harrison got out of the car and stretched, then looked across at the decimated building. The cat on the scaffolding looked back at him. 'Well. That's not good, is it?'

'Long story.'

Flynn and his dad did look alike, I found now. When Andrew smiled, as he was doing now, he had more than a hint of the Daniel Craig about him, and he and Flynn had identical grins. In fact, I could imagine that in his youth, Andrew, with long hair and a slightly more slender frame, could have been a dead ringer for his son.

'And this is Fee.'

'Right. Fee.' A hand came out to shake mine and, to his credit, he barely even looked at my scars or my hair, he looked directly into my eyes instead. 'You'd better call me Andrew.'

At that point my legs stopped tingling and gave way completely. I buckled at the knees and slumped towards the floor, only to be caught and held up by Flynn's dad, who managed the move without looking as though there were anything out of the ordinary in having to body-lift his son's girlfriends.

'Hello, Andrew,' I said, from my position of being held against his chest with his arms under my backside. 'Nice to meet you.'

'Shall we go up?' Flynn had also decided to treat this as a daily occurrence. He opened the door to the stairway and Andrew met the billowing smell of cod without any acknowledgement that this was in any way an odd way to go about a first meeting. He carried me up the stairs, pausing only to 'good morning' my downstairs neighbour, who was bustling about in her doorway, and put me down on the sofa.

My embarrassment had now reached epic proportions, and if one of the men had cracked a joke, or said anything about 'sweeping me off my feet', I would have turned into a small puddle of hot humiliated goo. But Andrew Mays-Harrison was an absolute pro and Flynn was used to me now, so we all pretended that this was perfectly normal behaviour and went on accordingly.

Outside, I could see the small crowd approaching the Bentley slowly, as though creeping up on a wild animal. 'Andrew, you might want to move the car...?' I began, cautiously. 'Double yellow lines and all that,' I finished, not wanting to damn my fellow Yorkshiremen by pointing out that cars of that rank were unusual in our tiny town, and it was going to find itself on the local Facebook page in very short order.

An airy arm waved. 'It's fine.' Then Andrew turned to me and his grin was so like Flynn's that I found I was smiling back. 'I play golf with the chief constable.'

'Yes,' I murmured weakly; the rich really were a breed apart. 'Flynn said.'

'So.' Andrew settled himself on the window ledge. 'What are we doing about the wine bar, then?'

It was that 'we' that did it, and I suddenly saw what Flynn had meant by being in his father's shadow. The calm assumption that owning a detonated bar was a family problem that they could put right together only went to show me how far from normal my own family were. His was suffocating, whereas I'd put so much space between myself and mine that I may as well have been in orbit.

'Not sure yet, Dad. We're waiting on the police deciding who they are going to charge and the thickness of the book about to be thrown at the culprits.' Flynn took a deep breath. 'And I'm not sure I want to stay around here, anyway.'

Andrew's expression didn't change. He blinked twice, his only indication of surprise. 'I thought this was your great experiment in independence?'

'I didn't say I wanted to take on another enterprise, did I?' Now Flynn looked almost mutinous. 'I don't need any help, Dad, truly. Fee and I are going to make a go of something. We just aren't quite sure what yet.'

To my surprise, Andrew came over and sat down next to me. Actually, he didn't so much sit as flump, and the frame of the sofa bed groaned a complaint. 'Right,' he said, sounding baffled. 'Right. Of course. Yes.' Then he glanced my way and winked, and I knew where Flynn got it from. 'I didn't think I'd be able to keep your wings clipped for much longer.'

'You don't mind?' Flynn sounded astonished.

'Of course not. You need to get out there and make yourself a proper life without having to look over your shoulder to check that I approve. I'm not a monster, Flynn, I'm your father and I want whatever you want.'

So, *this* was how proper families behaved, I thought, as the two men changed the subject with typical 'bloke' aversion to getting into anything sentimental. They were supportive and kind and they didn't mention money or where it was coming from once. They made my family look like aliens.

And later, after Andrew had left with a kiss on the cheek for me and a hearty back-slapping hug for his son, Flynn and I sat together and stared out of the window at the remains of the wine bar.

'What *am* I going to do?' Flynn mused. 'I suppose I could go into advising people on their businesses, but that's a tough gig.'

'You could write a book on cocktails?' I suggested. 'You're good at those.'

All the time, I was thinking that he was still fully functioning. The real question was, what was *I* going to do? Reluctant legs and a non-operational left arm weren't enough for me to retire myself from the world of work forever, and besides, I couldn't do that to Flynn. He may be the son of a multimillionaire, but I was damned if I was going to let that make a difference. What, after all, if he didn't stick around? I needed to be able to keep myself and, so far, my forays into the world of work consisted of shop work – because I'd been living at home and my parents liked the staff discount – the call centre and working in the bar. None of those had so far enabled me to do more than bob about under the surface of life. I needed something that would make me actual money. Something where I could demonstrate that I was the *me* that I'd pretended to be right at the beginning. Someone who could make things happen: *brave* Fee.

'True. Not sure many of them are my recipes though. Or even actual recipes, come to think of it. I usually just pour several types of alcohol in together, give it a shake and a stupid name and – well, people will drink anything. Incidentally, I'm really proud of the fact that you seem to have stopped drinking.'

He threw this in over his shoulder as he turned to my inadequate kitchen to begin the hunt for something to cook. Andrew had offered to take us both out to dinner, but I hadn't liked to say that I was likely to be fast asleep by half past six in the evening, some of my medication being somewhat on the sedative side. Flynn hadn't looked keen either, and we'd jointly and silently invented a previous engagement. Any previous engagement that prevented us being taken out for a meal by someone as rich and famous as Andrew Mays-Harrison would have had to have been of the nature of a summons from the Palace, but Andrew had wisely not enquired.

'You said I couldn't drink if I worked for you,' I pointed out.

'Well, yes, but I didn't mean you had to stop totally, only not drink when you were at work. I haven't seen you touch anything at all for ages.'

I *so* wanted to say that I had no need to drink now. I wanted to say that I'd beaten my demons, that having Dexter out of my life with his demands and his high-stress lifestyle, which had dragged me along with it, had meant there was no need to drink any more. I wanted to say that I'd regained a sense of self-esteem and realised that I didn't need the crutch of alcohol to prop me up, now that I had actual friends and a new life.

None of it would have been true. At least, it was true to an extent, and I hadn't felt the pull towards a couple of glasses of wine that would blur the edges and make the awfulness of my life fuzzier and more bearable, recently. But even so…

'I can't,' I admitted. 'The drugs they gave me at the hospital – you can't drink on them and I'd rather get better than drunk.'

'Oh.' He looked at me now, with his head on one side. 'But you didn't… I mean, you don't drink when you're working behind the bar either?'

'Oh no.' I pretended not to notice his slip into the past. 'I've got a really strict boss. I might have had the odd one or two some-times but between not being allowed to drink and not having time to drink, and then being hospitalised with nothing but weak squash and horrible water, I seem to have broken the habit. Plus, you know, the drugs make me woozy enough already.'

He smiled. Flynn had two grades of smile: one was a wide face-splitter that made his eyes crease behind the glasses and his mouth widen, the other was a softening of his expression, a kindness that came onto his face, hardly touching his features but making him look gentle and almost sad. The smile I got now was the second kind. 'Take it slowly,' he said, almost inaudibly. 'There's no rush.'

When he looked at me like that, taking in my puckered skin, the bruising that still darkened my skin all down one side of my face, the limp and useless arm and my decidedly wonky legs, but wearing such an expression of kind acceptance and almost-humour, I wanted to sweep him up and take him to bed and never let him leave.

The fact that I couldn't – limp arm, wobbly legs, etc. – was extremely frustrating.

'What did you think of my dad?' Flynn asked, clearing his throat. Our mutual exchange of looks had gone on a bit too long and the temperature in here was rising. I wasn't quite sure how sex was going to work now that I'd come out of hospital, and neither of us seemed to know how to broach the subject, so I was glad he wanted to get sensible.

'He seems nice. A little bit... brusque, maybe? But he obviously loves you,' I finished, trying not to sound jealous.

Flynn nodded. He put out a hand and touched the mottled side of my cheek that made it look as though I were turning into a lizard. 'He means well,' he said. 'But I don't want that life any more.'

I closed my eyes. Those gentle fingers soothed my skin, took away the ache. 'That life of having instant access to loads of money, a lifestyle that most people can only dream about, and never having to worry about paying the electricity bill? That life?'

He stepped in closer. 'It does have its advantages, I admit.' Now he cupped his hand gently along my jaw. 'But this life, you, friends, something *genuine*, that is what I really want.'

I opened my eyes for a second and took in the cluttered tininess of the three rooms. 'The stairs smell of fish,' I said, almost dreamily.

'I noticed that. Why?' Now he was touching my hair, the long bit on the top, not the shaved sides which had the texture of a nailbrush.

'I think it's the glue they used to stick down the lino.'

'Oh.' A pause. 'My dad will give me anything I want, you know. He seems a bit stuffy and a bit image-conscious, but really he just wants me happy. Actually, no, what he *really* wants is me taking over the Mays-Harrison empire so he can retire to lie on a beach in Bali, reclining on his billions, but he's not going to insist.'

I took a small step closer. Flynn smelled wonderful; he always smelled of clean, fresh clothes and the open air. I had no idea how he did it, when the rest of the flat smelled of damp plaster and frying electrical wire. 'Why are you telling me this?' I asked.

'I'm trying to impress you.'

I laughed at that, but quietly, because I didn't want to break the mood, which was becoming heavier and hotter with every second. 'It's working.'

'Because you, the club – even Fraser – are the closest I've ever got to anything that felt real.' Flynn was so close now that I could see myself reflected in his glasses. 'All my life I've been Flynn Mays-Harrison. It's affected how people treated me, how they saw me, how they *were* with me. You and the guys, you all treat me as though I'm one of you. You included me in the club for all the

Eddie-following stuff like I'm no one special, and you've no idea how wonderful that is when you've had a lifetime being my dad's son.'

I felt the light brush of his lips against mine and didn't murmur when he picked me up and laid me down on the sofa. There was something dark and haunted about Flynn since his father's visit, as though he needed to do something to make himself believe that he was a real person in his own right, that he didn't exist as an extension of his father, and if that was going to take the form of having wild – if somewhat limited, because of my only one arm and wonky legs – sex, then I was going to encourage this individualism with everything I had.

'I don't want the fact that I'm the son of a multimillionaire business owner to come between us,' Flynn whispered, sliding my T-shirt off over my head, but very carefully so as not to make my arm flop.

I *nearly* laughed about the hyperbole, but he was so earnest, plus, well, he was hot and he didn't seem to care that the left-hand side of my body was a little inert, and that the bruising came down over my ribs in colours that any artist would have given their brushes to have mixed. He was gentle, he was kind, but above all he was *thorough*, and the sex was both an affirmation and a breathless riot.

'Well,' I said, when I was capable. 'We must have your father over more often.'

There was a tentative knock on the door and Flynn and I looked at each other for a moment, wide-eyed. 'You don't think he's come back, do you?'

The tap was followed by an altogether more robust knocking, and Fraser's voice cheerfully calling, 'If you two are banging in there, can you get your clothes on and open this door?'

'Shit,' said Flynn, succinctly. 'It's the guys. I'd forgotten it was club night.'

He scrambled off the sofa and began pulling on his clothes, then looked over at me. I couldn't put my T-shirt on one-handed, so he carefully dressed me first, and then went to answer the door, jeans half done-up and his T-shirt on backwards.

'You *were* banging!' Fraser announced to the entire world as he came in. 'Knew it!'

Wren, passing me, suppressed a grin, and even Margot wiggled her eyebrows.

'Busted,' Flynn said cheerily. 'I knew that strip Scrabble match was a mistake.'

'Sssh,' I said, from the far side of the room. 'We were, in fact, reading improving literature and quizzing one another on the subject of seventeenth-century—'

'Banging,' Fraser interrupted and flung himself down on the sofa next to me. 'Wow, this place is small. Do you know, the stairs smell of...'

'Fish,' I finished. 'Yes, thank you, I did know, but it's cheap and... Well, no, it isn't anything else. Cheap, and cheap is good.'

'And you live at home with your mum, Fraser,' Wren pointed out. 'You're not exactly in a position to critique someone else's living arrangements.'

Fraser straightened importantly. 'I'm moving out,' he said. 'Minnie and her bloke helped me get one of the new places in the old warehouse behind the library. That one they've turned into flats.'

He was clearly almost bursting with pride about this.

'I thought that was sheltered accommodation for the elderly?' Margot dropped in, in her usual brusque way.

'There's flats for people like me, too.' Fraser didn't sound upset at all. 'As long as we helps out the old folks now and again –

bit of shopping, put up some shelves an' all – we gets cheap accommodation. And, you know, the neighbours aren't going to be playing grunge rock full volume 'til four in the morning like at Mum's.'

'That sounds great,' I said, pulling down the back of my T-shirt. 'That's really good, Fraser.'

He beamed at me. 'Some of those girls who comes in to do personal care are a bit tasty too,' he said. 'Might get to chat them up as well.'

'Aaaand we're back to our usual standard.' Flynn put the kettle on. 'It will have to be tea, I'm afraid, we're a bit short on the chardonnay, what with most of my stock being locked away behind an exploded building which we're not allowed to go into.'

Margot smiled and pulled a bottle out of her handbag. 'I brought supplies,' she said. 'I thought we could have a drink because Wren and I are off to Scotland on Thursday, so we won't be able to make next week's meeting.'

Flynn brought through my mismatched collection of drinking glasses and a cup of tea for me. 'Can't drink on the medication,' I explained, somewhat sourly, watching them pour themselves big glasses of what looked like a really classy wine. 'Besides, drinking is overrated. Look what it led me to.'

'Have the police made any progress in locking up your ex?' Margot peered at me over her glass.

I thought of the phones that had been hidden under my floor. 'There's been a bit of a development.'

'We're hopeful,' Flynn said. 'If he gets let off, we move up to Defcon Terrified and Australia.'

'If you need any legal help, I would be prepared to step in on the case,' Margot said. 'It's about time I got back to practising – I had to take time off around the divorce, but now that's all sorted, there's only the decrees to finish now.'

'And I could use all my journalistic contacts,' Wren added, clinking glasses with Margot. 'If you need me. I'm an absolute expert at forensic examination of social media.'

'And I can always punch him,' Fraser chimed in. 'If you needed me to. Or sit on him again. I liked that bit.'

I smiled at all of them. 'You are very useful people to know, thank you. We're hoping that the police will have enough to put him and his cronies away for a good long while.'

'Well.' Margot seemed mollified. 'That's good. Just – if you need us, that's all.'

'Thank you,' I said again, humbled by their wanting to help me.

'And I'm sure Annie would offer any assistance she may be able to render, too,' Margot went on. 'She's so very grateful for our support in the matter of Eddie.'

We all stared at her. 'She doesn't know, does she?' I asked. 'All the following and everything?'

'Oh, no no. Nothing like that, no, like she said when we all visited you in the hospital, she's incredibly grateful for the support we gave her when she suspected infidelity. She really does live her entire life wrapped up in Eddie.'

'Her choice though, surely.'

Margot frowned. 'She used to be an accountant, you know. Quite high-powered, apparently, but she gave it up because Eddie needed someone at home to organise him.'

We all inwardly digested the thought of Eddie, king of the pork products and the garden so regimented that the plants almost marched in step, needing organising.

'Houses take a lot of looking after,' Wren said reasonably. 'And if they were expecting to have children, perhaps it made sense. They have been married a long time, after all.'

'Plus, she makes a cracking hot pot,' put in Fraser, whose

concern with accountancy was clearly subordinate to his stomach.

The meeting broke up shortly afterwards, once everyone had finished their wine and reassured themselves that my recovery was ongoing. I had been nearest the blast, the others had been cushioned from the worst of the impact by furniture and the solidity of Fraser. It would, I thought, take more than a bomb to take down Fraser, who seemed to have the physical fragility of a combine harvester.

Flynn went across the road to sort out something to do with site security with a man in a very bright orange jacket who stood staring up at the scaffolding. I watched them from the window, leaning against the frame so that my legs didn't let me down again, and felt that awful sense of hopelessness come back over me.

What was I going to *do*? I couldn't spend the rest of my life reliant on Flynn. He would come to resent it, however much he said he wouldn't, and I really could not spend the next sixty or more years sitting down and reading, could I? Oh, I might manage the odd bar shift or some office work, and there was always the call centre again, as long as I didn't mind being humiliated on a daily basis, even though having the use of only one arm was going to hamper me somewhat. There was Flynn, all dark and lovely and willing to try to make a life with me – I had to be able to contribute somehow. I couldn't forever be the 'back-room girl', despite my ferocious amount of training in that direction during my growing up.

Then I thought how happy my parents would be if I had to go home. If Flynn got tired of me and replaced me with a fully working model, someone who could run up hills hand in hand with him – I had a vision of some advertisement-worthy couple chasing each other breathlessly to the top of a mountain and standing there with the wind in their hair and a look of ridiculously outdoors-inspired joy on their faces.

No. I had to do something. I stared around the flat. It was tidier since Flynn had moved in, so there wasn't a lot of inspiration, apart from the huge gap in my bathroom floor where we'd ripped up the floorboards. Hole in the floor, books piled up against the far wall because I hadn't got around to a bookcase. The Monday Night Heartbreak Club, all behind me...

I had the faintest glimmerings of an idea.

22

Two weeks dashed past.

Demolition work started on the wine bar and Flynn and I watched as skips arrived on the street, to the consternation of the passing public who gathered around them for a good ogle and gossip as work started.

'Are you all right?' I asked him, as he winced when some of the tasteful and carefully chosen artwork, thrown by a cheery man in a hard hat, slid into the skip, to be covered by a layer of brick.

'Apart from the fact that I'm watching all my attempts at starting up my own enterprise being hurled about by men in overalls?' He didn't look at me, keeping his eyes on the despoiling of his empire going on in the street below. 'Oh, and that lamp was imported from Japan!'

'Yes. Apart from that.' I touched his arm and he turned round.

'It's surprisingly okay, actually.' He gave me a smile. It was a little tight around the edges, but it was a good attempt. 'Of course, that's easy for me to say, isn't it, when I've got a dad who can bail me out until I find what I really want to do. What about you, Fee, how are you?'

We'd been going about life without asking any of the really important questions. Or mentioning love. After my blurting it out when I thought I might be arrested I hadn't repeated myself and Flynn was very quiet on the subject. We had fallen into domesticity together easily enough, but sometimes I looked at Flynn and wondered what he thought. He was very self-contained and although his eyes said he loved me his mouth hadn't followed suit. I supposed that his life as part of the Mays-Harrison empire had taught him not to blurt out his feelings in a stream of consciousness that would have made Fraser seem circumspect and thoughtful, but occasionally it might have been nice to have been given a clue as to what went on in his head.

His asking me how I was felt like a way in to a difficult conversation.

'I'm—'

My phone rang. The speaker had got dust in it during the blast and it now rang in a way that made it sound as though it needed a good cough and some fresh air. 'I'd better get this. You never know, it might be someone wanting to press enormous amounts of money upon me.'

'Don't, Dad is bad enough.' Flynn flung himself down on the bed. He hadn't even insisted on it being turned back into a sofa for the last few days, that was how bad things were.

'Ms Walker? This is the police.'

Despite the fact that I *knew* I hadn't done anything, my mouth still went dry and I felt my stomach squeeze. 'Yes?'

'We wanted to let you know that we have your ex-boyfriend on remand. Those phones you handed over had everything we could have wanted and more.'

All my innards now gave little leaps. 'Oh, that is good news!'

'The two men who planted the bomb are in custody too. They started out saying that they didn't know anything and the bag wasn't theirs, but since we got our lad banged up, they've changed their story. They suddenly remembered that he *did* give them the bag, and he *did* tell them where to leave it. Surprisingly, they've remembered a whole lot of other stuff too and they are so busy confessing that it's like a church on Sunday in here.'

'There was really *that* much stuff on those phones?' I asked.

'Oh yes. Looks like your ex thought it was his security; nobody was going to turn him in when they knew he had something on them, but now it's all out in the open, there are a lot of very worried people trying to make sure we get their version of events first.'

'Thank you for telling me.' I ended the call and told Flynn the good news.

'At least we won't have to move to Australia then,' he said, sounding tired. 'Bit of a shame really, it's great out there.'

'But you won't have to go to your dad for a job, will you?' I asked, trying to jolt him from the ennui that seemed to have pervaded him.

'We have to live, Fee.' He waved a hand from his prone position. 'Still, we've got this place and I can turn my hand to a few things.'

'You could ask...'

'No.' His tone was definite. 'No. I'm over being my dad's son. I know you love me for who I am, not for the money.' A slightly dubious look crossed his face. 'You do, don't you? I mean, you're not holding out for the inheritance and the houses and the hotels and all that?'

I laughed. 'Flynn, I fell for you as a barman; anything else is just window dressing. Of course you don't have to work for your father if you don't want to.'

Flynn sat up and took my hand, the non-floppy one. 'I love your confidence,' he said. 'Actually, I love everything about you. I don't want to be in Dad's shadow forever, but I've had a lifetime of it and I'm not entirely sure how I can break out. I've got a business degree and lots of experience, but it's all been as Flynn Mays-Harrison. As soon as people hear the name, they're fighting to give me chances, and I don't know how to go about standing on my own feet.'

These revelations, this insight into the way he was thinking, came as a huge relief. I'd been worrying that Flynn had been sitting on feelings he hadn't known how to express to me, and hearing him say that he loved me and that he was still thinking of the future gave me a burst of renewed desire to plan again.

I thought of my life, breaking away from my family, and felt a bit guilty about my wanting him to talk about feelings. Flynn had a lot of processing to do first. 'Can the angst about the future wait until later? We've got the club coming round at seven and I want to put some snacks out.'

Flynn, face buried in the depths of despair and the pillows, gave a muffled, 'It's only two o clock! How many snacks are you putting out?'

'Well, one of the people coming is Fraser.'

'True, true.' He hauled himself upright. 'And you're right, I'm wallowing. It's ridiculous. We're not going to starve and Dad isn't going to cut me off without a penny. If it means we have a roof over our heads and you can keep the private physio, I can suppress my need to be free and wild and run a bar that explodes under me.' He grinned and it rid his face of the last vestiges of unhappiness. 'You're important to me. Work – isn't.'

'Flynn, you know I'm perfectly happy with NHS physiotherapy.' I tried to sound reasonable. 'I'm better every day. Time will help.'

'They do great things, but I want you to have *more*.' He was frowning again. 'You might even get some use back in that arm with intensive sessions. Plus, we want you able to dance the fandango, don't we?'

He hadn't mentioned the plastic surgery again. He'd raised the subject briefly one night, when I'd been putting some of the prescribed cream on my scars, and I'd told him, in no uncertain terms, that the scars were going to remind me to stay away from people like Dexter for the rest of my life. I didn't want an artificial smile and eyebrows that I had to draw on for ever, for the sake of having a marginally less lopsided face. It sounded brave and it sounded as though I had embraced my scars, but in reality, the doctors had told me that, even with the best plastic surgery money could buy, I would never have smooth skin and an unmarked face. Skin grafts could only do so much and I saw no need for Flynn to lay out thousands of pounds just for me to have a smaller scar and a permanently surprised expression.

'Ah well.' Now he put his arm around me. 'I'm sure things will work out. Eventually. And there's the insurance money from the bar; when that gets paid out, it will help us get on our feet.'

'Unreliable though mine may be.' I sat next to him, wiggling my legs. 'Plus we've got each other.'

'And a flat where the stairs smell of fish and we have to sleep on a sofa bed.'

'But it's affordable,' I pointed out. 'It may not be designed by professionals but that's no good if you can't pay the rent.'

We sat in a slightly glum silence while the sun released a smell of old wood and hot cooking oil as it shone in through the windows. I leaned my head on Flynn's shoulder and he stroked the acceptable parts of my hair. Then I got up to go and put out the snacks.

* * *

'You're twitchy,' Flynn observed, watching me tiddle about with the crisp bowl for the third or fourth time. 'It's only the guys coming round, not the king.'

'I know.' I rotated the bowl again. 'It's more that... I've got an idea and I don't want to put them off.'

'By having the crisps at a forty-five-degree angle?' He watched me fiddle a bit more.

'Well...'

'Margot and Wren have only got eyes for each other, and Fraser will only have eyes for the contents of the bowls. Nobody is going to mind if they aren't centred.' Flynn put a hand over mine. 'Wow. You're actually shaking.'

I didn't want to tell him that my entire future – *our* entire future – might rest on the next couple of hours. I left the crisps alone and straightened the pile of books on the low table. I nearly went to the trouble of hunting out some coasters for the glasses and mugs currently lined up on the side in the kitchen, but thankfully I wasn't quite that bad yet.

'Is there something you need to tell me?' Flynn carried on watching me.

'Wait until the others arrive.' I neatened the throw over the back of the sofa for the millionth time.

'Oh. Okay.' He shifted and leaned back against the window, trying to look nonchalant. 'You're not... You're happy with our relationship, aren't you?'

The words came out very fast, as though he'd had them in mind for some time and had only just let them out. Like greyhounds let slip, the words had headed for the finish in a mass of phrases. Now that Flynn was letting some of those repressed feelings out it seemed there was no stopping him.

'What?' I left the throw and turned around slowly. Flynn was adjusting his elbows, still leaning. 'Of course I am. Why would you think I wasn't?'

He sighed. 'Sorry. I'm not good at these kinds of conversations. I wish Mum could have stuck around a bit longer and told me how this all works.' Flynn took a deep breath. 'I am, in my clumsy and not very practised way, trying to say that you've been a bit distant lately. Having been on the wrong end of a woman being... distracted, chiefly by working out how to scam me, I get twitchy around distraction. And then I don't know what to say or how to say it. Sorry,' he repeated.

I was so gobsmacked by his insecurity and his obvious attempt to feign nonchalance that I just stood with my mouth open and looked at him. Gorgeous, dark Flynn, with his quiet solidity and intelligence, like a black hole with a vocabulary. '*Seriously*?' was all I could say.

He shrugged. 'I thought, maybe, now that you're getting yourself sorted and that bastard of an ex is locked away, maybe you'd be having second thoughts. And I must admit to an uncharitable contemplation about just how attractive I am as a partner, now I've told Dad that I don't want to rely on him any more.'

I didn't like to say that I'd been having similar thoughts about him. Flynn and I *both* needed to learn to talk to one another.

'Flynn, it's not about the money. Well, it sort of is, because we've got to make a living, but...' I was aghast. 'It was *never* about who you are. I didn't *know* who you are.' I made my way over to him. He was averting his eyes now, concentrating ferociously on the dreadful carpet tiles. 'I honestly can't believe that you think that I'm the sort of person who would only be with you because of who you are.'

He shrugged again and twitched the cuff of his shirt. 'I don't.' Now he met my eyes and his expression was one of tortured wariness. 'I really don't. But I never know what you're thinking, Fee. You've got this kind of closed-off expression sometimes and it's impossible to read.'

'Of course I've got a closed-off expression, half my face was stitched up so tightly that I smile like only half of me is happy. And smiling hurts.' Of *course* I was closed off, I'd had a lifetime of being taunted by my brother for having emotions of any kind, and then bullied by Dexter if I dared show anything other than a type of wired ecstasy. Not showing any negative emotion had been beaten into me, and the positive ones had gone along for the ride. Showing how I was feeling was another of those things, like walking properly, that I needed to learn. 'I'm sorry. I've spent a lifetime keeping everything to myself. I'm finding it hard to realise I don't have to. And it feels as though you are realising the same thing. God, we're really crap at this "communication" thing, aren't we? Flynn, can you just trust me?'

'I love you,' he muttered to the floor again. 'And I know your life has been a bit unconventional this far. But I'm not this rich guy whose life has been all plain sailing up to now. I've got my own demons.' Those huge black eyes came back up to mine and held them this time. 'But if you can stamp on your demons, I reckon I can give mine a hard time too, don't you?'

He crossed the floor and his arms were suddenly around me in the kind of hug that was so tight it almost hurt. I put my obedient arm around him. My other one hung in its brace, my constant reminder of what had happened, limp and unavailable. 'Flynn, I will tell you what I've got in my head, but I need the others here first,' I said, muffled against his neck.

'But you're not dumping me.' He sounded a little bit lighter now.

'No. I am not dumping you.'

'I'm sorry.'

I stared at him. 'What on earth have you got to be sorry about?'

'Oh, I don't know. A ridiculous inability to cope with rejection? A predisposition to always fear the worst?'

'My ex blew up your bar! You didn't see that one coming, did you?' I could feel the smile beginning to make its lopsided way across my face. 'A little bit of fearing the worst is to be expected, under the circumstances.'

'True, true.' He moved back a little and I could see he was smiling now too, a complicated sort of smile that showed relief and guilt and self-loathing and despair all mixed together with that dark-eyed watchfulness. 'Life has taken a turn for the unexpected since I met you.'

I let those words sink in. *Unexpected.* I quite liked that. I liked the idea of being unexpected. Impromptu. Random. It made me feel less of a target.

'Here they come.' He glanced out of the window. 'They've all come together, again. Margot really does seem very fond of Fraser, doesn't she?'

'I think he's the son she's permanently glad she never had.' I rearranged the crisp bowls for the hundredth time.

'He's doing all right for himself now though.' Another glance. 'And he's looking incredibly fit.'

'Of course he is, he does nothing but train. I hope no beginners are going to look at his muscles and think they can do that in a few weeks. I mean, they can, he's living proof, but they'd have to have absolutely no other life at all.'

Fraser bounced about on the pavement waiting for Margot

and Wren, and then charged for the stairs to the flat like an over-enthusiastic dog. They followed more slowly, hand in hand and smiling.

'They're only getting fucking married!' Fraser said, bursting the door open like the Sweeney.

'They probably want to tell us that themselves,' I said, tactfully, but Fraser had seen the bowls of crisps and launched himself through the doorway. We waited for Margot and Wren and tried to look surprised when they held up their left hands, wearing identical engagement rings.

'There's no point in waiting,' Margot said, following our congratulations. 'We're both aware of how short and fragile life is.'

'Yeah,' Fraser said, around crisps. 'We could all have died in that explosion.'

'Thank you, Fraser. So, we decided—are you all right, Fee?'

Here was where I found out whether I had a future or not. 'I've had an idea,' I said.

Flynn grabbed my hand.

'Oh yeah?' Another handful of crisps went down and Fraser was looking around for more.

'Annie's coming in a minute,' I added, obviously surprising everyone. 'I think she should be part of this.' I looked at the clock. 'Any minute now.'

'Eddie's probably getting the car out,' Wren said, and the four of them nodded, as though they were privy to the extreme conditions that seemed to be involved in this action.

While we waited, I served more snacks, mainly to stop Fraser from bouncing on the sofa, and Margot and Wren outlined their wedding plans.

'We thought a small local ceremony,' Margot said. 'And we

would be honoured if you two would be our witnesses.' She patted my hand and smiled at Flynn.

'I'm giving them both away,' Fraser said happily. 'I offered to raffle them instead though.'

'And then we shall honeymoon in the Seychelles,' Margot went on.

'Here's Annie,' I said gratefully. The conspicuous consumption being discussed made me feel a little bit wobbly, when I lived this uncertain life in a cheap flat and, currently, with no job. Disability payments were slow in coming and I refused to let Flynn pay for everything, which meant I *had* to do something, and quickly.

Annie and Eddie came up the stairs slightly cautiously. They'd never been to the flat before and clearly thought they might be in the wrong place. We could hear them questioning each other all the way up and their evident relief when Flynn opened the door was slightly amusing.

'Nice to see you looking so well, Fee, dear,' Annie said. She was either lying or she didn't get out much, because, despite Flynn's assurances to the contrary, I still didn't look great. I knew I was pale, that the bruising was slow to subside and the broken cheekbone had made half my face swell, which was also slow to subside. I looked as though death would have been an improvement.

'We brought you these.' Eddie awkwardly jutted a bunch of hyacinths at me. 'From the garden.'

'Eddie's got it looking lovely, haven't you?' Annie said, with pride.

We all avoided looking at Eddie. I put the flowers in water and everyone sat down, apart from Fraser, who was still snaffling crisps and nuts from various bowls.

'I've had an idea,' I said. 'After what you said the other week about helping get Dexter put away. We don't need to worry about that any more, incidentally, the police have enough to lock him up for quite a while.'

Everyone made 'oh, that is a relief' noises. Flynn was watching me from the far side of the room, where he'd stationed himself by the window again almost as though he were preparing to jump. I wondered about his earlier insecurity. But then, he'd been wealthy all his life, girlfriends taking advantage of him must have become his default. It was no wonder he worried. But I was about to show that I'd thought about our future and I hoped he'd realise that it meant I was serious about earning my own money, serious about keeping us both without having to go cap-in-hand to Andrew. I'd had *enough* of looking to other people for my happiness. As to looking to other people for help – well, I was about to give that a try for the first time in my life.

I waved my one working hand at the stack of books that stood under the table.

'What?' Fraser said. 'We're not starting a book club, are we? I told you, I got dyslexia.'

'No. I got those a while ago, but I've been flicking through them.' I pulled a couple out. *The Practical Handbook for Professional Investigators*, and *Private Investigator Study Guide and Practice Test Questions for Private Investigator Exams*. Flynn was still staring at me.

'I thought you'd given that idea up,' he said. 'With you being... well, not as mobile as you were.'

'Plus, any bod's going to spot you following them in a crowd,' Fraser said. 'You wobble.'

My insides were burning with the acid of uncertainty. But I had to do it, I had to put myself out there and ask for their help. It didn't come naturally to me, and almost made me feel sick with the necessity of it, but I *had to try*.

I took a deep breath. 'I can't do it on my own,' I said. 'I know that. But – I thought, with your help, all of you...' I tailed off. Everyone was looking at me blankly.

'What, like driving you around?' Fraser asked.

'No, no, I mean – you all have your strengths. You all have things that could be helpful.' I turned to Margot and Wren, side by side and holding hands on the sofa. 'Margot, you've got legal knowledge. Wren, you said that you're the queen of investigative social media. Flynn is posh and has that confident thing that can get him in anywhere, and I could coordinate, do the background research work. Fraser, you could be the muscle.' The sick feeling had turned to a kind of burning urgency now. This was my hope for the future and I *knew* I could do it. I was just going to need some help. 'Annie, you are perfect for blending in with a crowd if we need to follow someone.' This was understating the case; Annie, with her short greying hair and cardigans, would be almost invisible in any gathering, other than that of a drug-fuelled all-night rave. 'And we might need you for forensic accounting, too. What do you all think?'

There was a long silence and I didn't dare meet anyone's eye. I was afraid that my vulnerability, my need, would show on my face. Finally, I had to do something, and looked up at Flynn. He was still over by the window. But he was smiling.

'That's what all the late-night sitting up was about?' he asked. 'I thought you were in pain. Regretting not taking up the offer of the rehab place and you didn't like to say.'

'No, Flynn.' I tried not to sound amused. It wasn't funny. Sometimes I *had* been in pain and using the books to distract me. I should have told him. Flynn wasn't Dex, he wouldn't have laughed and tried to persuade me into sex. Flynn wasn't my brother, using my fears and insecurities against me. I should have admitted that sometimes my legs tingled too much to let me sleep, and my arm got in the way when I tried to lie down. 'I was reading up on what I'd need to do to set up an agency. All the exams I'd need to take.'

Everyone else seemed to be holding their breath, as though they realised that I was sorting a lot of stuff out in my head. Even Fraser had stopped crunching.

Flynn left the window and crossed the room in two strides, to wrap his arms around me. He even *smelled* expensive, damn him. 'You could have said.'

I increased the hug. Some women, I mused, would have found his uncertainty unattractive. Some women wanted men to do the manly, 'I am in charge' thing and never express a moment's doubt or worry; not a second of anxiety or lack of confidence would be tolerated. I was not them. On the contrary, Flynn's self-doubt made me feel that we had a chance of being, if not equal, then more or less on a level playing field.

'I'm glad,' he said, into the slightly less bristly bit of my hair. 'I mean, obviously I'm not glad you are sometimes in pain. I'm glad that you haven't been regretting any of our decisions.'

'Yeah, yeah, lovely, now can we go back a minute or two?' Fraser tapped me on the shoulder. 'I wants to get this straight. You wants to start a private investigation agency – with us lot?' His face loomed into my field of vision. 'Seriously?'

I unwound myself from Flynn, who let me go without complaint. 'Yes.'

My heart was going at a ridiculous rate now. I felt stupid, small. However could I have thought it was a good idea? I opened my mouth to excuse myself, to say that it didn't matter, it had only been an idea, an idle thought, but then Fraser's face creased into a grin of almost planetary proportions.

'*Wicked*! I can be, like, undercover at the gym! Pretending to be a personal trainer when really I'm this ace detective!'

'Er, well…' I started.

'No, no, I think Fraser has a very good point.' Margot waded in. 'Having an ordinary day job will be perfect cover. And working with the public, Fraser will be ideally placed to pick up clients.'

'And me,' Wren joined in. 'I work for the local paper. There are *tonnes* of people with stories that the police aren't interested in, but who we could help out.'

'And Eddie and I would find following people quite exciting,' Annie said. 'A little interest for us, in our retirement.'

'Where do I fit in?' Flynn didn't sound quite as diffident as his words. 'Am I like James Bond's Q, the back-room boy with all the gadgets?'

'First line defence if we need a corkscrew and cocktail shaker,' Fraser said, still clearly very enthusiastic about the whole idea. 'Plus, like Fee said, you're our token posh boy for if we need to get into… err…' He was clearly racking his brains for the poshest place he could think of. 'Them upper-class places.' He had obviously given up on the specifics.

'You and I, Flynn…' I said, 'you and I are the power behind the outfit. We do the research and the telephoning and the boots-on-the-ground work. Er, if you want to, that is.'

Now Flynn smiled too. His smile wasn't quite as broad and unconsidered as Fraser's; he still held a hint of himself back, but he looked happy. 'I think I could get behind that,' he said. 'Plus, you know, I could just relax my principles a bit and get my multi-millionaire dad to help us out sometimes. And knowing my way around the tech stuff could be useful.'

His phone rang at that point, and he walked off outside the door to answer it. I noticed that his walk had a lot more spring in it, and he'd straightened his shoulders to the extent that he now looked a good few centimetres taller.

'You reckon we can make a go of it?' Fraser asked. 'Like, make money and stuff? Only, Minnie reckons it might be a while before our personal training business gets properly off the ground and I'm going to need cash for rent and food. Crisps are *not* cheap, you know?'

'I need to do some courses,' I said. 'Get proper accreditation and authorisations, so people hiring us will know that we stick to the rules and we know the law. But while I'm working towards getting qualified – why not?'

Margot and Wren looked at each other. 'Obviously I won't be doing it for the money,' Margot said. 'But I do like the idea of helping people. That's why I went into law in the first place, of course.'

'It would help bump up the wedding fund, though,' Wren said reasonably. 'If we want to go to the Seychelles.'

'We need to attract some trade.'

'We could advertise on social media. I have contacts.'

'It would be something to supplement the pensions.' Annie's eyes were shining now. I wondered if she had herself down as Miss Marple. Although I didn't remember Miss Marple having an omnipresent husband who seemed to struggle with Getting The Car Out.

I listened to them planning. Our current lack of clients wanting our services didn't seem to matter, as it stood. The idea was enough. I felt another of those waves of warm belonging wash over me again. These people, who'd been strangers not so long ago, were behind me. I really *could* do it, open my own agency, pay my own bills. I could make it. Flynn and I could make it.

Flynn came back in a few moments later. He looked cautiously optimistic, like a cat creeping in when it knows everyone has just sat down to dinner. 'Um,' he said. 'That was my dad. He wanted to check a few things with me, but then we got chatting and... turns out one of his employees has had their dog go missing in slightly mysterious circumstances. I think we might have our first case.'

* * *

MORE FROM JANE LOVERING

The next uplifting read from Jane Lovering is available to order now here:

https://mybook.to/JaneLovering14

ABOUT THE AUTHOR

Jane Lovering is the bestselling and award-winning romantic comedy writer who won the RNA Contemporary Romantic Novel Award in 2023 with *A Cottage Full of Secrets*. She lives in Yorkshire and has a cat and a bonkers terrier, as well as five children who have now left home.

Sign up to Jane Lovering's mailing list here for news, competitions and updates on future books.

Visit Jane's website: www.janelovering.co.uk

Follow Jane on social media:

facebook.com/Jane-Lovering-Author-106404969412833

x.com/janelovering

bookbub.com/authors/jane-lovering

ALSO BY JANE LOVERING

The Country Escape

Home on a Yorkshire Farm

A Midwinter Match

A Cottage Full of Secrets

The Forgotten House on the Moor

There's No Place Like Home

The Recipe for Happiness

The Island Cottage

One of a Kind

The Start of the Story

Happily Ever After

Once Upon a Thyme

The Monday Night Heartbreak Club